REAL
LIFE

REAL LIFE

BRANDON TAYLOR

RIVERHEAD BOOKS   NEW YORK
2020

RIVERHEAD BOOKS
An imprint of Penguin Random House LLC
penguinrandomhouse.com

Library of Congress Cataloging-in-Publication Data

Names: Taylor, Brandon (Brandon L. G.), author.
Title: Real life / Brandon Taylor.
Description: New York : Riverhead Books, 2020.
Identifiers: LCCN 2019022438 (print) | LCCN 2019022439 (ebook) |
ISBN 9780525538882 (hardcover) | ISBN 9780525538905 (ebook)
Classification: LCC PS3620.A93534 R43 2020 (print) |
LCC PS3620.A93534 (ebook) | DDC 813/.6—dc23
LC record available at https://lccn.loc.gov/2019022438
LC ebook record available at https://lccn.loc.gov/2019022439

Printed in the United States of America
5   7   9   10   8   6

BOOK DESIGN BY LUCIA BERNARD

I am allotted months of emptiness,
and nights of misery are apportioned to me.

Job 7:3

It was a cool evening in late summer when Wallace, his father dead for several weeks, decided that he would meet his friends at the pier after all. The lake was dimpled with white waves. People coveted these last blustery days of summer before the weather turned cold and mercurial. The air was heavy with their good times as the white people scattered across the tiered patios, pried their mouths apart, and beamed their laughter into each other's faces. Overhead, gulls drifted easy as anything.

Wallace stood on an upper platform looking down into the scrum, trying to find his particular group of white people, thinking also that it was still possible to turn back, that he could go home and get on with his evening. It had been a couple of years since he had gone to the lake with his friends, a period of time that embarrassed him because it seemed to demand an excuse and he did not have one. It might have had something to do with the crowds, the insistence of other people's bodies, the way the birds circled overhead, then dive-bombed the tables to grab food or root around at their feet, as though even they were socializing. Threats from every corner. There was also the matter of the noise, the desperate braying of everyone talking over everyone else, the bad music, the children and dogs, the radios from the frats down the lakeshore, the car stereos in the streets, the shouting mass of hundreds of lives disagreeing.

The noise demanded vague and strange things from Wallace.

There, among the burgundy wooden tables nearest the lake, he saw the four of them. Or, no, more specifically, he saw Miller, who was extraordinarily tall, the easiest to spot. Then Yngve and Cole, who were merely *tall*, and then Vincent, who just scraped under the bar of average height. Miller, Yngve, and Cole looked like a trio of pale, upright deer, like they belonged to their own particular species, and you could be forgiven, if you were in a hurry, for thinking them related. Like Wallace and their other friends, they had all come to this Midwestern city to pursue graduate studies in biochemistry. Their class had been the first small one in quite some time, and the first in more than three decades to include a black person. In his less generous moments, Wallace thought these two things related, that a narrowing, a reduction in the number of applicants, had made his admission possible.

Wallace was on the verge of turning back—he was uncertain if the company of other people, which just a short time ago had seemed somehow necessary, was something he could bear—when Cole looked up and spotted him. Cole started to flail his arms about, as if he were trying to elongate himself to ensure that Wallace could see him, though it must have been obvious that Wallace was looking directly at them. There was no turning back after all. He waved to them.

It was Friday.

Wallace went down the half-rotten stairs and came closer to the dense algal stink of the lake. He followed the curving wall, passed the hulls of the boats, passed where the dark stones jutted out of the water, passed the long pier that stretched out into the water, with people there, too, laughing, and as he walked, he glanced out over the vast green water of the lake itself, boats skimming its surface, their sails white and sure against the wind and the low, wide sky.

It was perfect.

It was beautiful.

It was just another evening in late summer.

AN HOUR BEFORE, Wallace had been in lab. All summer he had been breeding nematodes, which he found both boring and difficult. Nematodes are free-living, soil-dwelling microscopic worms, only about a millimeter when fully grown. His particular project was the generation of four strains of nematodes, which then had to be crossed together very carefully. It involved, first, the induction of a genetic lesion that was to be repaired in such a way as to yield a desired modification—the termination or amplification of genetic expression, the flagging of a protein, the excision or addition of a segment of genetic material—that was to be shuttled from one generation to the next, handed down like a gap or freckles or left-handedness. Then there was the simple yet careful math required to combine that modification with other modifications in other strains, changes that sometimes required a marker or a balancer: a tweak to the nervous system that gave the creature a rolling rather than sinuous behavior, or a mutation in the cuticle that rendered the nematodes thick like miniature Tootsie Rolls. There was also the dicey prospect of generating males, which always seemed to result in animals that were too fragile or uninterested in mating at all. And then, as always, the dissolution of the worms and the extraction of their genetic material, which had a way of revealing, after weeks of careful breeding and tracking of multiple generations, that the modification had been lost. Then it was a mad scramble, days or weeks spent backtracking through old plates trying to locate the modification among thousands of teeming progeny, the wild and fevered relief of locating—at the last possible moment—the golden nematode in the mass of wriggling animals, and then the resumption of the slow, steady breeding process, herding desired chromosomes and wicking away the undesired ones until the sought-after strain emerged at last.

All through the beautiful days of summer, Wallace had been working and failing to breed this one strain. An hour before, he had been in lab, removing from the incubator his boxes of agar plates. He had been waiting three days for this generation to roll into the next, just as he had been waiting months for this result. He would gather the babies, the fine, almost invisible hatchlings, and separate them, until at last he had his triple mutant. When he checked the status of his nematodes, however, the tranquil blue-green surface of the agar, uncannily like human skin in its soft firmness, was not so tranquil.

It looked disturbed, he thought.

No, not disturbed. He knew the word for it.

Contaminated.

Mold and dust, like one of those horrible re-creations of a volcanic event—whole civilizations frozen in ash and soot and coarse white stone. A soft pelt of green spores covered the agar and concealed at first an oozing bacterial film. The gelatin looked as if it had been scoured by the end of some rough brush. Wallace checked all of his plates in all of his plastic tubs and found shades of horror on all of them. The bacterial contamination was so bad that it leaked through the lids and onto his hands like pus from a wound. It was not the first time his plates had become contaminated or moldy. This had been common in his first year, before his technique and cleanliness improved. Before he knew to be vigilant, cautious. He was different now. He knew enough to keep his strains safe.

No, this level of carnage seemed beyond the scope of mere carelessness. It seemed entirely unaccidental. Like the vengeance of a petty god. Wallace stood there in lab, shaking his head and laughing quietly to himself.

Laughing because it was funny to him in a way that was difficult to clarify. Like a joke leaping unexpectedly from an entirely random arrangement of circumstances. In the past few months, for the first time in his four years of graduate school, he had begun to feel that he might be at the edge of something. He had gotten to the perimeter of an idea, could feel the bounds of its questions, the depth and width of its concerns. He had been waking with the steadily resolving form of an idea in his mind, and this idea had been pulling him through all the unremarkable hours, through the grit and the dull ache when he woke at nine to return to work after going to sleep at five. The thing that had been spinning in the brilliant light of the tall lab windows, like a speck or a mote of dust, had been hope, had been the prospect of a moment of brief clarity.

What did he have to show for all that? A heap of dying nematodes. He had checked them only three days before, and they had been beautiful, perfect. Into the cool darkness of the incubator he had placed them to sit undisturbed for three days. Perhaps if he had checked them the day before. But no, even that would have been too late.

He had been hopeful this summer. He had thought, finally, that he was doing something.

Then, in his in-box, the same as every Friday: *Let's go to the pier, we'll snag a table.*

It seemed to him as good a decision as he was capable of making at that moment. There was nothing left for him to do in lab. Nothing to be done for the contaminated plates or the dying nematodes. Nothing to be done for any of it except to start again, and he did not have it in him to take the fresh plates from their place on the shelf, to lay them out as if dealing a new hand of cards. He didn't have it in him to turn on his microscope and to begin the delicate work necessary to save the strain if it wasn't already too far gone, and he wasn't ready to know if it was already too late.

He did not have it in him.

To the lake he had gone.

· · ·

THE FIVE OF THEM sat in a curious, tense silence. Wallace felt like he had interrupted something by showing up unexpectedly, as if his presence somehow shifted the usual course of things. He and Miller sat across from each other, nearest the retaining wall. Over Miller's shoulder, a veil of delicate roots latched to the concrete, dark insects teeming in its recesses. The table shed burgundy paint like loose hair from a mangy dog. Yngve pulled gray splinters from bald patches left by the paint and flicked them at Miller, who either didn't notice or didn't care. There was always something vaguely annoyed in Miller's expression: a subtle snarl, a blank stare, narrowed eyes. Wallace found this both off-putting and a little endearing. But tonight, resting his chin on his hand, Miller just looked bored and tired. He and Yngve had been sailing, and they still wore their tan life vests open over their shirts. The tassels of Miller's vest dangled like they felt bad about something. His hair was a tangle of damp curls. Yngve was thicker and more athletic than Miller, with a triangular head and slightly pointed teeth. He walked with a permanent forward-canting posture. Wallace watched the muscles in his forearms tighten as he dug out more shards of weathered wood, rolled them into little bundles, and flicked them from the end of his thumb. One by one they landed on Miller's vest or in his hair, but he never flinched. Yngve and Wallace caught each other's eye, and Yngve winked at him as if his mischief were a private joke.

On Wallace's side of the table, Cole and Vincent had brought each other as close as possible, like they were on a sinking ship and were praying to be saved. Cole stroked Vincent's knuckles. Vincent had pushed his sunglasses back across his forehead, which made his face seem small, like that of a needful pet. Wallace had not seen Vincent in some weeks, maybe not since the barbecue that Cole and Vincent had thrown for the Fourth of July. That had been over a month ago now, he realized with a thrum of anxiety. Vincent worked in finance, overseeing chunks of mysterious wealth the way climate scientists tracked the progression of glaciers. In the Midwest, wealth meant cows, corn, or biotech; after generations spent providing America with wheat and milk and poultry, the Midwestern soil had given rise to an industry that built scanners and devices, a harvest of organs, serums, and patches sprung from genetic mash. It was a different kind of agriculture, just as what Wallace did was a different kind of husbandry, but in the end they were doing what people had always done, and the only things that seemed different were meaningless details.

"I'm hungry," Miller said, sliding his arms open on the table. The suddenness of the gesture, his hands sweeping close to Wallace's elbows, made Wallace flinch.

"You were right there when I ordered those pitchers, Miller," Yngve said. "You could have said something then. You said you weren't hungry."

"I *wasn't* hungry. Not for ice cream, anyway. I wanted real food. Especially if we're drinking. And we've been in the sun all day."

"Real food," Yngve said, shaking his head. "Listen to that.

What do you want, asparagus? Some sprouts? Real food. What even is that?"

"You know what I mean."

Vincent and Cole coughed under their breath. The table tilted with the shifting weight of their bodies. Would it hold them? Would it last? Wallace pressed against the slats of the tabletop, watching as they slid on slim, dark nails.

"Do I?" Yngve crooned. Miller groaned and rolled his eyes. The flurry of easygoing taunts made Wallace feel a little sad, the kind of private sadness you could conceal from yourself until one day you surfaced and found it waiting.

"I just want some food, that's all. You don't have to be so obnoxious," Miller said with a laugh, but there was hardness in his voice. *Real food.* Wallace had real food at home. He lived close by. It occurred to him that he could offer to take Miller home and feed him, like a stray animal. *Hey, I've got some pork chop left over from last night.* He could caramelize onions, reheat the chop, slice bread from the corner bakery, the hard, crusty kind, soak it in grease or batter to fry. Wallace saw it all in his mind's eye: the meal made up of leftovers, converted into something hearty and fast and hot. It was one of those moments in which anything seemed possible. But then the moment passed, a shift in the shadow falling over the table.

"I can go to the stand. If you want. I can buy something," Wallace said.

"No. It's fine. I don't need anything."

"Are you sure?" Wallace asked.

Miller raised his eyebrows, skepticism that felt like a slap.

The two of them had never been the sort of friends who traded kind favors, but they saw each other constantly. At the ice machine; in the kitchen where they took down abandoned plates and bowls from the shelves to eat their sad, brief lunches; in the cold room where the sensitive reagents were kept; in the hideous purple bathrooms—they were thrown together like surly, unhappy cousins, and they needled each other in the amiable manner of enemies too lazy to make a true go at violence and harm. Last December, at the departmental party, Wallace had made some offhand comment about Miller's outfit, called it something like the folk costume of the Greater Midwestern Trailer Park. People had laughed, including Miller, but for the next several months Miller brought it up whenever they were together: *Oh, Wallace is here, I guess the fashionista will have some comment*, then a flash of his eyes, a chilly, crooked smile.

In April, Miller paid him back. Wallace came into the department seminar late and had to stand near the back of the room. Miller was there too. They were teaching assistants for the class before the seminar, and it had run over, but Miller had left early while Wallace stayed behind to answer questions for the undergraduates. They stood against the wood panels, watching the slides crawl along. The visiting scholar was famous in the field of proteomics. Standing room only. It pleased a petty part of Wallace to see that Miller hadn't gotten a seat either. But then Miller had bent down close to Wallace's ear, his breath damp and warm, and he'd said, *Didn't they move your people up front?* Wallace had felt a cool, reluctant thrill at Miller's proximity, but in that moment it turned into something else. The right side of Wallace's body went numb and hot. When Miller looked down at him, he must have seen it on Wallace's face—that they were not this kind of friend either, that the list of things they could joke about did not include his race. After the lecture, among the jostling line for free coffee and stale cookies, Miller had tried to apologize, but Wallace had refused to hear it. For weeks thereafter, he had steered clear of Miller. And they fell into that chilly silence that comes between two people who ought to be close but who are not because of some early, critical miscalculation. Wallace had come to regret the impasse, because it precluded their discussing the things they shared: They'd both been the first people in their families to go to college; they had both been cowed upon arrival by the size of this particular Midwestern city; they were both unusual among their friends in that they were unaccustomed to the easiness of life. But here they were.

Miller's surprised silence, the dark caution on his face, told Wallace everything he needed to know about his offer.

"Well, all right then," Wallace said quietly. Miller put his head down on the table and groaned with exaggerated plaintiveness.

Cole, who was kinder than the rest of them and could therefore get away with such gestures, reached over and ruffled Miller's hair. "Come on, let's go," he said, and Miller grunted, then swung his long legs out from under the table and stood up. Cole kissed Vincent's cheek and shoulder, and another cold shard of envy darted through Wallace.

The table behind Yngve was filled by a league soccer team in cheap nylon shorts and white T-shirts on which they had drawn their numbers, loudly discussing what to Wallace sounded like women's tennis. They were all fit and tan and covered in dirt and grass. One of them wore a rainbow headband, and he pointed aggressively at another man, shouting at him in Spanish or maybe Portuguese. Wallace tried to make out what they were talking about, but his seven years of French gave him no purchase on the flurry of diphthongs and fragmented consonants.

Yngve was on his phone, his face caught up in its glow, more pronounced now that night was coming on. Darkness seeped into the sky like a slowly spreading stain. The lake had turned metallic and ominous. It was the part of a summer evening just past the blue hour, when everything began to cool and settle down. There was something salty in the wind, a charged potential.

"We haven't seen much of you this summer," said Vincent. "Where have you been hiding?"

"At home, I guess. Though I didn't know I was hiding."

"We had Roman and Klaus over the other night—did Cole tell you?"

"This is the first time I'm really seeing the boys all week, I think. It's been a little hellish."

"Well, it wasn't anything special. Just dinner. You didn't miss much."

If it wasn't anything special, Wallace thought, then why bring it up? He'd gone to their barbecue, hadn't he? But even there, he remembered, Vincent had said how good it was to see Wallace, how they never saw him anymore these days; he never came out with them or asked about them. *It's like you don't exist,* Vincent had said with a laugh, and Wallace had watched the thick vein down the center of his forehead engorge, wishing with a calm cruelty that it would rupture. Wallace saw Cole, Yngve, Miller, and Emma at the biosciences building almost every day. They nodded to each other, waved, acknowledged each other in a dozen small ways. He did not go out with them, it was true, not to their favorite bars or that time they'd all crammed into two cars and gone apple picking or that time they went hiking at Devil's Lake. He didn't go with them because he never quite felt like they wanted him there. He always got stuck on the edges, talking to whoever pitied him enough to throw him a bone of small talk. Yet here was Vincent, making like Wallace was the only reason he didn't spend time with them, as if they were not also to blame.

Wallace smiled as best he could. "Sounds like you had a great time."

"And Emma and Thom came over last week. We had a little lunch by the pool and went to the dog park. Scout is getting *huge*." Vincent's forehead vein bulged again, and Wallace imagined placing his thumb over it, pressing hard. Wallace made an assenting sound in the back of his throat like *Well, look at that*.

"Where are Emma and Thom? I thought they were coming," Yngve said.

"Getting Scout shampooed."

"How long does it take to shampoo a dog?" Yngve asked in exaggerated outrage.

"Depends," Vincent said, laughing, looking at Wallace, who

was not above much but certainly considered himself above making jokes about dog shit and so simply cleared his throat. Vincent drummed his fingers on the table. "Okay, but seriously, what *have* you been doing, Wallace? You think you're too important to hang out with your friends?"

It was a stupid thing to say. Even Yngve's eyes widened at it. Wallace hummed as if in deep thought, waiting for the flare of irritation and humiliation to subside. Vincent's expression was patient and expectant. Wallace saw a flurry of action at the next table: The soccer boys had started shoving each other, the white of the shirts glowing, so many bright rectangles falling across each other like in a postwar painting.

"Working, for one thing," he said. "That's the only thing, really."

"We love a martyr," Vincent said. "I suppose that's what we'll be talking about tonight. Our Lady of Perpetual Lab."

"We don't talk about lab all the time," Yngve said, but Wallace could only laugh, even if it was at his own expense. It was true: Lab *was* the only thing they talked about. No matter the subject, the conversation always found its way back: *I was running a column the other day, and you will not believe this, yes, I eluted before I finished my last wash. Someone didn't fill the tip boxes, so guess who spent four hours at the autoclave? Is it so hard to expect them to put my pipette back where they found it? They just come and take and never return.* Wallace could understand Vincent's frustration. Vincent had moved to town during their second year to be with Cole, and during the week they all were waiting for their final exam grades, he had thrown a holiday housewarming party.

Instead of drinking cheap beer and admiring the sleek chrome and leather sectional, they had huddled in a corner whispering about the 610 final, with its unexpected helix question at the end, and the 508 exam, which had included a question about free energy changes in various osmotic conditions that had taken Wallace five pieces of paper and calculus he hadn't even thought of since undergrad to solve. Vincent had spent the evening decorating the tree himself while they moaned and fretted, and Wallace had felt sorry for him. But it was automatic, this reflex to turn to lab, because as long as they were talking about science they didn't have to attend to other worries. It was as if graduate school had wiped away the people they'd been before they arrived.

For Wallace, at least, this had been the whole point. And yet he had begun to feel, this summer in particular, something he had never felt before: that he wanted something more. He was unhappy, and for the first time in his life, that unhappiness did not seem entirely necessary. Sometimes he yearned to trust this impulse, to leap out of his life and into the vast, incalculable void of the world.

"I work, too, but you don't see me talking about it all the time. Because I know it would bore you," Vincent said.

"Because that's a *job*. That isn't— What we do is different," Yngve said.

"You talk about it all the time because you don't have anything else to be proud of," Vincent returned. Wallace whistled. The voices from the other table rose in pitch and volume. Every so often, they gave a shout of either celebration or anger. They were all gathered around a phone now, Wallace could see, watching some kind of game. Now and then the bodies parted, and he saw the brightness of the screen for just an instant before it was lost to the cluster again.

"There's more to life than programs and jobs," Vincent was saying. Some noise from the lake, more playful shouts. Wallace looked out over the water, where the dark shapes of the rocks folded into the depths of the shadows over the water. There was music coming from some of the boats nearing the shore, but it all came together in a crackle like static at the start of a radio signal.

"I'm not sure that's true, Vincent," Wallace said. Yngve grunted in agreement. Wallace did not think, however, that he and Yngve were entirely in sync on this point. How could they be? Yngve's father was a surgeon; his mother taught history at a liberal arts college. Yngve had lived his entire life in this world of programs and jobs. For Wallace, to say that there could be nothing more than this meant only that if he should lose it, he might not survive his life. Wallace wondered if he had been too sharp with Vincent, and he turned to him to apologize, but just that moment, Cole and Miller were returning. The pale interior of Miller's thighs flashed. The skin seemed smooth and chaste compared to the rest of his body. His shorts were too short. The cords of his life vest jangled. Cole had a flat-footed, sweeping step and a smudged, puppylike enthusiasm. He and Miller carried white cartons of popcorn and something in a large plastic container: nachos drenched in oozy, rubbery cheese generously spotted with jalapeños. Miller let out an *oof* as he sat down. They had also purchased tacos, which Yngve snapped up, writhing in pleasure.

"Oh yes," Yngve said. "Yes, yes, yes. This is it, boys."

"I thought you weren't hungry," Miller said.

"I never said that."

Cole handed Vincent a small dish of vanilla ice cream. They shared another kiss. Wallace looked away because it felt too private to watch them.

"Do you want some?" Cole asked him, offering nachos, offering popcorn, offering food to Wallace the same way Wallace had wanted to offer food to Miller.

Wallace shook his head slowly, turned from the warmth he felt. "No, thanks."

"Suit yourself," Miller said, but Wallace could feel the weight of his gaze, its heat. He knew when he was being looked at, being watched, as if by some predatory animal.

"Are we still on for tomorrow?" Cole asked, unfolding a white napkin on the table.

"Yes," Wallace said.

The grease from the tacos soaked the napkin through until the wood was visible through its thin, translucent layers. Cole frowned, laid another napkin, and another. The aroma of food cut against the putrid sweetness of the lake. Dying plants.

"On for what?" asked Vincent.

"Tennis," the two of them said in unison.

Vincent grunted. "Why do I bother asking?"

Cole kissed Vincent on the nose. Miller cracked open the container of nachos. Wallace squeezed his hands under the table so hard they popped.

"I might be a little late," Cole said.

"It's fine. I have a bit of work to do anyway." Though it was not *a bit* of work. He felt sick just thinking of it. All that effort wasted. All the effort it would take to repair the damage, which very well could end up wasted too. Wallace had been doing well not to think of it, to set it aside for now. A wave of nausea pressed upon him. He shut his eyes. The world spun in slow, dark, slick circuits. Stupid boy, he thought. Stupid, stupid boy. To have hoped that things would turn out okay, that it would finally be his turn for things to come out all right. He hated himself for being so naive.

"That's *why* I'll be late," Cole said, laughing. Wallace opened his eyes. There was a metallic taste in his mouth, not like copper or blood—something else, silvery.

"You're working tomorrow?" Vincent asked. "We have plans, and you're working?"

"Not for long."

"Tomorrow is Saturday."

"And today is Friday, and yesterday was Thursday. It's a day. There's work."

"I don't work on weekends."

"Would you like a medal for that?" Cole asked, a wet streak of spite wicking across his voice.

"No, I don't want a medal. But I'd like a weekend with my boyfriend, for once, in the summer no less. Forgive me!"

"We're here now, aren't we? Yes? I am here. You are here. We all are here. We're here."

"What great fucking skills of observation."

"Can't we just enjoy the last bit of summer?"

"Wow, sure—*as it's ending*. Brilliant."

"There's a new year starting," Yngve said tentatively. "You know what that means."

"New year, new data," Cole and Yngve said together, their eyes filling with refulgent, desperate optimism. Wallace laughed a little at that. For a moment, he forgot himself, buoyed on their warmth, by their belief in what was possible. New year, new data. He didn't believe it for himself. It was just a thing people said sometimes. A way of getting by. He rapped his knuckles hard against the table.

"Knock on wood."

"God," Vincent said.

"Hey now." Cole put his arm around Vincent, but Vincent just shook him off. He dropped his dish on the table and ice cream leapt over the rim of the cup, splattering the table. A drop of white—lukewarm like spit—landed on Wallace's wrist.

"What would you do if you didn't have this? If you had to fend for yourselves?" said Vincent. He looked at each of them. Miller had raised his eyebrows. Yngve turned a little red. Wallace pinched some of Cole's napkins to wipe his wrist clean.

"Fend for ourselves? Excuse me, but you work in *finance*. Not exactly roughing it," Cole said.

"I didn't say I was roughing it. I'm just saying, what if you had to fend for yourself? Think for yourself? Plan your own fucking life. You'd be lost."

"I don't plan my life? My project? My experiments? Are you telling me we haven't planned our life together? We have *furniture*, Vincent."

"Because *I* bought furniture. When I showed up here, you were basically living in a frat house with these two," Vincent said, sharply motioning toward Yngve and Miller, who looked on stoically. "Plywood on buckets for end tables. Jesus Christ. You don't know anything about furniture, just like you wouldn't know the first thing about getting a real job, real health insurances, taxes. We can't even take a real vacation. Five days in Indiana—what a great time. Wonderful."

"We spent last summer in Mississippi with your parents, didn't we?"

"Yes, but your family *hates* gay people, Cole. There's a difference."

Wallace laughed and then clamped his mouth shut as tightly as he could. He again felt the edge of shame at seeing something private turning horribly public right before his very eyes. And yet he could not look away. They had begun this argument with smiles and soft feints at violence, but now they were snarling at each other. Cole had slid away from Vincent, and Vincent from Cole, which made their bench twist awkwardly. The food slid down the table, now at an angle. Miller caught the nachos before they hit the ground.

Cole smiled at Wallace. "Back me up. It's Mississippi."

"I'm from Alabama," Wallace said, but Cole closed his eyes.

"You know what I mean. Same difference."

"I'm from Indiana, and even I think it's pretty terrible," Miller said. "Vincent has a point."

"You're basically from Chicago," Cole said. "This is not—Vincent just hates my family."

"I do not hate your family. Your family is wonderful. Just deeply racist and wildly homophobic."

"My aunt is racist," Cole said to Wallace.

"His mother said their church is *struggling*. Tell them what the struggle is, Cole."

"A black family joined the congregation. Or tried to. Is trying to?" Cole said, putting his hands over his face. His neck was deep maroon.

"So don't tell me they aren't—"

"There were no black people in my church when I was growing up," Miller said. "Before I stopped going, anyway. It's Indiana."

"I mean, my family didn't really go to church," Yngve said. "Like, there were no black people in my town either. But my grandparents love black people. They say the Swedes are the blacks of Scandinavia."

Wallace choked a little on his own saliva. Yngve squirmed and returned to his taco.

"Anyway, there is more to life than your pipettes and epi tubes," Vincent said evenly. "You're all just playing at being adults with your plastic toys."

Cole was about to respond when Wallace opened his mouth, surprising even himself. "It is silly, isn't it? Still being in school like this. I wonder sometimes, what am I doing here? I guess it's not so silly. Lots of people think that. But still, I think about what it might be like to leave. Do something else. Something *real*, as you say, Vincent." He laughed as he talked. He looked past his friends to the soccer team, who had settled and grown closer and were now so transfixed by whatever they saw that they didn't even think to talk or move or drink their beers. Wallace dug his thumb into the top of his knee until it stung. "I guess I sort of hate it, sometimes, I guess. I hate it here."

The words fell out of him like the exhalation of some hot, dense space inside him, and when he was done talking, he looked up, thinking that no one had really been paying attention. That's how it was. He talked and people drifted in and out of concentration. But when he looked up, Wallace saw that each of them was looking at him with what seemed to be tender shock.

"Oh," he said, a little startled. Miller went on eating his nachos, but Cole and Yngve narrowed their eyes. Their shadows slid across the table. They felt close.

"You can leave, you know," Vincent said. His voice was warm on Wallace's neck. "If you're unhappy, you can always leave. You don't have to stay."

"Wait a minute, wait, hold on, wait, don't go telling him that," Cole said. "You can't just take it back if you leave."

"Doing things that you can't take back is what the real world is, babe."

"Listen to yourself. Suddenly you're a life coach? You're literally a telemarketer."

"You're so pretentious," Vincent hissed. "Like, to a terrifying degree sometimes."

Cole bent around Vincent to stare at Wallace. "Leaving will not make you feel better. Leaving is just quitting."

"You can't just decide what is too hard for someone else," Vincent said hotly. Wallace reached out and placed his palm against Vincent's back. He was sweating through his shirt. His body vibrated like a plucked string.

"Hey, it's all right," Wallace said, but Vincent hardly heard him. "Don't pressure him," he said to Cole. "What is this, a cult?"

"Where is Lukas, I wonder," Yngve said, loud enough that the soccer team heard him. "Do you know, Cole?"

"He's with Nate, I think," Cole said, but he was still staring at Vincent. Yngve flinched. Lukas and Yngve had been more or less in love with each other since their first year, but Yngve was straight and eventually Lukas got tired of pining and found himself a boyfriend who was in vet school. It was an odd but also correct choice, Wallace thought. Sometimes, at parties, when Yngve got very drunk, he said things like *Sleeping with a vet is like bestiality. Like, it's not even a real discipline.* Lukas would just shrug and let it go. Yngve had a girlfriend anyway. Wallace felt sorry for both of them. It seemed more miserable than was strictly necessary.

"Are they coming?"

"Not if they're smart," Vincent said.

The ice cream had turned to a white slurry. Gnats had left the vines on the retaining wall to dart with purpose through the dark at their food. Wallace fanned them away.

"You didn't have to come. You could have stayed at home," Cole said.

"These are my friends too."

"Now they are. Now they're your friends."

"What did you just say to me?"

Wallace glanced at Yngve, who looked terrified; and at Miller, who looked impassive, as if he were sitting at another table entirely. Wallace nodded at Cole and Vincent, but Miller just shrugged. Not surprising. In fact, Wallace himself knew better than to get involved in this sort of skirmish, but he felt bad, like it was his fault. Yngve nudged Miller, but his supreme apathy would not be disturbed. Vincent breathed hard and fast. Water rocked against the hulls of the boats tied near the shore.

"No one is quitting. No one is leaving. We're having a damn good time," Wallace said.

"Yeah, right," was Vincent's reply, but Cole cracked a smile. "Don't be such a crybaby."

"I'm not. No one's crying," Cole said, wiping his eyes with the heel of his palm.

"Poor baby, poor baby," Yngve said as he reached over and ran his hand through Cole's hair. "Are you gonna make it?"

"Leave it," Cole said. He sounded terribly small. He was laughing, but he was crying too. They all tried very hard not to see that, tried to pretend that the moisture in his eyes was something else. Poor Cole, Wallace thought, always so close to the surface. Watching him wipe at his eyes made Wallace's throat hot.

"Well, looks like he's going to pull through," Wallace said. These were his friends, the people who knew him best and cared for him most in the world. They were once more sitting in that awful, full silence, except this time Wallace was sure that it was his fault. He had caused the argument, him and his big mouth. But the funny thing, the joke of it that even he was only just now starting to understand, was that he had said only a part of the truth. Yes, he thought about leaving, and yes, he hated it here sometimes. But running through that feeling like hard, resolute bone was something else: It wasn't so much that he wanted to leave graduate school as that he wanted to leave his life. The truth of that feeling fit under his skin like a new, uncomfortable self, and he couldn't get rid of it once he acknowledged it. It was all the same, gray waiting, a fear of not being able to take it all back.

"You look like you've seen a ghost, Wallace," Yngve said, and Wallace tried to smile. He was breathless with the knowledge of it. Yngve did not return Wallace's smile. Cole tipped forward to look at him. Vincent too. Miller even, furtively, from his food, eating the jalapeños in big handfuls.

"I'm fine," he said. "Really." His throat was tight. There was not enough air. He could feel himself sinking under.

"You want some water or something?" Vincent asked.

"No, no. Yes. I'll get it," Wallace said, croaked. He stood up. Balanced himself with his hand as the world swung loose. He shut his eyes. There was a palm on his forearm. Cole reaching out, but Wallace pulled himself away. "Hey, don't worry. I'm fine."

"I'll come with you," Cole said.

"I said stay. Relax." Wallace grinned, his gums on fire. His teeth ached. He broke away from the table, but he could tell they were watching him still. He made for the lake. He would gather himself until he could once again present to his friends a reasonable semblance of happiness.

. . .

AT THE EDGE OF THE WATER, stone steps descended to the murky bottom of the lake. They were made from a kind of harsh, unfinished stone that had been smoothed by the water and the foot traffic. There were, two or three arm lengths away from Wallace, other people sitting too, watching the moon rise. And on the distant shore, past where the peninsula, furred with pine and spruce trees, hooked into the lake like a thumb, there were houses raised up on great stilts, the lights in the windows like the eyes of some large birds. Wallace had thought at times when he took the lakeshore path at night, looking through the scrim of trees, that all those houses did look like a flock of enormous birds crouching on the other side. He had never been over there himself, had never had a reason to cross the lake to that rarefied and separate part of town.

The small boats had come in and been set on their racks, draped for the night. The larger boats were taken out farther down, near the boathouse, where Wallace sometimes took walks in the other direction, to where the grass grew wild and the trees were denser and heavier. There was a covered bridge and a family of geese living there. Sometimes, he saw their big gray wings spreading out beneath him as they glided across the water. Other times, he saw them lazily and confidently striding in the shade toward the soccer fields and picnic grounds, like stern game wardens. But at this time of the evening the geese were away, and the gulls had returned to their nests, and Wallace had the edge of the water to himself except for the other anonymous watchers nearby. He glanced at them briefly and wondered what shapes their lives held, if they were content, if they were mad or frustrated. They looked like people anywhere: white and in ugly, oversize clothes, sunburned and chapped and smiling with large, elastic mouths. The young people were long and tan, and they laughed as they pushed on one another. Farther back, the great mass of people spread out over the pier like moss. The water beneath him splashed up a little, wetting the edges of his shorts. The stone was slimy and cool. A band was starting up behind him. Their instruments twanged as they whirred to life.

Wallace hugged his knees and put his chin on his arms. He slid his feet out of his canvas shoes and let the lake wash up to his ankles. It was cold, though not as cold as he had expected or would have liked. There was something slick in the water, something apart from the water itself, like a loose second skin swilling around under the surface. There were stretches of days when the lakes were closed because of the algae. It sometimes secreted neurotoxins that could be fatal. Or harbored parasitic organisms that clasped on to swimmers and sucked them dry, or gave them diseases that caused their bodies to tear themselves apart from the inside. The water here could be dangerous even if you didn't know it. But there were no warnings posted. Whatever was in the water was not yet at a level thought dangerous to people. The water stank more now that he was close to it, like alcohol, powerfully astringent and chemical.

It reminded him of the black water that had stared at him from the drain of his parents' sink all those years ago. Black and round, like a perfect pupil gazing up at him, smelling sour, like something gone bad. His father had also kept buckets of still water. *I'm saving that,* he'd say when Wallace tried to pour it out. Saving it the way one saved old clothes or bottles or pens with no ink or broken pencils. Because you never knew what might happen that would make the trash worth keeping. The water in the buckets was as dark as tar because leaves had fallen from the roof into it and had broken down. Sometimes, he saw the frail brown remnants of the stalks, after all the green had been eaten away. At the right angle, it was possible to see the writhing forms of mosquito larvae as they flitted just along the surface. His father had told him once that they were tadpoles. Wallace had believed him. He had cupped his hands in the slimy water and had squinted close, trying to discern the tadpoles. But of course, they had only been mosquitos.

Dark water.

There was a knot of tension high in his chest, something hard and coiled. It felt like a black ball stuck to the inside of his lungs. His stomach hurt too. He had eaten nothing but soup all day. The surface of his hunger was rough, like a cat's tongue. Pressure gathered in the backs of his eyes.

Oh, he thought when he realized what it was: tears.

In that moment, there was a body next to him. Wallace turned, for an instant expecting to see his father's face, conjured up out of memory, but instead, it was Emma, who had come at last with her fiancé, Thom, and their dog, Scout, a shaggy, happy thing.

She put an arm around his shoulders and laughed. "What are you doing over here?"

"Taking in the sights, I reckon," he said, trying to match her laugh. He hadn't seen Emma in a week or more. She worked two floors down, in a lab situated at the end of a long dark hallway. Every time Wallace had visited her—to go to lunch, or to drop something off—he had felt like he was passing out of the biosciences building and into some forbidden place, as if he'd gotten lost and had been sucked into some curious adjacent dimension. The walls were empty except for an occasional bulletin board where yellowed fliers and posters from the 1980s hung as though the opportunities they offered were still new. Emma and Wallace had become friends by virtue of the fact that neither of them was a white man in their program. It had been four years of shared looks over the tops of the heads of tall boys with their upright, sturdy confidence and loud voices and brash propositions. It had been four years of quiet conversations in that long dark hall, moments when it seemed that things might get easier for them. She smoothed her dark curly hair from her face and looked at him. He felt as thin as Cole's napkins in that moment.

"Wallace, what's wrong?" she asked. Her palm was soft on his wrist. He cleared the wet from his throat.

"Nothing, nothing," he said. His eyes stung.

"Wallace, what happened?" Emma had a small face with large features and an olive complexion that sometimes led people to think, in certain lighting, that she was not white. But she was white, if of an ethnic variety. Her grandparents on one side were Bohemian, or Czech, as it was called now. On the other side they were Sicilian. Her chin was keen like Yngve's, but it lacked a dimple. Her hand didn't fit all the way around Wallace's wrist, but she held him tightly just the same.

"It's nothing," he said again, and tried to mean it this time because he didn't know exactly what it was that bothered him. What could he say except that it was nothing?

"Doesn't look like it, mister."

"My dad died," he said because it was as true as any other thing, except when he said it, he did not feel relieved. Rather, it jolted him, like a sudden cry in a quiet room.

"Fuck," she said. "Fuck." Then, collecting herself, shaking her head, she said, "I'm sorry, Wallace. I'm sorry for your loss."

He smiled because he was not sure how to meet someone's sympathy for him. It always seemed to him that when people were sad for you, they were sad for themselves, as if your misfortune were just an excuse for them to feel what it was they wanted to feel. Sympathy was a kind of ventriloquism. His father had died hundreds of miles away. Wallace had not told anyone. His brother had called him. Then had come the social media posts from family members, those concerned and those just after information, that ugly, frothing spectacle of public mourning. It was strange, Wallace thought as he smiled at Emma, because he didn't feel a crushing sense of loss—no, when he thought of his father's death, he felt the way he always felt when someone didn't show up for lab in the morning. But perhaps that wasn't the truth of it either. He didn't know what to feel, and so he tried not to feel anything. It seemed more honest that way. A real feeling.

"Thank you," he said, because what else did one say when caught in the confines of someone else's sympathy?

"Wait," she said, glancing back over her shoulder at the table where the boys were sitting, now occupied with Scout, who was enjoying being petted. "Do they not know?"

"Nobody does."

"Fuck," she said. "Why?"

"Because it was easier, I guess. You know?"

"No, Wallace. I don't know. When is the funeral?"

"Weeks ago," he said, and she looked positively startled by this. "What?"

"Did you go?" she asked.

"No, I didn't. I had work," he said.

"Jesus Christ. Did the she-demon say no?"

Wallace laughed, and his voice skipped out over the water ahead of them. What a thought. That he might have told his adviser and she might have told him not to go. It was tempting to let Emma believe that because it was something Simone might have done. But then it would probably get back to Simone, and he'd have that mess to deal with.

"No," he said. "She's not that bad, you know. She wasn't even in town." Simone was tall and striking, a woman of terrifying intelligence. She was not particularly demonic. More like a constant hot wind that, after a while, wore Wallace down.

"Don't protect her," Emma said, narrowing her eyes. "Did she fucking say you couldn't go to your own dad's funeral? That's sick."

"No," he said, still laughing, doubling over and grabbing his stomach. "It wasn't like that. I just didn't have the time."

"It was *your dad*, Wallace," Emma said. The laughter in him died. He felt chastened by that. Yes, it was his father. He knew that. But the trouble with these people, with his friends, with the world, was that they thought things had to be a certain way with family. They thought you had to feel something for them, and it had to be the same thing that everyone felt or else you were doing it wrong. How could he laugh at the thought of not going to his father's funeral? How strange could he be? Wallace did not think he was strange. He did not think he was wrong or bad for laughing, either, but he made his face into a calm mask of quiet, still sadness.

"Fucking hell," she said. She was angry for his sake. She kicked at the water, sent it flashing into the night, drops of silver fading to black. She then put her other arm around him and hugged him. He closed his eyes and sighed. Emma began to cry a little, and he put his arms around her back and held her close.

"It's okay, it's okay," he said, but her crying only intensified as she shook her head. She kissed his cheek and hugged him more fiercely.

"I'm so sorry, Wallace. God. I wish I could change it. I wish," she said.

The size and scope of her sadness alarmed him. It seemed impossible that this display of grief could be entirely sincere, that her body shook in his arms because of a loss she felt he must have felt. He wanted to cry for her sake if not for his own, but he couldn't. People at nearby tables began to hoot and holler at them, clapping and blowing kisses.

Emma growled at them, but they could not hear it. Only

Thom stood with his back straight, like he sensed something wrong. When Wallace looked back at him, Thom was scowling, glaring. Thom knew that Wallace was gay. He knew that there was nothing between him and Emma. So why was he staring so hard? It was like someone had told him a joke but he hadn't gotten it. He could be stupidly unironic, to the point of self-parody. He had messy hair and wore hiking boots year-round, even though they lived in the flat part of the state and he was from the middle of Oklahoma. Thom was all affectation all the time. He was getting a doctorate in literary studies, and he was strapped to the drowning enterprise of academia. Still, Wallace liked Thom more than he disliked him. He gave Wallace reading recommendations. He talked to Wallace about books the way the others talked about college football and hockey. It was just that every so often, in moments like this, he could be found staring at Wallace and Emma as if he wanted to decapitate them both.

"Well, that's enough of a show," Wallace said.

"No, not yet." Emma kissed him on the mouth. Her breath was warm but sweet, like she'd been sucking on candies. Her lips were soft and sticky. The kiss was brief, but the noise it drew from the nearby tables was deafening. Someone swung a flashlight beam at them, and there they were, kissing down by the water, like something out of a movie. Emma, naturally dramatic, flung her arm back and fell across his lap.

Wallace had never been kissed before, not by anyone, not really. He felt vaguely like something had been stolen from him. Emma laughed against his knees. Thom came down to the water's edge with Scout's leash fisted tightly in hand.

"What the fuck was that?" he asked Wallace, sharply, meanly. "Do you just go around kissing other people's partners?"

"She kissed *me*," Wallace said.

"I kissed him," Emma said as if that explained it. Wallace sighed.

"Emma, we've talked about this."

"He's gay," she said, sitting up now. "It doesn't count. It's like kissing another girl."

"Well, I appreciate that," Wallace said.

"See?"

"No, Em. It's not okay. It doesn't matter if he's gay—no offense, Wallace—"

"I mean, I *am* gay."

"You're still kissing other people," Thom went on. "That's not okay."

"Don't be such a puritan," Emma said. "What, are you a Baptist all of a sudden?"

"Don't make fun of me," Thom said.

"His dad died. I was being a good friend!" She had stood up now. The edge of her skirt—some floral thing, probably rummaged out of someone's closet and sold for pennies—was damp. Wallace sucked in a breath. Thom looked at him.

"Your dad died?"

"He died," Wallace said, with a faint singsong quality.

"Man, I am so sorry." Thom drew him in for a hug. His skin was hot and flushed. His dark beard bristled against Wallace's neck. He had hazel eyes that seemed brown in the evening light. "I had no idea. That's really hard. I'm sorry."

"It's okay," Wallace said.

"No, it's not. And *that's* okay," Thom said, patting Wallace's back with what to Wallace seemed like self-satisfaction. Scout licked Wallace's hand, passing her tongue over palm and knuckles. He crouched down to ruffle her ears. She jumped up and put her paws on his shoulder. She had a woody fragrance like a lime tree. Emma and Thom shared a conciliatory kiss while Scout licked the inside of Wallace's ears.

The three of them walked back to the table, which had grown cramped and boozy. The pitchers of beer had arrived, and a cider for Wallace.

"I ordered it for you," Miller said.

"How thoughtful," Wallace said dryly despite himself, but Miller only nodded.

Fat hornets swam in lazy circles overhead. They occasionally dove for the sweet beer and cider, but Yngve, a conservationist at heart, had been trapping them beneath a cup and walking them to the edge of the pier to release them. By the time he came back, new hornets were buzzing nearby.

"I hate bees," Wallace said.

"They're actually not bees," Yngve tried to interject.

"I'm allergic to wasps," Wallace said.

"Bees and wasps are not—"

"Me too," Miller said. He yawned and stretched. He rubbed his eyes with his hand, which was salty and messy from the popcorn and nachos. He jumped up right away, nearly upending the table. Wallace saw the empty tub of nachos and knew immediately what had happened.

"Shit," Miller said.

"Oh no."

"You okay?"

"No, Yngve. I am not okay," Miller said and was gone, up the stone path, away from them.

"I'll go," Wallace said, before Cole could.

AMONG THE CLUMPS of white people, Wallace saw: a large red man whose golden body hair was lit by the high-wattage lamps at the concession stands; two small boys with toy cars they ran around and around the smooth surface of their table and up the arms of their vaguely tired, athletic parents, whose faces were tight in the sort of mean way that fit people carry; several tables of frat boys all in tank tops, their skin so healthy in the milky dusk light under the trees that they almost glowed with possibility; and groups, here or there, of older people, their bodies and lives gone soft, here to recapture some bit of the past like coaxing fireflies into a jar. The band on the stage, the whole lake at their backs, played something that sounded to Wallace like a Caribbean swing, but as if out of time, on a delay. They wore Hawaiian shirts, and they looked to be about Wallace's age, with shaggy blond hair and keen noses, each so like the other that they could have been siblings. Several torch lamps had been lit throughout the sitting area, but the concession stands had powerful high-wattage lights that pooled in front of them, and it was like emerging from night into day when you stepped up to order overpriced beer, or decent soft pretzels, or brats. Wallace waited in line behind the man with the golden shoulder hair, and when it was his turn at the concession stand, he asked for a small bottle of milk. It cost him $3.50, and the attendant, a scraggly bearded boy with a flat nose, looked at him skeptically as he dug around in the cooler under the counter for the bottle.

Wallace glanced around looking for Miller. He hadn't been far behind him as they'd left the stairs that came up from the concrete path below. The hallways in the union were visible to Wallace because they were lined with glass, and glowed with soft, yellow lighting. The floors were made of a kind of marble that Wallace associated most often with banks. Under the wide, dark cloak of the oak tree at the center of the pavilion, some people had gotten up to dance. He watched as they snapped and swung their hips in a stiff, jerky little dance. Two of the old men were trying their best to get the women to dance, but they only shook their heads and smiled in embarrassment. At the next table were a few younger women, students. They had the boxy musculature of athletes, and large square heads. Their laughter was deep and serene. Two of them got up to dance with the old men, and their friends clapped for them, and it was like a wave, suddenly, everyone at every table turning to look at them and clapping, and the band began to play more vigorously, the music scraping through the air like a shovel through gravel. It wasn't pretty. It could scarcely be called music, Wallace thought, but the pairs went on dancing, and soon they were joined by others, and two frat boys got up and did a parody of the dance, but then they seemed to get shy and to turn away from each other and let their thick arms fall by their sides. But then Wallace came back to

himself. A shadow fell on him through the glass, and he saw
Miller walking down the hall, to the bathroom. They passed
each other on opposite sides of the glass, him outside, Miller
inside, but Miller didn't see him or pretended not to, as if in
a dream.

WALLACE FOUND MILLER at the sink, splashing water up into
his eye, getting it all over his shirt and chin in the process. He
winced and cursed softly under his breath the whole time. They
were alone.

"Hey, let me help," Wallace said.

"I'm so stupid," he said. "I completely forgot that I hadn't
washed my hands."

"Happens," Wallace said, setting the bottle of milk aside. It
was cool from the ice. He rinsed his hands under the tap. The
bathroom smelled like beer and antiseptic. It didn't smell at all
like piss. The lighting was dim. It felt too clean to be a bathroom,
which made Wallace uneasy. The countertop was some sort of
cheap black stone. The plastic bottle was sweating. Miller regarded it through narrowed eyes. The mirror was tall and con-
cave. Wallace had to look away from their reflection. "Can you
crouch a little, bend down?"

Miller didn't move at first. Wallace thought he'd done it
again, exposed himself. But slowly, Miller did begin to move,
like he'd made up his mind about something, and he bent his
knees and turned just a little so that his face hovered over the
sink. He was perfectly vulnerable. Wallace twisted the cap from

the milk bottle and held it over Miller's eyes. His hands shook. A drop of milk fell from the lip of the bottle and landed on Miller's cheek, just below his eyelashes. Wallace swallowed. He watched Miller breathe. He watched Miller wet the corner of his mouth. Water dripped from the tap.

"Here we go," Wallace said. He poured just a little of the milk into Miller's eyes, watched it run in a white stream across the bridge of his nose into the sink. Miller closed his eyes. "You can't do that. You have to keep them open." Miller grunted. He opened his eyes. The milk struck the inside of the sink with a soft tapping sound. He poured half the bottle into Miller's eyes, and then thoroughly wet two paper towels. He squeezed the water into Miller's eyes, which were brown with little blue rims on the outside. The whites of his eyes were already starting to redden. The water ran into Miller's eyes, and he again closed them instinctively, but then he opened them after a moment. Wallace blotted Miller's thick eyelashes with the paper towels, filled them with more water, rinsed, blotted again.

"Okay," Wallace said, "there, there."

"Come on. Don't make fun of me."

"I'm not," he said. He tried to be gentle as he washed Miller's eyes, reapplying water each time, rinsing, dabbing. "I did this to myself one time. I picked peppers with my grandparents and rubbed my eyes when I got sleepy," Wallace said, laughing a little at himself, at how miserable he'd felt, his eyes swollen like grapefruits and so tender. He looked down at Miller, saw his sunbleached hair, his long eyelashes. Wallace felt like he'd been kicked in the stomach. Miller was staring at him; of course he was. Where else would he look except up, and who was there but Wallace to intercept his gaze? Of course he was staring. "All done," Wallace said. He dropped the bottle into the trash under the sink.

"Thank you," Miller said. "It's not so bad. Just hurt like hell."

"It's like that. It always hurts worse than you expect, even if it doesn't do any real harm."

They stood at the sink, the faucet dripping little bit by little bit. Wallace's hands were damp and cool. Miller's eyes were puffy and red, as if he'd been crying. Miller leaned away from him, against the wall, which had the effect of making him seem shorter. The music coming through from the outside was soft and nonthreatening, like the caress of wind through the trees. Wallace twisted the damp paper towels in his hands. Miller reached for them, his large hands opening and then closing around Wallace's fingers.

"Are you really thinking about leaving?" Miller asked.

"Oh," Wallace said, laughing nervously because he could appreciate, in this moment, how silly, how ridiculous he had sounded before. "Who knows? I think I'm just clenched up."

"I think we're always clenched," Miller said after a minute, and he squeezed Wallace's fingers. "I think we're always tight until we get what we really want, and maybe even then, too. Who knows?"

"Maybe," Wallace said.

Miller pulled on his hand and Wallace let himself be drawn in. They didn't kiss or anything like that. Miller just held him until the sound of the music changed. It was time to go back out to their friends. They held hands until they reached the sliding door that opened into the night air, and then, tentatively, reluctantly, they became separate people again.

"See you there," Miller said to him, raising his eyebrows.

"See you there." Wallace made his way back through the crowd, his body buoyant but raw. Some inner surface had been agitated. When he sat back down, they all asked him where Miller was, and he could only shrug. "He said he'd be back."

"How is he?" Cole asked.

"He's better. He was too tall to reach the faucet, so you know, for once being short paid off."

"Poor guy," Emma said.

"He's fine," Wallace said, lifting his cup of cider. It was tart, and a little lukewarm. There was the bitter, chemical taste of the plastic. They were all looking at Wallace. Emma's eyes were wet. Cole kept peeking at him furtively, and Vincent kept swallowing thickly. Yngve was looking at him over the surface of his beer. Scout rolled between Thom's legs. Her collar tinkled faintly like a little bell.

"What?" he asked. "Is there something on my face?"

"No," Cole said. "We just . . . Emma told us about your dad. I'm so sorry."

Wallace had known this would happen, and yet he felt a momentary flare of anger at Emma. Things moved through the group in this way, information sliding around as if through an invisible circulatory system, carried on veins made of text messages, emails, and whispered conversations at parties. He wet his lips, and he could still taste Emma there. The flare did not subside, but it gave way to resignation.

"Thank you," he said neutrally. "Thank you very much."

"It must be so hard," Yngve said with a shake of his head. His sandy brown hair flashed in the light. His sharp features softened, except for the point of his chin, which always made him look boyish. Yngve had spent the summer before graduate school climbing a mountain after the death of his grandfather, a benevolent Swede.

"Yes," Wallace said. "But life goes on."

"That's true," Thom said from the end of the table. "Life goes on. It reminds me of my favorite novel."

"Oh god," Vincent said. "Not again."

"'And all the lives we ever lived and all the lives to be are full of trees and changing leaves.'"

"That's very pretty," Wallace said.

"Don't encourage him," Emma said. "He'll go on all night."

"*To the Lighthouse*—it's actually a line misquoted from a poem," Thom said proudly. "It's one of the best books I've ever read. Changed my life in middle school."

Vincent and Emma and Cole all shared a look. Yngve was back studying the grain of the wood through the pale yellow of his beer.

"I'll have to check it out," Wallace said. He looked up, and Miller was coming back to them. He had another pitcher of beer.

"Here we are," Miller said. He sat across from Wallace again, but did not look at him. Wallace felt a little hurt by that, but he understood, could understand, the awkwardness of such things.

"I should get going," Wallace said. "This has been wonderful."

"No, don't go," Emma said. "We just got here."

"I know, my love, but before that, I was marooned with these goons."

"So you don't love us," Cole said. "I see how it is."

"Are you okay?" Yngve asked. "Do you want me to walk you home?"

"I live across the street. It's a short commute. I appreciate it."

"I guess I'll leave too," Miller said, which drew a startled silence from the table. "What?"

"Why are you leaving us?"

"Because, Yngve, I'm tired. I've been in the sun all day. I'm a little drunk. I want to go home."

"Then let's all go together."

"No, you stay," Miller said. Wallace was already getting up from the table, hugging Emma and Cole and Vincent. They all smelled like beer and salt, sweat and good times. When they shook hands, Thom gazed into his eyes for a long time in what Wallace guessed was an attempt at solidarity. "Wait for me," Miller said.

"You live in the other direction," Wallace said, pointing.

"But we have to leave through the same entrance."

"Okay then," Wallace said.

Miller repeated Wallace's good-byes, and they walked out to the street together. Overhead, there were a few bright stars in the sky. The music swept the air, echoing through itself into a blurry medley of indistinct sounds. People were getting into and out of cars, so there was a bit of activity. Wallace and Miller stood under an overhang, half in shadow.

"Why did you leave like that?" Miller asked. "Was it me?"

"No," Wallace said. "I'm just tired."

Miller searched his eyes for the truth. He was worrying the corner of his lip. "I'm sorry about the bathroom."

"Why? It's okay."

"No, it's not. I shouldn't have. I feel like I took advantage of something."

"Oh," Wallace said.

"I'm not into guys," Miller said. "But I see how you look at me sometimes, and it's like, does he hate me? Does he like me? And I hate the idea of you hating me. I do."

Wallace was silent. He could still see the water from here, the way it was lighter in the distance and darker near the shore.

"All right."

"I don't know what to do about it," Miller said, balling his fingers into a fist. He looked like he was about to cry, but it was only the moisture from before.

"There's nothing to do."

"Is that true?"

"It's okay," Wallace said again, meaning it, wishing it to be true. "We just held hands. It's junior high."

"I don't know. God," Miller said, stepping toward Wallace and then away.

Wallace sighed. "Do you want to come back to my place?"

Miller regarded him suspiciously. "I don't know if that's a good idea."

"Well, I'm tired and I'd like to go home."

"I'll walk you there."

"Great," Wallace said. The desire to be at home in his bed was overpowering. They walked the block down the street, passing a large circular apartment building, and a small bar on the corner, which was bumping music loudly. Some white people were out front smoking. He felt their eyes follow him up the street. Miller walked close by, their elbows and then fingers brushing occasionally, which made Miller look down at him. Wallace, to his credit, did not return Miller's gaze. What was this life, currently? What was this strange place into which he'd been thrust? He now regretted walking to the lake. He now regretted going with his friends. Not because Emma had told everyone about him, but because now something that had previously seemed simple had turned messy, difficult, complicated.

HE TOOK MILLER up the stairs to his one-bedroom apartment. The window had been left open, so the apartment smelled like the lake and like summer evening. It was cool because of the fan going in the bedroom. Miller sat at the counter and watched as Wallace made them coffee in the French press, which was a minor novelty to Miller.

When there was no avoiding the topic, Wallace climbed up onto the counter and sat with his legs crossed, coffee warm in his hands. Miller was picking at the edge of a piece of paper.

"So what's this all about, Miller?"

"I feel bad," he said. "I feel bad about the bathroom, about that thing I said in April, about all of it. I feel like a shitty friend. A bad person."

"You aren't."

"I just wanted to be clear. I'm not into guys. I'm not gay, or whatever. I just, I don't know."

"It's okay. You were being a good friend."

"I'm not so sure I was. I was being stupid. I saw you kiss Emma, and I thought—well, you know."

"Yeah, I'm not sure if I get what you mean by that," Wallace said. He drank from the coffee. His sink was full of dishes from earlier in the day. "You saw Emma kiss me and thought—what? Well, if we're all kissing people we're not attracted to, maybe I can try it?"

"No . . . yes. I guess it was something like that. And then you got up to leave, and I thought, Oh fuck, I've done it now."

"That's very kind of you."

"I do want to."

"You want to what?"

"Kiss you," Miller said.

"Oh."

"Is that wrong?"

"No. It's not. But you know, you just said you didn't."

"I do. I want to. I shouldn't. But I do."

"Okay," Wallace said.

Miller squinted at him. The apartment was dimly lit by the kitchen light and whatever light came in through the broad living room window that overlooked an alley.

"That easy, huh?"

"What can I say, I'm easy."

"You're so bad at jokes," Miller said, rising from the stool and coming toward him. He blotted out the kitchen light, and so

Wallace was completely in his shadow. He could feel the warmth of Miller's breath on his cheeks. Miller reached up with the tips of his fingers and pressed them to Wallace's lips, used his thumb to make space between them. Miller was looking down at him intently, not nervous or shy. He had done this before, that much was evident, been in such a position of power, control. Even so, there remained a bit of restraint, an awkwardness. There was a hitching quality to the way he drew his thumb back across Wallace's lips. Wallace closed his mouth around Miller's thumb and sucked the salt from its rim slowly, tenderly. "Why are you like this?" Miller asked.

Wallace did not answer. He pulled on Miller's shirt and sat more upright so that their bodies touched. Miller standing between his legs, bending just a little, and then, their lips coming into contact, the passing friction of it, the heat, the flicker of dampness. Wallace had been kissed only twice now, but he couldn't understand why it had taken so long to get to this point of intimacy, which felt so good that he was afraid of losing it.

Miller kissed him again, and Wallace involuntarily made small mewling sounds, which only encouraged Miller to kiss him more. Wallace felt as if he were being searched for something, as if each kiss, pressed to a different part of his mouth and jaw and cheek, was meant to yield some sort of answer to a question that wasn't being asked. Miller's hands were on his hips and then on his sides, going higher and higher until they arrived at his jaw, where they stopped. The sailing had roughened them, made their texture exciting on Wallace's skin. His kisses tasted like beer and ice, cold and sharp. He bit Wallace's lip.

"I'm enjoying this," Miller said. "More than I thought I would."

"That's nice," Wallace said. It seemed to be the wrong thing to say because Miller frowned and then went to pull away from him. But Wallace wrapped his legs tightly around Miller's waist, stilling him. "Hey, where are you off to?"

"You didn't seem that into it," he said. "I don't want to make you do anything you don't want to do."

"I'm into it plenty," Wallace said, and he guided Miller's hand between his legs, where he was hard. Miller gasped a little, jolted in surprise as if remembering that Wallace was a man like him, but he was not chastened by this. He wrapped his hand around Wallace tightly, maybe a little too tight, and pressed his lips to Wallace's neck.

"I don't—I don't know how to," Miller said.

"It's okay," Wallace said. "It's not too hard."

Miller laughed. "I'm not a virgin. I just . . . This is . . . Well, you know." He made a vague motion with his hands.

WALLACE'S BEDROOM WAS STILL DARK, except for the open window, which was blue-black from the streetlight below.

Wallace shut the blinds and the room was darker, shades of gray layered over each other, but this was his room. He knew its dimensions perfectly, and he knew that Miller was standing at the edge of the bed. He came up to him from behind, catching Miller unawares, and pushed him. Miller's body resisted at first, just a little catch, and then he landed on the mattress with a bemused sigh. Wallace climbed onto the bed next to him, and they lay that way for a long time, or what seemed like a long time, the edges of their bodies just barely touching.

Wallace couldn't remember the last time he had lain with someone this way, in that nearly innocent configuration that comes before sex when both parties pretend to want everything other than that, letting their bodies wind up to the point of unbearable tension. He reached for Miller first, his hand against Miller's chest to feel the rhythm of his heart, its fast, hard beat.

They kissed again, the slow, downward sweep into desire. And then they came out of their clothes, shedding them like skins, so that when they touched again, they were bare and quivering like small, naked beings new to the world.

"Get under the sheets," he told Miller, who obliged him. When they touched, it was so impossibly tender and fearful that Wallace could have wept for the boy he'd been at seven or eight, when he was touched for the first time, neither tenderly nor fearing that the touch might do him harm. Wallace was determined to give Miller what nobody had thought to give him, determined that at the end of this, whatever it was, Miller wouldn't learn to fear his body or what it could contain. Miller's fingers dug into his hair as his head bobbed between Miller's thighs. He took Miller deeper into his throat, and there was the final, strangled gasp.

They fell asleep sore, covered in minor scratches and bruises. They fell asleep tangled together. They fell asleep, but Wallace did not dream. He skimmed beneath the surface of waking, gliding along a vast silver sea of light, viewing it from below, the world passing him by, passing over him.

Miller's body was so warm and heavy against him. Hard in odd places that felt unfamiliar to him. While Miller slept, Wallace traced his fingers along the bones of his hips, through the sparse pubic hair above his cock. Sailing had indeed changed Miller's body, not that Wallace had been familiar with it before. But there was something about its underlying firmness and the residual softness of his stomach and thighs. It was a body in transition. Miller's chest hair was soft and curly. Asleep, he looked sweet, gentle, like a little boy in a grown man's body. There was vulnerability in the way he had his hand draped over his face, a peace and depth to his sleep that suggested to Wallace a level of comfort, of innocence.

How long had it been since Wallace had slept well and easily? How long had it been since he had felt beyond the world's grasp? Miller made a small sound in his sleep and rolled over, seeking out Wallace's warmth. Wallace lay back down next to him and let himself be enfolded. The hum of the fan fell in and out of his perception. Would their other friends wonder where Miller had gone when they arrived home and found him not there? He shared a place with Yngve. It would be unusual if he stayed out. It wasn't his habit. Even if he and Wallace were friends, it would be unusual, but well, there was tomorrow to worry about that.

Wallace got out of bed and went into the kitchen, where he poured himself a tall glass of very cold water. He drank it slowly, letting it numb his tongue and throat, until swallowing was hard and his thirst felt both sated and unquenchable. His stomach expanded. He almost gagged, but he kept drinking. Down and down and down, swelling, welling with water. He refilled the glass, right up to the brim. He drank it. His lips were red. He kept drinking. He drank four glasses back-to-back, and he went into the bathroom and threw up. Up came the water, the semen, the kernels of popcorn, the sour cider, the soup from lunch, all of it churning and orange in the bowl. His throat was raw and burning with acid. He trembled as he braced himself against the toilet bowl. The stench drew more vomit from him, a heaving, clenching retch.

He felt empty when it was done. He blotted the vomit from his mouth, brushed his teeth, and went back into the living room. He sat at the edge of the couch and folded his legs under himself. Outside, the moon was a perfect white circle. The world was still and quiet. He could see into the building across the alley, into the lives of the people who lived there. One of their lights was on, and there was a man ironing at his kitchen table.

The sounds from the other apartments in the building gave a texture to the silence of Wallace's apartment. He heard someone singing off-key to a song that was popular that summer. And then, farther off, a ringing sound, not like a phone, but like water hitting a pipe.

Wallace was nervous about his friends finding out about Miller, not because he was ashamed of it, but because he was afraid Miller would be and wouldn't want to do it again.

One blow job in the dark. That was it.

"Where are you?" came a voice from the other room.

"I'm out here," he said, his throat still hot.

Miller came dragging out of the bedroom with Wallace's comforter wrapped around him. He sat next to Wallace. He smelled sour from sweat, but still very good, pleasant.

"What are you doing out here?"

"I didn't want to wake you up."

"You couldn't sleep?"

"No," Wallace said, smiling a little. "But that's nothing new."

"Why?"

"Why what?"

"Why can't you sleep?"

"I don't know. It's been hard since my dad died."

"I'm sorry," Miller said. He nodded as he said this, and then he kissed Wallace's bare shoulder.

"Thank you," Wallace said.

"Were you two close?"

"No, not really—that's the crazy thing, isn't it? We didn't even really know each other."

"My mom died two years ago," Miller said. "She had breast cancer for a long time, and then it was in her liver and then it was all over her body. She died at home."

Wallace put his head on Miller's shoulder. "I'm sorry," he said.

"What I know is that it doesn't matter if you didn't know them or they didn't know you. My mom was a real bitch. She was mean and hateful and a liar and spent my whole life tearing me down. But when she died, I really . . . I don't know, your parents aren't people until they're suffering. They aren't people until they're gone."

"Yeah," Wallace said. "That's it. Or some of it, anyway."

"My mom died, and I thought, Oh shit, oh shit. Because I had spent so long hating her, resenting her, and then she was suddenly facing this thing she couldn't beat, and I just, I really felt for her."

"Did you say good-bye or anything?"

"I was there every day," Miller said. "We played cards and argued over television and she made fun of the music I liked and I cooked for her and she told me she loved me." Miller's eyes had begun to darken, cloud with tears, but none fell. "And then she was gone."

"I'm sorry," Wallace said, stupidly, lacking anything more significant to say.

"I can't tell you what to do about your dad. I can't tell you what to feel, Wallace. But I'm here if you need me. I'm your friend if you need me. Okay?" He took Wallace's hand and Wallace let him. They kissed again, tenderly, faintly, briefly. It seemed silly to them, and they laughed. But then Miller lay on top of him and drew the blanket over their bodies, and Wallace, for the first time in a long time, let someone inside him. It hurt at first, like it always did, but that pain and the joy of his body remembering its keenest pleasure was enough to get him hard again, and through it. Miller was easy on him, but he knew what he wanted, and he pursued it relentlessly. They were both breathing hard by the time it was over.

THEY WIPED THEMSELVES clean in the bathroom light. Wallace felt like a beaten egg, frothy and messy. There was a throbbing heat inside him, like a private little sun glowing. Miller looked at him with clear, sober eyes.

"I'm not going to lie to you," he said. "I am very confused by all of this. I don't know what to do about it."

"That's fair," Wallace said, choking back hurt. "It's fine."

"No, let me finish. I don't know what I'm doing. It's all probably wrong. But I liked this. It was good. Don't beat yourself up."

"I'll try not to take it personally."

"Wallace."

"Okay—thank you for your candor."

"Forget it, forget it."

"No, let me try again."

But Miller was already leaving the bathroom and going into the kitchen. Wallace followed him.

"Hey, where are you going, come back, I'm sorry."

"Can I have some water?"

"Sure," Wallace said, but his cheeks and neck were hot because he remembered from before, the drinking and throwing up. He poured Miller a glass, the same one he had been using. He watched Miller drink, the flex of his throat, the swallowing action. He thought of his own mouth on the glass, the transference of his taste to Miller's lips. Did he taste him there?

"Stop watching me; I'm getting self-conscious," Miller mumbled around the glass.

"I'm sorry," Wallace said, and made a show of looking away, back into the building across the alley, to where the man was still ironing at the sink. Had he seen them fucking on the couch?

"More please," Miller said. Wallace lifted the carafe and poured the last of the cold, clear water into the glass. Miller watched him as he poured, and he watched Miller watch him. The water level rose and rose until it was almost overflowing, spilling down their fingers. But it didn't. Wallace stopped just short of that point, the point at which the water wavered on the very cusp of the container that meant to hold it, the point at which things swell to an unbearable height before giving way, the point at which something must either recede or break and extend.

"There," Wallace said. "Enjoy."

"Thank you," Miller said, and he drank it all in one big gulp with his eyes closed, as if in ecstasy.

2

The other labs on the third floor of the biosciences building are empty, as if after the rapture. Strangely, it's also not dissimilar from catching a glimpse of someone undressing when they think they are alone, the twin thrill and shame of the voyeur. The air carries the salty scent of yeast media. Wallace's mouth waters. Below him, the atrium is filled with gauzy light. Dry yellow vines wrap around the railings, the floor glossy with wear. If he jumps, he thinks, he will plummet, a slow sweep through empty space, a horrible way to die. He feels, momentarily, the heat of the impact, the ghostly wet of his skull collapsing. The illusion of weightlessness gives way. The elevator slides shut with a rebounding clang.

It's a little after ten a.m. on a Saturday.

At the end of the hall, light spills out of Simone's lab. Katie stands at the table centrifuge. It is an enormous gray machine, emitting a high whine that rises in pitch until it bleeds into the mechanical noise of the lab: rattling cages and clinking glass beakers strapped to agitators, mewling coils behind the incubators, the dull roar of the air conditioner overhead. Standing there is like being in the peristaltic system of some large animal, amid the sounds of a body adjusting itself. Katie does not look at him.

She's blond with quite small features, as if someone had wiped away her original face and painted in its place a delicate, miniature facsimile. She balances a green ice bucket on her hip and she's slapping a pair of pale blue nitrile gloves across her thigh. Impatience. Boredom.

Wallace walks quickly by her, as if he might slip her notice, but she says, "Let's get this shit done."

"Let's get it done," he says gingerly. He's been caught, he knows. From up the lab—for it is really three rooms linked end to end, two benches per bay and five bays per room—a chorus of *Let's get it done* comes back at them. The others sweep in and out of his line of sight as he makes his way to his bench. They are all here in this bright cluster in the middle of a cool dim building, for a moment its vibrating core. A minor comfort.

In the lab, there are only women: Katie, Brigit, Fay, Soo-Yin, and Dana.

Katie is almost feral with a desperation to graduate; she emits a kind of raw and blistering energy. They all look away from her. She is their senior, just ahead of Brigit and Fay. Brigit is a natural, curious and dynamic, but with a preternatural memory that feeds on whole bibliographies of developmental biologists. Fay is awkward and nocturnal, short and so pale that when she pipets, you can almost see the shadow of blood sweeping up her forearms to her muscles. Her experiments are precisely designed if inconclusive, with minuscule error bars, something Wallace admires to the point of envy. Once, in lab meeting, Simone commented that Fay was trying to deduce some subtlety too fine to matter. Soo-Yin lives in the small lab among the chemical reagents and the tissue culture closet. There she plates thousands of tiny cultures, clumps of grayish cells that grow and divide, or else die, in pools of brilliant red media. Wallace once found her there, like stumbling upon a spirit in a myth. She had been dabbing tears from her eyes with her bare forearm, dabbing and pipetting simultaneously in one unbroken motion. She had a heavy scent to her, like salt water. The youngest is Dana, taken in the year after Wallace. Their adviser has not taken another student in some time. Every couple of months, the group hears whispers of rumor: retirement, migration to the Ivy League, leaving for an adviser position in government, consulting work. Rumors as insubstantial as they are numerous and temporary.

For the most part, the lab is quiet. Clipped questions dart through its cool, bright air: *Do you have any 6.8 Buffer? Did you make new TBE? Where is the DAPI? Why are we out of scalpels? Who forgot to order dNTPs?*

Two floors up, in Cole's lab, Wallace has heard they play Frisbee together on weekends and sometimes visit each other outside the lab. Most of Cole's lab came to his barbecue with Vincent, and when he asked Cole about it, Cole gave him a look of profound confusion: *Of course I invited them! They're my lab!* When Katie showed up with Caroline, then just a few weeks postgraduation, Wallace went to stand in a corner with them. He was drawn to them out of a kind of loyalty, although the room was full of people he knew better and liked more. Caroline and Katie talked, but only to each other, not to him. Caroline let out a sigh and said, "Here we are again." And Katie nursed her wine, looking through the glass out onto the patio, where the grilling was happening, watching a fifth-year swim lazy strokes in the pool. They languished there for hours, no more than a handful of words passing among them, but instead of making an excuse and heading off to find a friend, Wallace stood there with them the entire night—even after Caroline, having drunk perhaps too many beers, started scowling openly. Even after Katie rudely told Vincent that the meat looked undercooked and she wouldn't be having any. He stood next to them because he had felt no impulse to leave.

Today, the other desk in Wallace's bay is empty. This would not be the case, he thinks, if Henrik were still here. Henrik would be striding from his desk to his bench and back again, half starting a dozen tasks before settling finally on one. Henrik was a thick-necked former football player who had attended a small college in central Minnesota, where he studied chemistry and also was a tight end. It was Henrik who taught Wallace to dissect, to do it in the dish rather than on the slide because it gives you more time and range of motion; how to wait for the worms to grow still; how to time everything just right so that you could cut through a mass of nematodes, severing their heads in a single stroke, fifty at a time. He taught Wallace the perfect angle at which to slide the slender needle into their germlines, that mass of beautiful cells, like roe. He taught Wallace many things, including how to put slides together for presentations and how to calm down right before, running your hands under cold and then warm water. (*Get the temperature up, Wally, bring the heat.*)

Sometimes, Wallace saw Henrik's face when he closed his eyes, or heard his voice, warm and Muppet-like, silly sounding, a man who would always be a boy, perhaps. There was something vigorous and rough about him, like he might wrap his arm around your neck and dig his knuckles against your scalp at any moment. But there were moments, too, when Henrik drew to his full height and towered over you, moments when you were suddenly aware of his strength. Wallace had once watched him fling a five-gallon jar to the ground in a rage because someone had left the lid off. Another time, Wallace had been inoculating colonies, and Henrik shoved him aside and slammed the gas off and said, "That's not right, that's not aseptic technique." He slapped the wooden spindle from Wallace's hand so that it clattered with a pathetic little noise on the bench top. During lab presentations, everyone in the room could feel Henrik's body in the dark, as if they were all keeping one eye on him, waiting, waiting. It was strange to hear him raise his voice because it didn't lose the Muppet quality. It just sounded like an unhappy Kermit, shouting down conclusions that he thought were facile or uninteresting: *What is this, a goddamn campfire? The data do not support it! They don't! They don't support it!* Wallace was always a little ashamed when Henrik made him jump. It made him think of the days when he was young and his brother used to clap his hands in front of Wallace's face, suddenly and really hard, then call him a sissy for flinching. *What you jumping for? You think I want to hit you?* Wallace hated the way his body reacted to Henrik. Against his will. Again and again, like hands clapping at the edge of his nose.

But Henrik is gone now, at Vassar running his own lab, teaching undergraduates the same way that he taught Wallace. Is it envy that Wallace feels? There's a bit of dust on Henrik's old desk, a green highlighter; it's no shrine. Wallace swivels back to his own desk, piled with papers: protein alignments, plasmid library forms, strain sheets, some articles he's been meaning to read for months. His computer is asleep; an amber-tinted version of himself glints back at him. His coffee from yesterday is covered in a skin, the creamer gone rancid. He is dithering, he knows. He can't bring himself to look at his bench, though he knows he must, and so finally he lifts his head and forces himself to look, to really look, to see.

Wallace's is one of the larger benches in lab, inherited four years ago from a departing postdoc who had left for Cold Spring Harbor to study stem cells in the gut of mice. The bench is wide, black, and smooth, made chalky from years of sliding the hexagonal bases of Bunsen burners or the hard feet of microscopes across its surface. A set of blond wood shelves is set farther back on the bench to divide it from the bench on the other side, Dana's bench. Bottles of fluids, colored and clear, sit in stubby white plastic racks like peering children. Tools, implements, stuck into every open space, jeer at him. And on the open space of the bench are the towers of plates, the agar dishes solemn and silent, like some miniature slum. His microscope is dark, waiting, and Wallace feels its weight like an albatross or a warning.

Katie watches him over her shoulder in an act of indifferent surveillance, and it is then that he remembers *the other thing*. Among Wallace's ruined experiments: immunostaining and immunohistochemistry data he had been tasked with generating, because it is the one experiment that Wallace can do better than anyone else in the lab. Like a savant or a trained circus seal, to hear Simone and Katie tell it: a perfect seven hundred dissections in under eight minutes, a precise accounting, all variables and conditions marked and measured, the microscopy penetrating and clear. Wallace's talent is not for looking, exactly, so much as it is for waiting. He can pass hours in the embryonic dark of the microscope room waiting for the confocal to take its z-projections, slicing in micrometer-width sections through the bulk of the germline, each cell a perfect kernel through three channels of fluorescence. That his gradients are clearer, sharper than even Katie's, does not reflect a superiority on his part—a greater mind, for example—so much as it demonstrates that Wallace has the time to burn, time for the idle stupidity it takes to sit in front of a scope and wait for hours. Sometimes an entire day passes without him leaving the dark, pausing only to change the slide, look for more germlines, focus the beam of the laser as he waits for a shape to emerge. Simone asked him to perform this task for a publication meant to sit at the heart of Katie's thesis, and he agreed because they so seldom turned to him for things he felt equipped to handle. And he was preparing to do that, aging the nematodes just so—and it's now, watching Katie watch him, that he understands why she's so irritated with him. Those worms are gone now too, lost to the mold and the contamination. It's not the worst thing in the world. He can restart the experiment. But it is lost time, which is precious to Katie. She is closer to the end than he is. She expects more from her hours, can expect more. Bitter regret, then. Katie turns from him, pops open the centrifuge. The brown sediment of pelleted cells. She slots in another.

The machine cries softly again.

AT HIS MICROSCOPE AT LAST, Wallace slides plate after plate under the objective. Only mold, like a cotton field in late fall, dark and muddy, prickly with stalks. Clumps of bacteria. Bad enough, these terrible environmental conditions. Bad enough the pits in the agar through which the nematodes sometimes slither and find themselves pressed flat to the plastic base of the dish, which sucks all the moisture from their bodies. But there is also something more worrying to Wallace: dead eggs. Nematodes whose germlines are fisted and gnarled. On some plates, tiny larvae struggle, winking glyphs. Their numbers are smaller than he expected, as though there was some other, underlying problem at work even before the carnage took hold. Some invisible calamity. They are not just drenched in spores, which makes it hard enough. The mold has made them sterile, their bodies filled with vacated spaces, as though their delicate reproductive tissues have been puffed with air. Vacancies in the body cavities. Unusual morphology. He knows it when he sees it. There is a chance that his strain is sterile, that the combination of genetic modifications has rendered a nonviable organism; it will die out. This might be an answer to a question. Or it might be the result of contamination, mere noise. He will have to be careful. Even more careful.

Picking twelve worms from fifty plates means six hundred plates, all of which have to be passaged multiple times to free them of the mold, which means something like eighteen hundred plates. And on top of that, more screening. This is why he fled— the weight of the work it will take to fix this. It feels impossible in the way only possible tasks can seem, when you know that despite the scale of what you must do, it's not really beyond the realm of possibility to do it, and so it feels impossible because you know you must. For a moment he's tempted by the notion of giving up, starting fresh, not trying to make heads or tails of the mess before him. He looks from the scope at the stacks of plates. They creak when he adjusts them. He could throw them away. Wallace rests his forehead against the eyepiece of his scope.

"Goddamn. Goddamn. Goddamn."

Henrik would know what to do, Wallace thinks. Henrik would say, *Get to it. What are you waiting for?* Wallace reaches for his pick, a glass capillary melted around a flattened segment of titanium wire. He holds a metal striker over the burner, turns on the gas, strikes. The rotten, faintly sweet smell of natural gas, then, ignition, orange glow, a few sparks dissolve, fire. He burns the end of the pick to sterilize it. He takes a fresh plate, coats the end of his wire in *E. coli* to use like glue, and slides under the objective one of the old plates. It's like staring down through the top of a canopy. He waits for signs of movement, rotates the glass in the base of the microscope to change the angle of light so that things shift into curious metallic shadow, searches, waits, searches, rotates, waits, searches.

At last he sees a worm, the briars of spores stuck to its back, and he sends his pick down through the air, lowers it like the claw machine, and taps it gently, softer than gently, and up the worm comes, from its world into the air, swimming back up, attached to the pick. He sets it down on a clean plate, all that open space; it's surreal.

One worm.

Five hundred ninety-nine to go.

He lowers the pick. Begins.

THE ANIMALS ARE NOT DEAD—this is a relief. He expected worse. They are more sterile than he anticipated, shriveled oocytes and empty sperm ducts, which magnifies the task. These he burns in the flame like an angry deity.

Brigit, in soft gray clothes, sweeps past Wallace into his bay and pours herself into Henrik's old chair.

"Wally," she says, exasperated. "Mom's in a mood today."

"She's pissed about my plates, I bet."

"Tough break." Brigit is full of compassion. She has always been good to him, in an uncomplicated sort of way. She gives off no sense that she expects anything for her kindness or feels she is treating him in any remarkable way. Which is perhaps what seems so remarkable to Wallace, who is not accustomed to uncomplicated offers of help, to generosity. Brigit tosses her legs up on Henrik's desk. She folds her hands smoothly across her stomach. "Funny thing about that, huh?"

"What?" Wallace asks, glancing back at her from the scope. Something in her voice catches inside him, a note of cool suspicion.

"No, nothing," Brigit says. "It's just funny how your plates got ruined that way. I mean, and out of nowhere, yet everyone else's in that incubator was— No, I've said too much." She puts her arm over her eyes, feigns being overwhelmed, sighs.

"What do you mean, their plates are fine?" Heat and the low murmur of fury. He rotates fully on his chair. Brigit is a little shorter than Wallace, dark haired and freckled. She is Chinese American, from Palo Alto, where her mother is a cardiologist and her father took early retirement from one of those primordial tech start-ups eaten by Google. She had been a dancer before she settled on science—bad ligaments, she said—and she retains a gummy flexibility, much solidity beneath the softness of her good nature. Her expression at the moment is one of conspiratorial glee. They have a tendency toward gossip, these two.

"Nothing concrete. No. Not at all, but I heard from Soo-Yin, who as you know has plates on the racks right below yours, that her plates were totally fine. In the clear. Not even a *mote* of dust."

"That makes absolutely no sense," Wallace says. He sounds hoarse even to his own ears, his voice a pitchy jangle. Brigit raises her eyebrows and shrugs. But then her expression tightens, closes slightly. She drops her feet from the desk and rolls in the chair to him. Up close, the harsh light of the lab throws a glare across her dark hair, caught up in a messy bun.

Her voice is low when she speaks. "I think someone fucked with your plates, Wally. I'm not saying I saw anyone. Or anything like that. But I wouldn't be surprised. Because Fay saw *you-know-who* here late all week, and you know that *you-know-who* hates working after five sharp."

"*You-know-who* being Dana?"

Brigit shushes him loudly, makes a big show of looking around pointedly. "What do you think?"

Dana, who comes from Portland or Seattle or some more minor city out there. Once, in her early days in lab, Wallace saw her running her protein preps through the wrong column. She had used the kits for a DNA purification. He went up to her and said, as casually as he could, "It looks like you've got the wrong box there—it's an easy mistake, they look so similar, I know."

Dana put her hand flat on top of the blue-and-white box and frowned at him.

"No, I don't," she said.

"Oh," Wallace said. "Well, it just says DNA prep there, on the side, I mean."

Dana, her eyes hazel and wide like a cat's, had pressed her tongue to the roof of her mouth three times in quick succession, a disapproving sound.

"No, Wallace," she said, her voice slow, steady. "I'm not retarded. I think I'd know if I were using the wrong kit."

Wallace stood there, a little shocked by the intensity of the response, but it was her bench, her experiment. She could do what she wanted. So he backed away from her, his face hot.

"Okay, well, if you need anything."

"I won't," she said.

He watched her for the rest of that day. He was in his second year then, she her first; they were young and still finding their way. What did Wallace know? After all, he'd always felt a little uneasy in the lab, a little uncertain. And he thought everyone felt that way. Insecure. Unwilling to ask for help because it meant baring your belly. He had wanted to say something to her about that, that he knew it could be scary to say you didn't know something, but that people wanted to help, mostly. He had wanted to be a good lab mate, a supportive person. But instead Dana had drawn a thick, dark line between the two of them. He was one way. She was another. She was gifted. He was not.

But at the end of that day, Dana stood staring at her columns, wondering what had gone wrong. She stood there, staring at the printout of the purity readings, which made no sense, of course. The spec reading said that there was no protein at all in the tube. But she couldn't understand why. Hadn't she followed the directions? Simone stood at the end of her bench looking at the data with her. She waved Wallace over, and he went shyly. Night had been falling in a smooth dark veil beyond the window. He saw all three of them reflected there in the light of the lab.

"Do you know anything about this, Wallace?" Simone asked.

"About what?"

"Dana's results. She says that you mixed up the kits."

Wallace frowned and shook his head. "No. I think Dana was using the wrong one."

Simone turned the box around and pointed, and Wallace saw there in the neat print that the kit was the protein one. He felt an inky, slippery feeling inside.

"Did you maybe put the DNA purification reagents in the wrong box when you were doing those simultaneous cleanups? Wallace, you have to be careful."

"I didn't," he said.

"Well, these numbers don't make sense otherwise."

"And you tried to warn me," Dana said with a high yet flat tone. She shook her head. "I guess maybe you felt like you'd messed up."

"You have to pay more attention," Simone said. "I know you want to be ambitious and get things done, but you have to be careful."

Wallace swallowed thickly.

"All right," he said. "All right."

Dana put her hand on his shoulder and said, "You know. If you need anything."

Wallace looked at her. He looked at her, and tried to understand what sort of person she was, but all he saw were the flakes of dead skin collecting in the gingery hair that grew between her eyebrows.

Simone had him sort out the reagents again, in front of her. She made him sort them into two neatly divided groups on his bench. And when he was done, she made him do it again, just to make sure, just to make sure.

"She wasted her whole day on it, Wallace. Her whole day. We can't lose that kind of time because of carelessness." Simone stood at the end of his bench and watched him sort out the reagents and the columns, their neat white bottles, again and again. He could have done it with his eyes closed. Because he was careful. "This isn't to punish you. This is to make you better."

Still, even for Dana, ruining his plates on purpose seems excessive. She is not entirely malicious, just lazy and inattentive to detail.

"How late?" he asks Brigit. "I've been here till midnight at least. Every night."

"Two a.m.," Brigit says, and Wallace jerks up from her.

"No way."

"Like I said, I didn't see anything. That's just what I heard."

"What sense would that make?"

"It doesn't have to make sense. She's *gifted*," Brigit says, spitting out Simone's favorite word for Dana but meaning the opposite. Wallace laughs. Gifted is the sweetness meant to make the bitterness of failure palatable—that a person can fail again and again, but it's all right, because they're gifted, they're worth something. That's what it all tracks back to, isn't it, Wallace thinks. That if the world has made up its mind about what you have to offer, if the world has decided it wants you, needs you, then it doesn't matter how many times you mess up. What Wallace wants to know is where the limit is. When is it no longer forgivable to be so terrible? When does the time come when you've got to deliver on your gifts?

Brigit pushes up from the chair and kicks it back under Henrik's desk. She sighs, stretches. He can hear her bones realigning, the joints popping. "I just thought you might want to know."

"I don't know if I feel better," he says, and she puts her arms around him in a loose hug.

"Hang in there, Wally," she says. Katie passes the end of his bay swirling another large beaker, but seeing the two of them, she turns on her heel, pivots, and is gone.

"Like I said," Brigit says. "In a mood."

"She's not the boss of me," he says.

"Maybe not. Maybe so."

Brigit backs out of his bay, waves. He salutes. He is alone again.

It makes no sense for Dana to have ruined his stocks. They are on different projects, in part because of something that happened the last time they worked together. To help Dana learn the techniques of their lab, Simone had thought it would be a good idea if she worked with Wallace on a project that required the generation of various oligo strands of DNA. But Dana, who is a genetics student, felt that she should be the one in charge of designing the oligos, despite having little practical experience in the technique. Though Wallace had already designed at least two hundred successful oligos, Dana would not listen to him as he tried to describe his strategy for designing, his thoughts on optimal annealing temperatures, targets in the genomes, what was feasible to clone and knit together using enzymes, screening methods, competent cell lines. He tried maybe twenty different kinds of interventions, pressing on her stubbornness at different junctures in the process, but all of it rebounded on him. She did not want his assistance.

Unsure what else to do, he went to Simone. At a point when they should have had, say, twenty oligos ready for injection, Dana had slowed their progress to the point where they had none. "Wallace," Simone said, "maybe you should try a different tone. Are you being a little presumptuous?" And when he said no, she said, "Are you *sure*? Because Dana is bright, bright, bright. Don't talk down to her." When it came to the injections, Dana was clumsy and sloppy. She skewered the animals with the needle, which she could not load because she kept pricking her finger with it, requiring Wallace to load it himself. She was also slow in getting the animals loaded onto the sucrose pad and dabbed with levamisole and buffer, which kept them sedate and hydrated, so her worms turned into hard pralines right there on the slide. He tried to help her. He talked softly, quietly. He waited even when he knew the animal was dead. Once she turned to him with such a look of pride on her face that he thought she'd finally done it, but when he looked at the animal under the scope, he saw that it was beyond dead. Its insides had ruptured out and backed up into the needle end itself. It was awful, a gruesome death.

At last, tired of their failed collaboration, he asked to be given a different project—and, it was true, Dana maybe did not take it well. But that was two years ago. These days, on any given week, Dana shows up to lab for a handful of semi-productive hours. She hasn't settled on a project. Her mind is rangy, restless. But worse, failure causes her to discard things and people. Every time a project does not go according to her expectation, she scuttles it like a decommissioned watercraft. Her lab presentations are an amalgam of half-chewed ideas. Her fingernails are bitten raw, and there's a chafed, bruised feeling to her.

Still, it makes no sense that she would brutalize his plates. There is no material gain in it for her, and her selfishness has always seemed pragmatic to Wallace. It would be a pointless, essentially lazy move.

His head hurts.

People can be unpredictable in their cruelty.

The thought startles him. He thinks swiftly of that awful time last year when he had to take his preliminary exams and spent three months unable to get out of bed or to eat or to bathe regularly. Those three months were a long, dark slide into something amorphous and cold. He spent all that time watching old doctor shows on the internet and lying in bed watching the light on the walls change. When he did manage to pry himself out of bed, he sat in the tub for long hours and felt afraid and small. He spent hours wondering what he would do if he failed. Not even the humiliation scared him as much as the utter drop into the unknown. He'd have to leave the program. He'd have to figure out a different thing to do with his life. That's what paralyzed him all those months. It was impossible to do anything.

Then, one day in late September, Henrik came to Wallace's apartment and pressed the buzzer until Wallace relented and let him in. Once upstairs, he dropped a stack of research articles and notebooks and markers on Wallace's floor and told him to get to it. For hours every day, Henrik taught Wallace everything he'd failed to learn. They covered cell signaling, gradients, morphology, protein structure, the composition of cell walls, the entire lineage of the gonadal tissues in flies and nematodes, yeast screens. Technique after technique Henrik diagrammed, patiently and then less patiently, and when that failed he slapped his thick palm on the table and shouted, *You have to learn this, Wallace. Get it together.* Wallace sat there listening. Taking notes. Reading the articles every night until the text swam before his eyes. He lost five pounds, then ten pounds, then fifteen pounds.

Henrik started taking him to the gym. Forcing him to jog and to read, to recall at any moment some obscure fact of nematode embryological development. To recall the degradation machinery of certain proteins in certain tissues under certain conditions, and then other conditions, other tissues, scenarios swinging open and closed like a door on loose hinges. Wallace got to know the way light moved through Henrik's beard. And through his thick hair. The long slope of his mouth. He learned to read Henrik's temper the way mammals on doomed islands learn the slow, unwinding signs of an eruption.

On the bleak December afternoon when Wallace passed his preliminary exams, like a firing squad more than a test, the first person he looked to at the celebratory lunch was Henrik.

But by then Henrik was already looking away, out the window.

They spoke sparingly at Simone's annual holiday gathering. Three days later, Henrik left for a tenure track position at Vassar. And then Wallace went to the departmental Christmas party and made that comment about Miller and trailer parks.

Wallace misses waking up at three in the morning and finding Henrik curled up in his living room, asleep, the heavy sound of his snoring, the bulk of his body almost deforming Wallace's cheap couch. He misses their meals together, the almost angry way Henrik ate. He misses, maybe, also, other things, the weight of unnamed feelings moving through him. And those feelings were transmuted into something cruel and mean.

There was an economy to it, even when you couldn't see it at first, a shadow calculation running underneath all their lives.

In the end, it doesn't matter who did this. In the end, none of it matters.

Back to work, then.

THE KITCHEN IS EMPTY. Wallace beats his palm against the reluctant handle of the faucet until it gives way, and the water comes out too hard, too fast. It strikes the basin with a sound like a protest, as if upset at Wallace's force. He runs the water into a battered gray pot and sets it on the electric range. The stove groans to life. The abandoned, mismatched mugs crouch in the back of the cupboard like children in foster care. Wallace presses his face to the warm glass of the window. Below him, the main street splits around a Lutheran church. Leisurely traffic. One vein of the street trails delicately around the biochemistry complex, and it ends at the boathouse and the botanical gardens, where in springtime there are fund-raising parties at which wealthy white people fling bits of bread at koi and talk in hushed, slurred voices about the changing demographics of the university. When Wallace was a first-year, he was invited to a welcome dinner at those very same gardens. At one point that evening, he was herded over to a heavy, bearded man who smelled like sweat and oak leaves. *This is Bertram Olson, Wallace. He's the one who endowed your first-year fellowship.* And there, in the descending darkness, holding a sweating glass of ginger ale, Wallace suddenly comprehended just what the object of the welcome dinner was. *Welcome. Here is the person who pays your stipend. Please worship him.*

Wallace considers himself fortunate in this way at least. His stipend is generous, twice what his mother made as a housekeeper, and it affords him a general material ease: He can afford food, rent, and other items like his laptop and his new glasses, which cost almost a thousand dollars. It's not very much money. But it's the most he's had in his entire life, and more still, it's consistent. It comes every month, can be depended upon. The water comes to a swift gray boil, and Wallace pours it over the chai that he purchased from the overpriced grocery store downtown. Money is always on their minds: who got the big departmental fellowship (Miller), whose adviser had a grant rejected (Lukas's), which lab receives private research dollars (Wallace's), whose project is likely to translate well to industry (Yngve's), who will grab the job at Brandeis (Caroline), who will take the job at MIT (Nora, a postdoc in Yngve's lab), who is maybe leaving for Harvard (Cole's adviser), for Columbia (Emma's adviser), for UT Southwestern (no one). They discuss the lives and fates of faculty the way one might track the paths of minor planets. Careers move in orbits, fixed by certain factors. One typically stays at the level of their graduate or postdoc institution, or goes one step lower. It's difficult to migrate across tiers. Fellowships lead to good postdocs, good postdocs lead to good grants, good grants lead to faculty positions at institutions that are more or less commensurate with the stature of one's first faculty adviser. It all rises and falls on money. Wallace's stipend now comes from a moderately prestigious, nationally recognized research fund. Simone is considered senior in their field. They enjoy a path forward, into the future, that is level and good. It is for this future that he has worked his entire life. For the alignment of these particular advantages.

Yet *the terms*, Wallace thinks. The terms of all that luck. The cost.

The tea is a compromise. He wants coffee, but coffee would make the work difficult. When he started in the program, Wallace went through three triple cappuccinos every day before three p.m. just to stay awake. During the afternoon seminars he found himself dozing, drifting off to the sound of talks on deep sequencing and protein NMR. Professors kissed the backs of their teeth and spoke in that smooth, glossy voice popular in certain widely circulated videos on arts and sciences. Everything was *I'm going to tell you a story*, or *Today, I'm going to share with you three intriguing narratives* or *I'd like to walk you through how we got from* here *to* here. And in the rigid chairs of that auditorium, where there was no cell service or Wi-fi, where all the wood was blond and the walls were covered in an undulating wave of wood panels and the floors in acoustically favorable carpet, Wallace drifted as if floating in waters he could not swim. He drank more caffeine than he ever had in his whole life, and he spent his afternoons with hot, forceful diarrhea.

Wallace drank so much coffee that the world seemed a little brighter for it, on the verge of turning convex, as if every fragment of light were reaching out for him. And then, one day, Henrik gave him a piece of advice: *Caffeine is a stimulant*. This was mystifying to Wallace. It seemed like a fake aphorism. Henrik said it to him every time Wallace returned from the basement café with a cup of coffee, whenever he and Henrik were in the elevator together returning from a seminar at which Wallace had helped himself to one complimentary cup after another. His heart fluttered. His mouth went dry. His fingertips grew stiff and swollen. He felt as if he were being squeezed through his skin like sausage from its casing. He was startled by strange sounds in the middle of the night when he was working in lab alone. One day, during his dissections, his hand convulsed wildly, a sudden shooting spasm, and he dropped the scalpel. It landed with a soft, sick sink into his thigh. Not terribly deep, but enough, and Wallace knew, in that moment, exactly what Henrik had meant.

The white tiles are an ocean of light in midafternoon, and gray pages shift under Wallace's tender eyes. He presses his thumb to the knuckle of each of his fingers, eliciting a solid crack from the joints. A bird rests on the flat white ledge outside. It's pecking at the inside of its wing. Small, round thing, gray feathers and white belly. Its head is small, nearly indistinguishable from its body. Just a round ball of fluff. The bird's shadow hops along the floor, and Wallace watches until it's gone, vanished into the air. On his way to lab, Wallace stopped at the library and found that book that Thom had mentioned.

He reads in lab on Saturdays, when it's less likely that Simone will be around. In Wallace's second year, Simone came into the kitchen and found him reading and eating cup ramen. That day a strong storm had been blowing through the area, and the world had turned an eerie shade of aquamarine. Simone stood standing at the window watching the wind and the rain, the sallow glow of the streetlights below. She turned to him with a restless, angry look and asked sharply, *Do you not have better things to do than reading Dr. Seuss or whatever the hell that is?* And Wallace set the book down very slowly and gave a weak, defenseless shrug. *It's Proust,* he said. *He's French.*

Wallace is thirty pages into the novel when there's a shadow pressed to the corner of the page, as insistent as a thumb. Miller's impassive expression, his eyes distant and cool. There is accusation in his gaze. Messy hair. A gray sweatshirt, the shorts from last night, miles of tan leg, the coppery hair like down.

"You left me."

"I left a note," Wallace says.

"I read it."

"Well, don't cry about it."

Miller grunts, but there is a smile. Wallace is relieved, an uneasy buoyancy like drifting out to sea.

"I'm just saying you could have woken me up."

"You looked peaceful, though," Wallace says. Glossy with condescension, he settles back into the stiff purple booth with more confidence than he feels. Miller has a giant's natural indifference to the world, hanging back, watching from under the rims of his eyelids. Wallace wavers. The edges of his body tingle, like the electric range coming to life. A whine spreads through him, coils heating. Some inner surface goes slick and hot.

"Still," Miller says, "you didn't have to bail on me. *In your own apartment.*"

"Do you want to sit?"

"I can."

Wallace makes room on the seat, drops the canvas bag to the other side of himself. Miller's skin is warm. They're thigh-to-thigh. The sticky sweat of the plastic cushion beneath them, Wallace shifting to make room, the dampness of his skin pressed to Miller, who is dry and not quite so warm. They tuck their arms tight by their sides. They are sitting closer than is exactly necessary. Wallace glances down at Miller's bony ankles. The bare, pale cartilage at the back of his feet. Remembers too the salty taste of Miller's skin, so different from his own, the bodies of others somehow always so different, as if made from rare elements, strange metals. Miller pops his knuckles, glances back over his shoulder at Wallace. A look—shame or something else. He puts his head down against the inside of his shoulder. A shy boy, then, Wallace thinks, shy and watchful.

"How are you?" Miller asks. Disappointment. A conventional question. All that playful teasing gone to waste.

Wallace puts his elbows on the table, which rocks sharply, dangerously. The tea shifts. Sloshes. Miller's eyes widen just so, and Wallace holds his breath until the table and the cup and the whole world steady themselves.

"Are we strangers now?" Wallace asks. *"How are you?"*

Miller frowns. The disappointment sharpens. "How are you" is the kind of question you ask in a doctor's office. There is no meaning in "How are you." But perhaps that is why Miller asks this question. A soft reset. A denial of sorts. Wallace runs his tongue around his mouth, thinking it over. Trying out different answers. Miller's frown goes taut. The edges of his mouth pull and then relax. A sober, dark light in his eyes.

"I didn't say that. I just asked how you were, because of last night, I mean. You know."

"Is this junior high?" Wallace asks. "You're an adult. Say it."

The exasperation on Miller's face lights Wallace up. A silver thrill, a frisson of pleasure.

"Don't be obnoxious, Wallace," he says. "Come on."

A reward then, Wallace thinks. He will be generous. He kisses Miller's shoulder, rests his face against its solid shape. It is a relief to rest his eyes, if only for a moment. Miller's large hand on his thigh then. Cool and dry, coarse. A low laugh in his body.

"Hey now," Wallace says, but Miller has already taken his hand away.

"What are we doing?"

"I don't know. You tell me." The crinkling plastic. The wood frame beneath them groaning. Wallace slides away; his skin sputters. Miller slowly rotating the mug with this thumb on the handle.

"I was just trying to be considerate. That's why I asked."

"Is that what this is, then? Your consideration?"

"Don't be a brat."

"Don't lecture me," Wallace says in another momentary flare of pride, of cantankerousness. Miller briefly looks stricken, but he recovers, turns more fully on Wallace, which puts his back to the rest of the kitchen. They are in a corner. The sun streaks across the bridge of his nose, under his eyes, everything bright and golden. They are close. The room a chattering gray static. Miller's eyelashes seem so painfully soft. Wallace presses his palm over Miller's eyes, feels the edges of his eyelashes tickle his hand. There is another current, relief at not being watched, seen up close that way. Miller's face a gentle boy's face again, sullenly patient. Another reward, Wallace thinks. Gets up on his knees. The cushion sinks deep under his weight. He steadies himself with a hand on Miller's shoulder.

"What are you doing?" Miller asks, the edge of concern. Wallace hums, resists answering. Feels the tension in Miller's body. He is the taut coil now, winding under Wallace's hand. He levels their faces, aligns their lips and noses and eyes. Stares into the blank dark ridges of his own knuckles over Miller's eyes. Miller shifts more. Surely he feels Wallace's breath. The press of his body. Asks again, "Wallace. What are you doing?"

Wallace almost laughs. Almost says, *Exercising agency.* Almost says, *Let me tell you a story.* But he says none of this. Closer now. Their lips touch. The soapy aftertaste of toothpaste. Sharp alcohol of mouthwash. The deeper, more stubborn residual flavors of sleep. No coffee for Miller. Wallace tastes Miller's lips. Their soft cupid's bow and then their corners. Then deeper through the lips into the mouth, a damp warm cave.

Enough, he thinks. Retreats.

Miller does not open his eyes right away. Wallace feels a little pulse of worry, that he has gone too far, too fast. That he has erred, miscalculated. But then, the slow upward sweep of Miller's eyelids. The angular shard of sunlight across his eyes now.

"Your hands smell good," he says.

"It's the tea. Have some." Wallace presses the lip of his cup to Miller's mouth, and with his eyes set firmly on Wallace, he drinks. The throat works it down, swallows. "Good boy."

"Blow off tennis," Miller says. Wallace sets the cup down, holds his breath.

"Can't."

"You *can*," he says.

"Sorry."

"What about after?"

"Let's play it by ear," Wallace says, feeling gummy. His knees shake. Miller's breath smells like the chai, like Wallace's hands.

"Let's," he says.

Wallace gets up. Takes his book, the bag.

"Well, work beckons," he says, coming around the table, but Miller reaches out, takes his hand.

"Wallace."

"Don't be stupid about it," he says. "Let's be smart."

Miller drops his hand. The sunlight striking the back of Wallace's neck and legs prickles.

"Sure," Miller says with a grunt. "You bet."

A WORM, proceeding through a series of gathering and unlatching motions, pulling itself along.

Nematodes are transparent. It is one of the features that make them an ideal model organism, amenable to microscopy. Other features include a facility of genetic manipulation, a small, manageable genome size, a short generation time, and the ease of handling. They are quite hardy creatures, in fact. Capable of self-fertilization. At a certain point in larval development, their germlines switch from spermatogenesis to oogenesis. *Even the little boys get to be young women*, Simone likes to say.

One worm on a single plate can give rise to thousands of

progeny after just a week or so. When food is scarce, they cease reproduction to some degree. Though whatever fertilized embryos there are undergo development and hatch inside their mothers. They eat their way out, eventually rupturing the cuticle to enter the world, sometimes with fertilized embryos of their own inside them. It reminds Wallace sometimes of creation myths.

The worm he selects just that moment is severely bagged. There are dozens of smaller worms inside it. She's old. She's dense with bodies. Yet she's still alive. She's no mere vessel. No good to pick starved animals. Their descendants are born with a signal for disaster going off in their bodies.

Wallace can still taste Miller. It was a mistake to kiss him again. Strange that he has become a person who *kisses*. The coppery taste of shame at betraying oneself. Nausea, as if he must now explain this change to some higher power, some greater authority. He is surprised at himself, at his traitorous body. His mind a tumult, hazy and dark shapes opening, turning upon themselves. The ghost of Miller's warmth in his bed, the morning light dulled by the curtains, the pale rise of his hip, his curly hair, the room sour with sweat and beer. A swirl of dark hair on his chest. Regret. At having left him in bed this morning or at having left him in the kitchen? Both. Neither. Oh, Wallace, he chides himself. There are more important things.

The lab is bright and quiet. He hangs to the side in his chair to stare down the length of the lab, finding no one else. At the far end just bluish shadow, stillness. The part of the day when the others recede and there is just him in the quiet and the dark, and the world outside is vast and blue and beautiful. Outside, there are birds in the pine tree across the street. Small, dark birds fluttering near the top of the tree. How strange to be a bird, Wallace thinks. To have the world beneath you, that inversion of scale, what is small becoming large, what is large becoming small, the way a bird can move where it wants in space, no dimension unconquerable. He feels a small mercy at being left alone. The others will return at night, descending like a dark flock upon the building, pushing their experiments and nudging their projects toward completion in small, painful increments.

The quiet is really the amassing of noise. The protests from the agitating machines like the cries of an unruly populace. In this building, he is outnumbered. But the noise soothes something in him. When Wallace was very young, he kept his fan on all the time, even in winter, because its regular rhythm made something about his life easier. When he turned the fan toward the wall, it sounded like the ocean, or like the creek, when you were approaching it from the south through the pine forest at the edge of his grandparents' farm. He worked on math and science homework that way, getting better and better at it until he was the best student in the whole state of Alabama at doing long division in his head and estimating the weight of a bowling ball in metric units. When the fan in his room was going, he couldn't hear his parents arguing about who had taken the last Natural Light from the fridge or who had eaten the last piece of fried chicken or who had let the greens burn on the stove, a charred mess stuck to the bottom of their one good pot. He couldn't hear his brother and his girlfriend next door, the constant rap on his wall drowned out by the seascape. He could, if the window was open, hear the baying of wild dogs in the woods, their lonesome yips and howls rising up out of the trees like ghosts or birds. He could hear the echoing crack of rifle fire and the explosion of canisters tossed into the burning barrel out back. It wasn't the world outside that he had needed to drown out, then, but the world inside, the interior of the house, which had always seemed so much wilder and stranger to him than anything he found walking alone in the woods.

And when he got older, he turned on the fan to drown out the snores of the man his parents let sleep on their couch because he had nowhere else to go and he was their friend, after all. Sometimes Wallace wonders if the fan was also the reason he didn't hear when the man got up in the middle of the night, walked into his room, and shut the door.

That old anger rolls over in him. His vision swims briefly. He hasn't thought of it in years, and yet there it is, the sound of that door closing that first night. The finality of it as the bottom of the door swept across the gritty hardwood, a scraping sound. Something awful. That jittering thud and the retreat of gray shadow as his room was sealed in darkness. Deep, inky darkness. Why does it return to him now? All these miles away. These years. His previous life cut away like a cataract. Discarded. But here, found stuck to the bottom of his mind like a piece of garbage. Here. In this place. Alone in the lab. He almost jumps at the fright of it, the wholeness of the memory. His body remembers. His traitorous body.

His father is dead—his father who did nothing for him.

Dead, for weeks now. Wallace forgot it. He managed not forgiveness, but erasure. They seem so much the same to him.

His father. A sizzling, glowing wire of hatred. Wallace's vision is dimpled, as if pinched from the corners and pushed inward. This life drawn carefully across the other, former life. He does not think of it. Turns his mind from it entirely. They are again as strangers might be, faces fleetingly familiar in a great stream of faces. It is the kindest thing that he can do for himself and for them. There can only ever be a tenuous claim on the lives of others.

"Still working I see," says a voice—Dana's, he knows, before he even looks up.

"Some of us have a lot to do."

"And some of us are self-important," Dana says. She hoists herself up onto Henrik's old bench. Her angular athleticism, her ascetic thinness set against her wide face. Her fingers raw and flaking. She digs into the corner of her nails, extricates a flap of skin, and chews it off. White gristle. A trickle of blood. They are silent. They watch each other. She's staring at him from under her eyelids. She manages to look down and up at the same time. Her sweatshirt is loose, threatens to swallow her. A girl with a shell. She might vanish into it and leave them all behind. Her insult doesn't get under his skin because the casualness of her voice is thin and reedy, a desperate feint.

"Is there something that I can do for you, Dana? I'm busy," he says as he turns back to his bench. He adjusts the plates next to his scope. He has lost his appetite for work. His hands are no longer steady. A tremor winds its way up and down his fingers. His knuckles ache.

"Come on, don't be that way." A cool laugh. Wallace stretches his fingers. The smell of gas, the low blue flame burns on.

"I'm not being a way, Dana. I'm just busy. Perhaps you have heard of this thing called *research*. It requires *work*. Are these terms familiar to you?"

"You sound like Brigit. You two are such a weird little cult."

"*Friendship*, Dana. It too might be an unfamiliar concept for you."

"Admit it," she presses on. "You two are so cliquey. You hardly talk to anyone else. You're, like, the only two people in lab. And you talk so much shit about the rest of us."

"We're friends, Dana. We enjoy speaking to each other."

"I heard what you two were saying. I know what you two talk about when I'm not around," she says quietly.

Wallace spins so that they face each other again. He is surprised to find her looking down into the space between her thighs. Her scalp is red, dry. It is a curious position for her. As if someone set a stuffed animal on a shelf and left it. The blank vacancy of her body. He feels a flicker of sympathy, the memory of last night, being discussed like an object of communal fascination.

"Even if we did talk about you. How would you know?" he asks, though the answer is obvious. Gossip cuts both ways. Allegiances shift. He is not the only one with allies. Dana doesn't rise to the bait. She's back to chewing on the ends of her fingers.

Wallace's hands sting just watching. "I don't think you ruined my plates, if that's what you're worried about," he says.

A moment of silence. The flame hisses as it writhes in the air currents. It's a soft, fluttering sound, fire turning back on itself. So deep is the silence in that moment that he can hear the impurities in the stream of gas burning.

But then a strange thing happens: An animatronic jerkiness shifts her shoulders, her arms, her legs, as if electricity were independently bringing parts of her to life. Low at first, a whisper, but then almost immediately louder: laughter. Her head tosses back suddenly so hard and fast that he worries for a moment that she will strike the shelf on Henrik's bench. But she doesn't. Just laughter. She grips her stomach, her thighs. Her eyes fill with tears.

"Oh my god, listen to you. How arrogant can you be? Do you think I care what you think?" Dana dries her tears. "I cannot believe this. You actually think I care what you think."

"I don't understand," Wallace says, feeling more tired than he has felt in his entire life. "I don't want to. Leave me alone."

"Yes, Wallace. I ruined your big experiment because I don't have enough things to do. That's me."

"I said that I *didn't* think that you did that, Dana. You don't have to be so ridiculous."

"I *hate* you, Wallace. And do you know why? Do you know why I hate you? Because you walk around like you're so important because you spend all of your time working. You dump all of your precious little time into this lab, and into these dumb little experiments that don't matter, and you have the nerve to say to me, *Some of us work.* Imagine, *you*, saying that to *me.* Of all people. You aren't Katie. You're certainly not Brigit. And yet you think you have a right to lecture me."

Wallace can smell his own blood. He touches the end of his nose to see if there is blood there, but no, he isn't bleeding. There is just the metallic sheen of blood coating everything. Its heat. Its bitterness. He can taste it too.

"Oh, no one could lecture you."

Dana sits up straight. The laughter is gone, though the room rings with its ghost.

"You know what I think, Wallace? I think you're a misogynist."

The word flicks by him, a shooting dart of silver. There's a momentary grit of bitter regret at the back of his throat.

"I am not a misogynist."

"You don't get to define what misogyny is to a woman, asshole. You don't get to."

"Okay," he says.

"So, if I say you're a misogynist, then you're a misogynist."

Wallace turns from her. There is no arguing. This is why he keeps to himself. This is why he speaks to no one and does nothing.

"Fucking gay guys always think that they've got the corner on oppression."

"I don't think that at all."

"And you think that you get to walk around because you're gay and black and act like you can do no wrong."

"No, I don't."

"You think you're fucking queen of the world," she says, slapping her palm on the bench, which makes Wallace jump.

"Dana."

"I'm fed up with your shit. I'm fed up with you always talking down to me and treating me like I'm beneath you. I'm tired of it."

"No one did that to you, Dana. No one has done anything to you except try to help you, but you won't be helped because you have to prove yourself."

"I have to prove myself because you and men like you are always counting me out. Well, fuck it, women are the new niggers, the new faggots."

A sour, wet taste spackles the roof of Wallace's mouth. The world is momentarily illuminated by something coarse and bright. He blinks. He grips the back of his chair to keep himself still, steady, even. He thinks of Brigit, her warmth, her kind voice.

Dana pants like a winded, wounded animal. She has worked herself up into a froth, into a violent anger. She is making fists over and over, her small hands turning to hard white knots. It isn't sympathy he feels. They are beyond that now. But it is the first part of sympathy: recognition. White foam sticks to the corners of her mouth. Her eyes flash and narrow. He recognizes himself in the futile, thrashing heat of her rage. The unfair thing, he thinks, is that she is afforded this moment to vent herself. She will be fine. She will be all right. She is *gifted*, and he is merely Wallace.

None of this is fair. None of this is good, he knows. But he also knows that the point is not fairness. The point is not to be treated fairly or well. The point is to get your work done. The point is results. He could say something to her, but at the end of the day, it doesn't matter because no one is going to do his work for him. No one is going to say, *Well, Wallace, it's okay if you don't have your part of the data. You were being treated poorly.* And there is the other thing—the shadow pain, he calls it, because he cannot say its real name. Because to say its real name would be to cause trouble, to make waves. To draw attention to it, as though it weren't in everything already. He tried once, with Simone, to talk about the way Katie talks to him as though he is inept. He said to Simone, *She doesn't talk that way to anyone else. She doesn't treat them like this.* And Simone said, *Wallace. Don't be dramatic. It isn't racism. You just need to catch up. Work harder.*

The most unfair part of it, Wallace thinks, is that when you tell white people that something is racist, they hold it up to the light and try to discern if you are telling the truth. As if they can tell by the grain if something is racist or not, and they always trust their own judgment. It's unfair because white people have a vested interest in underestimating racism, its amount, its intensity, its shape, its effects. They are the fox in the henhouse.

Wallace does not talk about it anymore. He learned his lesson in third year, when, after he had passed his preliminary exams, Simone pulled him into her office to debrief. She sat behind her desk with her legs crossed, a beautiful winter day lying white and smooth behind her, all the way to the lake, that blue-white churn and the trees like delicate woodwork in a diorama. He felt good about himself. He felt, for the first time since coming to grad school, like he was finally doing what she always urged him to do—catching up—and he imagined that he saw pride in her eyes. He was excited. He was ready to begin in earnest—to really begin. And she asked, *How do you think that went?* And he said, *Oh, well, I thought it was okay.* And she shook her head grimly. She said, *You know, Wallace, that was . . . frankly, I was embarrassed for you. Had that been another student, it might have gone differently. You might not have passed. But we talked a long time about what was feasible for you, what was reasonable for your abilities, and we decided we'd pass you, but we are going to watch you, Wallace. No more of this. You need to get better.* She spoke as though she were bestowing blessings. Bestowing beneficence. Bestowing irrefutable grace. She spoke as though she were saving him. What could he say? What could he do?

Nothing. Except to work.

And now the work has been turned on him. His work is an insult to them. She hates him because he works, but he works only so that people might not hate him and might not rescind his place in the world. He works only so that he might get by in life on whatever he can muster. None of it will save him, he sees now. None of it *can* save him.

Wallace reaches over and shuts off his flame, for a moment thinking that he's pushed the dial too hard, that he's broken it and the room will fill with gas. But the handle holds his weight. He then turns back to Dana, this panting, miserable girl. Her face is red. Her eyes gleam. He steps closer to her on the bench. The soles of her shoes press flat to the front of his thighs.

It isn't hatred. He does not hate her. Because she matters so little to him. It would be like hating a child. It would make him like his parents, who had certainly, in some way, hated him. And he does not want to be like them. But he cannot bring himself to be good. To be generous.

"Fuck you, Dana," he says finally, and it feels like a relief, so much so that he is briefly thankful to her for the gift of it. "Just, totally fuck you." A rush of air buoys him. He collects his racquet bag from the low storage on the floor, and all the time she is staring at him as though she has been slapped.

He rises. Another look passes between them. She looks like she's on the cusp of saying something, but he turns, leaves. Away through the blue shadow that has taken the lab now that the lights have turned off. His motion doesn't trigger them, as though he is a natural part of this place or a ghost.

Dana shouts after him, that she's not done, that he doesn't get to end a conversation before she's had her say. She is shouting after him because she doesn't know what else to do with her fear and her anger, and soon her shouts turn to sobs. But Wallace is already crossing the hall.

The light in the hall is too bright, searing. His steps echo. He walks hard. He's got a heavy step. His mother used to make fun of him for that. *You're so heavy footed; you never look down.* He does look down now. Sees the thin shawl of his shadow on the tiles. Passes the kitchen, passes Miller's lab door.

"Hey," Miller calls after him, but he does not stop. He can hear Miller's steps after him, which only spurs him on, past the posters of experiments, past the fliers advertising employment opportunities, past the familiar bulletin boards with their cartoons and silly sayings, past the row of lockers where, in the eighties, people used to store their belongings. He is walking so fast that his feet are slipping over each other. He's back at the stairwell that overlooks the atrium by the time Miller catches him. "What's going on?" Each word is deliberate, drawn out.

"Apparently, I'm a huge misogynist," Wallace says.

"What? Come on. What was all that shouting about?" Miller's eyes are kind and concerned. He takes Wallace's arm in his hand, and it's like before, in the kitchen. Wallace can feel himself vibrating, with anger, with fear—who can say?

"Nothing," he says. "Nothing."

"Don't do that."

"Don't do what? Tell the truth? It's nothing."

"It's obviously not."

"Well, it's not your problem," Wallace says, and he snatches away from Miller. "I'll deal."

Miller is both angry and annoyed. He reaches, Wallace avoids.

"Come on."

"No, I'm fine."

"No, you're not." Miller takes his hand and pulls on him. They go into the library on the third floor, into one of the little rooms with doors that lock. Miller makes Wallace sit on the table and he steps between his legs. He is not letting him get away. The room smells vaguely dusty and like dry-erase markers. The carpet is hideously purple. Miller smells like his shampoo and soap. His eye is still puffy from last night, with the peppers and the nachos at the pier.

"I'm mad," Wallace says when it becomes clear that Miller isn't going to say anything or initiate the conversation. He's got his arms folded over his chest and there is a patient look on his face.

"Obviously."

"She said women are the new niggers and faggots."

"I'm not even sure what that means."

"She hates me."

"Seems likely."

"You aren't helping," Wallace says.

"I'm sorry it's so bad," Miller says, and he kisses Wallace softly. "I'm sorry."

"Stop being nice to me. You hated me too, just the other day, didn't you?"

"I didn't hate you. I didn't understand you—I don't understand you—but I never hated you," Miller says. How strange, Wallace thinks. A strange thing to say. He can't look at Miller. Feels weirdly exposed. The table is cheap and yellow, laminated plywood. He wants to get down. Miller won't move. Wallace pulls at the hem of the gray sweatshirt.

"I hate you. I hate you a lot."

"I know," Miller says. "Do you feel better?"

"No," he says at first, and then, shrugging, "Well, maybe some."

"Good." There is another kiss and then another, and then Wallace is sliding his fingers through Miller's hair, and Miller is biting at the side of Wallace's neck. The table creaks beneath him as he shifts to get closer and then to get away.

"Please do not give me a hickey. I am not prepared to explain to anyone."

"Oh, shit, I forgot," Miller says.

"Yeah, well. It's been real." Wallace pushes at his chest, and Miller, remembering where they are and who they are, steps back.

"I am sorry, Wallace. You shouldn't have to put up with that."

"It's fine," he says. "You know, everyone has shit to deal with."

"They do—but, well, you're one of my people and I'm sad you have to deal with it."

"Thanks," Wallace says, touched to be someone's person, to be thought of so tenderly.

"I guess you're playing tennis after all."

"It's a date."

They don't know what else to do with their bodies except the obvious thing, which is intractable at the moment. So Wallace kisses Miller's cheek, which makes Miller blush.

"Off I go."

"Okay."

Wallace is going down the steps when he looks up and sees Miller watching him. He thinks again of a bird, the matter of scope, how everything below it, all the big and towering world, is both flattened and shrunken. How he must look to Miller from above, the distortion of distance and light falling down through the skylight at the top of the atrium, how he must appear half in shadow, half lit. Looking up, he sees Miller's height diminished, an illusion of the angle. He lifts his hand, waves. Wallace waves back.

"Call me later," Miller says.

"Okay." The answer to the question from before, the one he asked himself by leaving Miller in the kitchen—if he could withstand the possibility that last night was all he needed—is no. He knows this for sure now as he goes farther and farther down the steps, can feel Miller getting farther and farther away, higher above him. There will come a moment when he passes directly beneath Miller's sight line, when they will be the closest that they possibly can be, and to someone looking from even higher up, they will appear identical, one laid over the other.

But there is a difference between entering someone, being in someone, and being with that person. There is an impossibility to the idea of simultaneously existing within them and beside them, the fact that when you get close enough to someone, you cease to be discrete entities and instead become a single surface, glittering in the sun.

"I mean it," Miller says, his voice wafting down. "You better call, or text."

"I will, thanks, Dad," he calls back, walking backward, laughing.

"Don't call me that."

"Sure thing, Dad."

"Wallace."

"Bye."

"Bye."

Their voices are twinned echoes that grow apart until there is only silence, or that clash into each other until their energy is spent and they are subsumed into the quiet. Either way, Wallace is gone, and Miller is gone, and the atrium is still and warm.

The agitating machines beat on, beat on, beat on.

3

Wallace is at first surprised to find the courts deserted, but then he remembers the game at the stadium, a structure barely discernible at this distance, a soft white hump like the back of a whale. Music, dull and empty, pulses into the air, and Wallace knows that soon the streets will fill with drunk people in red-and-white-striped clothes, lolling from one side to the other. They will spill in a red wave across the campus and into downtown, and their voices will crowd the air like shouts from some sinking ship. It's the worst part of the weekend. How permeable everything and everyone becomes. It takes only one glance to provoke a person into conversation or worse.

Last weekend, Wallace had been standing in line at the corner store behind a group of tan boys who smelled like beer and sweat. The boys were all wearing sunglasses, and now and then one of them would run his hands around the insides of his shorts, and occasionally Wallace saw a flash of hip, the tawny fur of pubic hair, a tumescent shadow between the legs. One of them turned to him, pushed his sunglasses up just enough for Wallace to see his bloodshot eyes, and said, "Bro, what are you doing here? We told you to wait." Wallace blinked at the boy, not knowing what to say or what to do, but the boy just stared at him in amused annoyance as though Wallace were the one who'd made the mistake. The boy's friends hooked their arms around his neck and pulled him, and the boy shouted after Wallace, "No, no, we can't leave him. He's got the hookup. Don't you have the hookup, bro?" And all the people in the store turned to look at Wallace, who had only wanted to buy some soap and deodorant, who could have picked a better time and better day, certainly, but had chosen that moment and so had been marked out in some way. It could be that way.

The heat has not broken. Wallace sits down on the bench. He takes his racquet out of the yellow sleeve. The courts are blue with crisp white lines, made from recycled rubber or cement or some similar substance. They are the slowest courts he has ever played except for the soggy green clay where he first learned the game on weekends with his friends in undergrad.

There is a row of trees populated by crows calling to one another. Wallace moves to the hot surface of the court and begins to stretch, first his legs and then his back, bending this way and that, trying to unclench, to release. He breathes deeply, trying to let go of Dana. He pictures her on a boat sailing farther and farther away. The court is burning the undersides of his thighs, but the pain feels good, soaking into him like water through a shirt. The knot in his spine is unfurling. His bones crack. He stretches as far forward as he can, and his stomach presses against the tops of his thighs. He doesn't have the build of a tennis player. He is not lanky like Cole. He is chubby, at best, fat at worst. This is the most rigorous exercise he gets all week.

He often thinks of the boys he sees rowing on the lake, how perfectly efficient their motion is as they draw themselves over the placid silver surface of the water. He sees them often when he's out there walking, can hear their calls in the trees; sometimes he stops and stands on the edge of a slippery rock, marveling at the speed, their shining arms, their muscles flexing in perfect unison.

Cole comes jogging along the fence. He's breathing hard.

"Sorry sorry sorry," he says. He bends over, clutching his side. "Whew, it's a scorcher out here."

"Yep, it's something," Wallace says. "It's okay. I'm not doing anything else today anyway." He lies back on the court and pulls one thigh up to his chest, holds it until there is a sweet ache in the muscle.

Cole tosses his bag on the bench and joins Wallace on the ground to stretch. There is something agitated about him as he stretches out his long pale legs, which are already turning red from the sun. His eyes avoid Wallace's. The coarse concrete scratches the back of Wallace's neck.

"You okay?"

"Fine. Yes. No. Yes."

"Oh—well."

"It's nothing," Cole says, sitting up. "I just . . . Fuck. I don't know."

"Okay," Wallace says. He sits up too, slowly. Cole lies back down.

"Are you on that app?"

"Which app?"

"You know the one." Cole flushes as he says this, looking away to the trees and to the long, winding sidewalk that slopes down to the lake.

"The gay one, you mean?"

"That's it. Yeah."

"Oh, yeah, I guess, sometimes." Wallace deleted the app some weeks ago, but this feels like a minor point. Cole has always made sure to mention that he is not on the app and that he's relieved to have found Vincent before the advent of such technology. Geolocation, finding the nearest queers for fucking or whatever. Wallace always has to keep himself from saying that Cole would have done well on the app. He is tall and good-looking in an average sort of way. He is funny and quippy, gentle. He is also white, which is never a disadvantage with gay men. But Wallace says none of these things because to say them would disrupt Cole's view of the average gay man as shallow and kind of stupid—they are shallow and kind of stupid, but no more than any other group. Wallace only deleted the app because he had grown tired of watching himself be invisible to them, of the gathering silence in his in-box. He wasn't looking anyway, but at the same time he wanted to be looked at the same as anyone else, to be seen.

"I saw Vincent on there last night."

"Oh? What were you doing on there?"

"I suspected he was on there. So I made a fake profile."

"Isn't that . . . ?"

"I know, I know, but I had to see if he was there. And he was there. Can you believe that?"

"Is that something you two talked about?"

"No. Yes. I mean . . . We said we'd think about it, you know? Opening things up. I don't know why I'm not enough."

"Maybe you are," Wallace says. "It's not about things not being enough. Maybe he just . . . wants something different. I don't know."

"But why would he sneak around to do it?"

"I don't know."

"That's what kills me, Wallace. That he snuck around."

"Has he?"

"Not that I know of. Fuck. I don't know. We're supposed to be thinking about getting a dog, you know? We're supposed to be thinking about getting married. Settling down. And now he wants to open everything up."

Wallace lets out a slow breath. He claps his hand on the back of Cole's shoulder.

"Come on," he says. "Let's hit a little."

WALLACE AND COLE have been playing tennis together since their first year of graduate school. They are an evenly matched pair: Wallace's backhand is a decent, flowing one-hander and Cole's forehand is smooth and easy. Wallace hits his forehand with a looping swing and Cole's backhand is piecemeal, barely keeping itself together. When they play, it's a matter of just a few points here or there, but Cole typically comes through with the win because his serve is more consistent and when he needs it he can lash an ace out wide, leaving Wallace scrambling, flailing.

They have played each other a number of times—so many, in fact, that each knows what the other will do even before the ball has landed on their side of the court. For example, Wallace knows that if he kicks his second serve up to Cole's forehand, baiting him, Cole will swing out and probably sail the shot long. Cole knows that this is the tactic, but he thinks that this time will be the time he slaps the winner up the line.

They start at the net, just a few volleys to get their bodies used to tracking the ball in the sun. Back and forth they send the ball across the net, easy, controlled. Wallace prefers his forehand volley and so he's deft at meeting the ball out front on that side. He can put it to either side of Cole's body, warming up both wings. Cole is less adept at this part. He prefers the telescopic blasting from the back of the court. But this will let them talk a little more. Cole's eyes are red-rimmed, and his voice is thick and foggy with moisture.

"I mean, would you open things up if you had a partner?"

"I don't know, Cole. I think that sort of thing depends."

"I don't. I think some people want it and some people don't, and you can get to wanting it if something goes wrong. What the fuck went wrong?"

"You said you had talked about it maybe."

"We did."

"Did he say why he wanted it?"

"He said he was tired of waiting around for me on weekends and at nights and on holidays, that all I could think about was bacteria and drug discovery and my next paper. He said he wanted something too—more intimacy. We are fucking intimate."

"That's a lot," Wallace says. "I mean, it's a lot to take in."

"Yeah, so he says, 'I'd like to open things up. I'd like to discuss it with you.' You know what he's like, with that neutral voice. That shrink voice he got from his mother."

"I didn't know his mother was a shrink."

"She isn't. She's a high school counselor. His dad's the shrink."

"Oh," Wallace says. The ball comes faster, so he takes a step back from the net. Cole is striking the ball beautifully today, hard and flat. Wallace is having a hard time keeping up. His racquet flutters a little in his hand. He slides his grip up, flexes his fingers.

"It's true. Things haven't been great, or perfect, for a while. But I didn't know it was this bad." Cole shakes his head in disgust, slaps the ball into the bottom of the net.

"You know," Wallace says, though he has no idea where he's going with this, only that the look on Cole's face makes his stomach hurt, "I think that it's probably a good sign that he expressed, um, a want? A need? It's probably good that he said something?"

"But the minute I said no, he turned around and hopped on a dating app? What's the point of communicating if you don't listen?"

"Yes, you are right, yes. But perhaps he did it because *he* didn't feel heard?"

Cole looks up from the net, and his eyes are cold. His mouth is a grim line.

"So it's my fault?"

"No, Cole, that's not what I mean."

"Because that would be a fucked-up thing to say, Wallace."

Wallace tries to find some inner bead of calm, some granule of peace. He sighs. Sweat burns the edge of his vision.

"Cole, all I'm saying is that Vincent is a person too. And you aren't the only one in your relationship with feelings."

"I'm not ready to be on his side!"

"I am not asking you to be on his side, or to forgive him or whatever. I am only saying that maybe you're still okay. Maybe all this means that you're okay." Wallace tries to smile through the tension in his jaw and his neck. If he can, then perhaps it is true that they are okay, that they will be okay. If he can smile, then he might believe it and then Cole might believe it. That's all he wants, after all. That's all that matters here, he realizes. Cole's feelings.

"I don't know."

They go to the baseline, and Cole decides to drop in by sending the ball hard to the service line. It bounces up nice and high, and Wallace is able to send it back with good depth and spin. There's a pleasant shape to the ball, an arc that puts it right in front of Cole's service line. It's easy to rally this way, putting just enough force into the shot to send it over the net, but not enough heat to do real harm. The best players in the world could do this for hours with no mistakes. Cole often sends a ball into the net or off to the side, and Wallace has to move quickly to save it, catching it in the air and sending it back nice and easy.

He is surprised that there is so much trouble in Vincent and Cole's relationship. They have been together going on seven years now. When Wallace first met Cole, they had sat next to each other on a log at an introductory bonfire. The heat was on their thighs and their faces, and Cole was telling him how much he loved tennis. There was no mention of a boyfriend or even that Cole was gay, but there had been something in the way their eyes met, the way Cole reached over and put a hand on Wallace's knee, the insistence of those fingers kneading the surface of his skin, that had caused Wallace to hope.

That whole first year was an elaborate flirtation. He and Cole went everywhere together. To dinner, to lunch, to play tennis. They spoke quietly in Cole's van after they had been rained out, cold and soaked. There was a moment, the world a gray streak, when they looked at each other and found a possibility of something. Cole leaned toward him, across the center console, smelling like sweat and rain, his full lower lip plush and red, and Wallace tilted toward him out of instinct, two bodies in motion. But something stopped them. Some force rendered them still right before contact, and Wallace got out into the rain. He didn't hear if Cole called after him, and maybe that was for the best.

Some months later, at the end of that first summer, at the start of second year, he was walking home from grocery shopping, his hands full of food, thinking of calling Cole and patching things up, when he saw a group of his friends walking in the opposite direction. He waved with his hands full, and they waved and came up to him. Cole and Emma and Yngve, and Vincent, who at the time was unknown to him.

"Hi," Wallace said.

"Hey," they all said in turn. Then Vincent stepped up to him, stuck out his hand, and said, "Hi, I'm Vincent, Cole's boyfriend." And Cole looked away in shame.

Their relationship has always seemed so steady to Wallace. They are so steadfastly even-tempered—except, perhaps, for last night, when Vincent seemed, yes, a little on edge. Had he been cruising even then? Had he been on the lookout for something passing in the night? There is a cruising ground near the lake, a sloped hill covered in downy trees. At night, all you have to do is let yourself be sucked into the darkness of the unlit running path. You walk and walk on soft soil until you bump up against something hard and firm, another man out there looking for something in the dark.

A shot skids off the sideline, and Wallace scoops it up off the bounce, sends it cross-court to Cole's forehand. Cole should send it back cross-court but closer to the middle, but he won't. Wallace can see it now in the way he's winding up, drawing his racquet back and a little down. He's going to shoot it straight up the line for a winner. Sure enough, Cole swings out, hits the ball squarely in front, and sends it hurtling low over the net and into the doubles alley.

If there is anything he does not enjoy about Cole, it's the erratic nature of his tennis, how even during warm-up, kind as he is in daily life, he's only thinking about himself. The goal of warm-up is just that, to get the body going, to get the shots ready for the set or match. It's not about practicing winners. It's not about showing off. Wallace would be content to hit the same forehand one thousand times in a warm-up. It's boring, but he likes it, the consistency. He hates to miss.

"You think you might want to play a set?" Cole asks over the net.

"Sure. We can."

"Great. First serve in?"

"Sounds perfect."

He bunts the ball back over to Cole, and he lines up at the baseline to receive. Cole is bouncing the ball, eyeing the box. His toss rises slowly from his hand, and he reaches up for a serve. It misses horrifically, into the fence, which rattles. He tries again. Another misfire, this time flat into the court in front of him. Wallace clucks the roof of his mouth, but he knows that once Cole's serve gets going, this same randomness will make it difficult to read and return.

Cole wipes sweat from his brow in frustration, rolls his shoulders two hard times. Then he tosses the ball up, and this time he strikes it perfectly. The ball shoots down into the corner of the service box, no spin or anything, just low and darting. Wallace chips it back with his forehand and the floating slice drifts toward Cole, who puts it away for a winner.

On the next serve, Wallace connects with a beautiful return, sending the ball up the line and away from Cole. The geometry of tennis is simple in many ways. You want to hit to where your opponent isn't, but in order to make a space where they are not, you sometimes have to hit to where they are. You are trying to outmaneuver them. But because he and Cole know each other's game so well, the maneuvering is always in minor gains, little turns in momentum. A winner here, an error there, an ace, a return winner. Cole manages to hold serve after digging himself out of two break points. They change ends.

Wallace takes two balls to the line. His arm is getting there.

There is a small pain in his shoulder, the pain of remembering, recollecting, redefining form. His serve is mostly conservative. He spins it in rather than going for broke. He is a master of angles, slicing it wide or bending it into the body. For his first serve, he catches Cole going the other way and clips the outside of the line. The next serve is a double fault. And then a kicker that draws an error. He holds to fifteen. They each hold serve after that, the set score going higher and higher, matching hold for hold. There is the usual tension at a deuce point where Cole is playing wall-to-wall defense, scrambling, digging balls out of the corner, rushing the net, ready to put away anything that even remotely looks short, and by some bit of magic, Wallace manages to loop a winner by him cross-court, a dipping, vicious angle.

After, they sit on the bench side by side, sweating profusely. Wallace sucks lukewarm water from his bottle, and Cole chews on a banana.

"Are you coming to the dinner thing tonight?" Cole asks.

"What dinner thing?"

"Oh. We didn't tell you? That's probably because you left last night. We're having a dinner thing at the boys' house."

"Dinner thing" usually means a party at which everyone stands around eating a variety of baked vegetables doused in dark sauces. "Dinner thing" also means standing in the corner looking out the window at the nearby street.

"Maybe not," he says.

"Please come. Especially after this shit with Vincent, I need someone to be on my side."

"Who isn't on your side?"

"No. I just . . . Nobody else knows except Roman, and I think he's the one who got Vincent thinking about opening things up in the first place."

Roman is the attractive French student who is a year ahead of them, who is also gay and also in an open relationship, with an equally attractive German named Klaus. Roman has always been closer to Cole and Vincent than he has ever been to Wallace, for reasons that are abundantly clear to Wallace but that Cole pretends not to understand.

"So you want a gay civil war at the dinner thing. Okay."

"No, not a gay civil war. No wars."

"I don't know, Cole." Sweat stings his eyes. He's pleasantly sore and buzzed from the set. The score is tied. Maybe he finally has a chance to win a set off Cole.

"Okay, but please come. Besides, you can laugh at Yngve trying set up Miller with some girl from his rock-climbing group."

Miller's name sits like a stalled train in his mind.

"What?"

"I forget her name, but Yngve says she's nice. So that should be good for a few laughs."

Wallace blots sweat from his face with his towel, but holds it still for several long moments. He's trying to catch his breath, but it's almost impossible because the towel is not letting any airflow through.

"Oh," he says, muffled. The hurt surprises him more than anything else.

"You look like someone shot your dog," Cole says.

"I don't have a dog," Wallace says. He towels off his hands, and takes up his racquet. "Let's go."

Cole lets the banana peel drop into the trash can beside the bench and picks up his racquet too. The sunlight and the heat are fanning out over them, pressing into their bodies. Wallace can feel it on his skin, like fizzy water. He's darkening, as in boyhood when he had worked alongside his grandparents in their garden, his skin going from brown to a clay red color. Soil and clay.

Wallace is standing at the baseline preparing to serve. Cole prepares to receive, deep knee bend, weight loaded. Wallace's palm aches. The racquet feels stiff and awkward as he bounces the ball. The vibrations jar his wrist. Miller and the girl from the rock-climbing group sitting side by side at dinner. Laughing. Eating their baked vegetables. Talking about what, Wallace wonders. The things people talk about when the world thinks they belong together. Who knows what affinities unlock between such people? How easy it must be. He's not shocked at not having been invited. He's not particularly offended by it, even. But now he's in the impossible situation of having to either justify his absence or explain his presence to Miller. He's been bouncing the ball too long, can see that Cole is getting anxious over there. Serves him right.

Wallace slices a serve up the middle, sending it spinning away from Cole, who lunged the other way. Cole looks back behind himself, a little shocked at the speed of the ball, the severity of its spin. The next serve bounds into his body. Wallace grits his teeth as he stalks up to the line again. Another slice, this time into the forehand for a weak reply. Wallace is already leaping forward, taking it on the rise, hitting the ball with the full weight of his anger. He has nudged ahead in the set, but he doesn't feel like he's winning anything at the moment. He also doesn't feel as if he's expended the urge to do harm, to vent his frustration and fury.

"So what are you going to do about Vincent?" he asks as they're changing ends. Cole chokes a little.

"Oh, I don't know. I can't bring it up, right? He'll know that I was on there too, but I was only on there to find him. It just seems so stupid."

"Yeah," Wallace says. "But you can't not say something. You have to acknowledge it."

Cole is silent, taps his racquet against the net, making its shadow flutter on the court's surface, like a net dragging the blue sea. Wallace presses: "Unless you don't think it's worth it."

"No, I do. I just . . . I'm more hurt than anything, you know? I'm hurt he lied. I'm hurt he's doing it behind my back."

"Do you think you'd ever want to open it up?"

"I don't know, Wallace," he says tightly.

"I just mean, you know, if you're not going to be working fewer hours or whatever anytime soon."

Cole is really whacking at the net now, and it's shuddering under the force of his blows. He's got his face screwed up in frustration. Oh, Wallace thinks. Oh no. What has he done?

"I'm sorry. It's none of my business," he says. "I'm sorry for prying."

"No, you raise a good point. I just don't know what to do."

"If he's not cheating, if he's just looking—"

"Looking is cheating, Wallace." Cole's voice is sharp, hot like pressing your hand to a knife that's been left in the sun. The anger in his eyes is adamantine and gleaming. Wallace swallows thickly.

"Well, sounds like you have to talk to him, then."

"I don't know how," Cole says, shoulders slumping. "I don't know how to begin it. Fuck."

They're done with tennis. Cole drops on the bench and puts his face in his hands. He's not crying, but he's breathing hard. Wallace takes the edge of the bench and puts his hand on Cole's shoulder. He's drenched in sweat and hot. It's like the time in first year in the van in the rain, and Wallace feels the edge of that distant ache surfacing in him.

"It'll be okay."

"I don't know if it will."

"It will be. It has to be," Wallace says, catching a rising tide not of confidence, but of desperation to see his friend through this at whatever cost. "People do this. They fight. They hide things, they argue. It means you're in something that's worth giving a damn about."

Cole's eyes are wet when he looks up from the curve of his palms. There is moisture on his cheeks, sweat or tears, Wallace is not sure. His lips crack open a bit, and there's a sad, soft sound coming out of him.

"Hey," Wallace says. "Hey."

"No, you're right. I have to put on my big-boy pants, or something. God, it's hot out here."

"It is," Wallace says. "We can go to the lake if you want." Cole considers it, stares out at the empty courts. The roar from the stadium is audible. A car glides by. The crows are back at it in the trees overhead. The shade cast through the fence is coarse and riddled with tiny holes of light, like standing beneath mesh and staring up into the sky. A single bead of sweat glides down the curve of Cole's ear. Wallace is tempted to catch it on his fingertip, to say, make a wish, but that doesn't work for water. There are no wishes to be found in salt water, no magic there at all except, in some cases, the way it turns to stars when dispersed, as from the tip of a finger with a breath.

"Okay. I'd like that. Okay." They rise from the bench with stiff muscles and aching joints. Their bodies have cooled and hardened. They've been running from side to side under the sun for a little over an hour, and having come so suddenly to a stop, they can feel their blood cooling in odd places. It gives the world a kind of tilting, buoying quality as they exit through the gate at the fence and walk along the cool grass. It tickles their ankles, and they walk close enough together that their elbows collide with a meaty thud. They pass beneath the shade of the trees, crow calls fading. Up ahead, the world narrows, darkens. The sidewalk fades into crushed blue gravel and then yellow dirt. The air is immediately cooler when they enter the shade at the corner of the boathouse.

THE LAKE IS A SHIMMERING immensity ahead of them, going all the way out to the peninsula and beyond, to the other shore.

They can make out the shape of a couple of far-off boats, blurry in the distance. Behind them, the boathouse has its doors rolled up; muscular men are drawing cloths and sponges over the rowboats, polishing hulls, scraping off lake gunk. Some rhythmic, driving song on the radio. The air fizzes with humidity this close to the water.

Cole and Wallace turn left, away from the direction where Wallace lives. Through the thatch of trees and shrubs, the lake is intermittently visible. Their shoes slide and scrape. Occasionally a bicyclist shoots by, a blur of white or red or blue. Cole, for a few paces at least, puts his head on Wallace's shoulder. Wallace loops an arm around his back. Whatever words Wallace might have for Cole in this moment feel inadequate to the task of righting him, solving this problem for him. He's said all he knows how to say. He feels shitty for having dug around in the wound, prodded his friend this far. Cole's body is warm against him, slippery with sweat, but since the sweat is cooling, drying into a husk, he's a bit easier to hold on to as they go along.

"I didn't know it would be like this," Cole says. "I had no idea it'd be this hard."

"Like what?"

"When I first moved here. I was lonely all the time. Vincent was still at Ole Miss. I was stuck here all alone. I missed him so much I thought I'd die. I thought it'd be easier once we were in the same place. I thought it would fix things."

"It didn't?"

"No," Cole says, and he reaches up to wipe at his nose with his wrist. "No, it didn't. I mean, for a while it did. It was great being with him again, here. But I don't know. It's not the same."

"You're not the same," Wallace says.

"What do you mean?"

"Just that we're never the same. We're always changing."

"Maybe so," Cole says.

The trees drop back and there, out to the right, is marshy yellow grass and dark water. There is also a narrow channel that runs out to the lake, but this is a small swamp. Herons move among the grasses, and large gray geese sun themselves on the bank. Ancient black wood juts out of the water like a jagged tooth, or a claw from some large underwater animal. Gray gulls circle overhead, and Cole tilts back to stare at them, shielding his eyes.

"If it's hard, you know, maybe that means something too."

"We've just put so much time in this thing. We've put so much love and blood into it. And Roman comes along and fucks it all to hell."

"How did he get involved, anyway?"

"You know how it goes. Vincent wanted him and Klaus over for dinner. We get to talking about relationships, monogamy, being queer, which is fucking ridiculous. We're gay, not queer."

That Cole is going on again about how normal he and Vincent are—how regular-gay they are—is not entirely shocking. This is a common topic for him. Cole resents Roman, Wallace knows, because Roman is not only French and good-looking, but he also possesses the sort of deceptive charisma that can make even an open relationship appeal to Mississippi boys raised on Communion and the Holy Ghost. And haven't they scraped this far from Sodom and Gomorrah in the public's opinion by virtue of their normalcy, their adherence to traditional values? Cole doesn't see how turning back the clock, how embracing hedonism is going to get them anywhere.

It's all the same to Wallace. People do what they want even when they shouldn't, even when they know better. The compulsion to take and take and take is a natural one, the urge to expand; desire will out, he thinks.

Cole does not notice Wallace's silence. The water's surface ripples with the passage of birds swooping low, snatching up insects. He picks up a rock and flings it out over the yellow grass. A dozen or so birds erupt into the air, their wings gray and brown, their bodies darting like arrowheads. Cole lets out a groan of frustration.

"And then, we're having coffee after dinner," Cole continues, "and Roman turns to Vincent and says, 'You know, nothing is better than fucking someone while my boyfriend watches.'" Cole's French accent is terrible, offensive and hilarious. Wallace tries not to laugh. It's bubbling up out of him. "Can you believe that? Can you believe that fucking homo said that to my boyfriend? In front of my face. He said that."

"I wonder if that's true," Wallace says. "I wonder if he really feels that way."

"I'm not letting someone fuck my boyfriend in front of me. I'm not letting anyone fuck my boyfriend at all. Except me."

Wallace bites the tip of his tongue, which is already so raw today. He swallows down what he wants to say: that a person doesn't belong to you just because you're in a relationship, just because you love them. That people are people and they belong only to themselves, or so they should. Miller can do whatever he wants with whomever he wants, is the thought that flashes through Wallace. He has a jealous heart. Love is a selfish thing.

"What does Vincent think?"

"Well, after that fucker left, we talked about it. We're doing dishes, and he turns to me and says, 'Babe, what did you think about what Roman said?' I lost it, Wallace. I fucking lost it."

"But what does Vincent want?"

"So, I say, 'I'm not a fan.' Vincent has this look on his face. Just . . . You should have seen it, Wallace. He looked like he'd missed his bus or his train or whatever. He looked like he was standing on the wrong side of the lake trying to see if the boat was coming back for him." The look on Cole's face is sad but angry. He's remembering it, slipping back to that night in their apartment. "And I just knew that he was going to do something like this. Get on that app, look for something."

"But what did he say?"

Cole licks the salt from above his lip. He looks back out over the water, to the grass drifting, sighing in the wind.

"He said, 'But don't you want to know?'"

"Know what?"

"That's it," Cole says, laughing. "That's it. That's what he said. 'But don't you want to know?' What the fuck are we missing out on by being together, Wallace? Can you tell me that? What are we missing out on?"

Wallace crouches low and sits on the grass next to the trail. His body is humming. Cole sits down next to him, but then he lies back and puts his arm over his face. The world in all its vastness is still and quiet. Even the birds sit suspended on their perches. A cricket crawls to the end of a yellow piece of grass and beats out several long cries. Then it's swallowed by a heron. Wallace watches that bird's enormous eyes as it bends its long neck down to see the bug on the grass. To the bug, the eye must seem so large, impossibly large. And the eye must see the bug as so infinitesimal as to be inconsequential and yet still be able to discern all its architecture. The heron claps its beak over the grass, taking the cricket into its body.

Cole sighs. "I just want things to be like they were. Like when we were at Ole Miss, making plans. This was never in the plan. We only ever wanted each other."

"Plans change. That doesn't mean they're bad or broken. It just means . . . you want something else."

"But I don't want something else. I don't want anyone else. I want Vincent." Cole sounds petulant. Wallace is twisting green grass, making a tiny hole in the ground. Cole's voice is riddled with cracks. The air is cooler by the water, but the heat of the day hasn't broken open yet, is still present, gauzy on their skin.

"I know, Cole. But you haven't lost him. You're still together. You can still make it work."

"But what if he doesn't want me back? What if he's found something else?"

"Don't borrow trouble," Wallace says, struck by these words because they do not belong to him but to his grandmother. He can hear her at the kitchen table, stirring the batter for corn bread, singing to herself. He feels momentarily ill, dizzy with memory.

"I can't help but to, it seems. All I have is trouble."

"That's not true," Wallace says as he sprinkles the blades of grass on Cole's stomach. "You have a boyfriend. That's more than some of us have."

"My boyfriend is looking for a boyfriend."

"You don't know that. You haven't asked him."

"What are you on there for, on the app, I mean?"

"To pass the time, mostly. Curiosity, maybe?"

"Do you ever hook up with people from there?" Cole slides his arm down to look at Wallace, and Wallace shakes his head. That's the truth of it. He's never been with anyone from the app.

"Nobody's barking up this tree," he says.

"That's not true."

"Oh, be sure to send me their address, then."

"I mean it. You're good-looking. You're smart. You're kind."

"I'm fat," Wallace says. "I'm average, at best, on a good day."

"You aren't fat."

"No, *you* aren't fat." Wallace drums his hand on the flat of Cole's stomach, which is softer than he thought it would be. He leaves his hand there, startled. Cole does not push it away.

"I thought about it," Cole says. "In first year. I thought about it. You probably know that."

"Let it alone," Wallace says, more words from his grand-mother.

"If I had known—"

"It would have been a mistake, anyway."

"I still think about it, you know. I do. I want you to know that."

Heat at the back of Wallace's throat. The world is blurry. His eyes sting. He takes his hand from Cole's stomach and lies down too. The grass is itchy on the back of his neck; dirt is in his hair. Cole's body smells like the ocean, or how Wallace imagines the ocean must smell.

"That's just your loneliness talking," Wallace says.

"No. Maybe."

"I thought about it, too, for a long time. And then I stopped."

"Why?"

The clouds over them are white and thick. A cool wind comes out of the west, draws a hand across the grass and makes it whisper. The herons are moving through the stalks slowly, turning them over for more bugs, or a fish caught sleeping.

"You get tired of listening to yourself whine about the same old things."

Cole does not laugh, though Wallace does after he says this.

"And then your boyfriend shows up. What do you do then?"

"I guess that's true," Cole says.

"I know you're just saying that part about thinking about it to make me feel better, maybe. You think I need to hear it, but I don't."

"That's not it."

"I think it is, Cole. You're too nice sometimes." The water rustles against the shore, but because they're lying down, they can't see the lake entirely. The geese are immobile, sitting near the edge of the water. "You get to feeling sorry for people, and then you say things like that."

"I don't know," Cole says. "Maybe you're right about that too."

"Do you really want me to come to the dinner thing tonight?"

"Yes."

"Okay," Wallace says. "I'll be there."

There is an audible sigh of relief from Cole, air going out, but Wallace feels as if that same air is pressing closer than ever on him. At the dinner party, he'll see their friends. He'll see Miller. There is also the matter of the strange woman, the rock climber, whom he imagines as a tall, leanly muscled woman, very tan, with blond hair and expensive teeth. He imagines her voice fluty, with just enough crass humor running through her to make her interesting.

But he knows that Cole needs him there. He isn't going to see Miller. He isn't going to make a fool of himself. He's going for his friend. He's going to help Cole get through this. Yet—Miller looms, or rather, the prospect of seeing him again, and he is thrilled by it.

"We spent the whole time talking about me," Cole is saying. "I didn't even think to ask how you're doing."

"What do you mean?"

"Your dad. You thinking about leaving. How is everything— are you okay?"

Wallace is momentarily confused and then it comes back to him—that Emma told everyone about his dad dying after he and Miller went off to the bathroom. He is again in the situation of having to articulate the curious shape of his grief, which does not bear the typical dimensions of such a loss. He doesn't feel flattened by it. Instead, there's a small channel in him going from his head to his feet, a channel through which a cold substance is churning at all times, cooling him from within, like a second circulatory system. There is something to it, isn't there? Something beyond his grasp.

"I'm okay," he says instead. Cole rolls over and looks at him.

"Are you sure?"

"Yes," he says. "I was just at the end of a very long rope yesterday, that's all."

"Is it the she-demon?"

"No. One of my lab mates ruined some experiments, and I just couldn't deal with it." There's a smile on Wallace's face, one that bears no heat. He's watching the clouds again.

"I hope you don't leave," Cole says. "I hope you stay. I need you."

"I don't think I'll leave," Wallace says. "I don't have any skills to live in the world."

"Me either."

"But sometimes I'd like to live in it—in the world, I mean. I'd like to be out there with a real job, a real life."

"Vincent has a real job and look what it's done to him."

"Is that fair?" Wallace asks. "Do you think his job is the reason he downloaded a gay sex app? Or do you think it's something more elemental?"

"I think my boyfriend is trying to cheat on me, is what I think. And I think I want my friend to stay and not throw his life away."

"Persuasive."

"I think so," Cole says, half-joking, half-sincere. Wallace would like to be able to gaze out at the clouds and parse their slow language for signs and omens, but that would require a belief in a higher power, a higher order of things. There are shadows on the dark water, and in the distance, a hush upon the trees on the peninsula, a cessation of movement, the breeze gone now. What is the thing that Cole is really trying to persuade him of—going to the party or staying? And hasn't he already made up his mind about staying? And going to the party?

Wallace rolls over onto his stomach and puts his chin against his folded arms. Behind them are soccer fields and dormitories. The grass is very green and very straight, bordered by sharp yellow signs and fence posts. Farther back, hazy in his vision, is the gray solidity of the gymnasium, and figures flickering in and out of view, people drunk from the game or because it is Saturday, wandering far afield of the stadium. The sun is hot on his lower back, where his shirt has come up, and he can feel it stinging, digging in, a purplish bruise on his skin gathering. Cole is making some dull, digging sound of his own, into the earth, as if to hide.

"If Vincent leaves me . . . I don't know what I'll do," he says. It's the sort of the thing you can say only when you're looking away from it, offhand, distracted, the way you might casually notice a piece of furniture. It's the sort of thing you say with a laugh, a soft roll of the shoulders. That's the only way to express the inconsolable grief of it, the fear that begins down in the tripe, in the guts, in the core of who you are and what you want and what you need—it's the truth, and for a moment, Wallace almost turns to him to comfort him. But he does not. To do so would be to break the spell, to cause Cole to crumple in on himself. His voice is streaked with moisture, a windowpane in the rain.

"You aren't there yet," Wallace says. "You'd know if you were."

"I just don't know what I'd do, Wallace. I don't know."

"You do know—you'd try to hold on. But you aren't there yet."

"Trying. What good is trying?"

"You have to try. You always have to try."

"What if we're there, but I don't know we're there?"

"You'd know. You just would."

"But how do you know I'd know?"

"Because I know you."

"What if you don't?"

"Oh, stop playing at somber," Wallace says. Stop playing at morose, at mystery, as if you aren't living every moment of your life on the surface or just below it. Cole is one of those fat fish that circle near the underside of a vast plain of ice in winter, showing their scales through the dull frost, the whites of their bellies. He is as native to solemnity as Wallace is to decisive action.

"I'm not playing. I'm serious. What if you didn't know me at all? Then what would you say?"

"Who are you?" Wallace replies quickly, laughing, his stomach pressing flatter to the ground. His own weight is making it harder to talk so low to the earth. "I guess I'd ask, 'Who are you?'"

"I have no idea, some days, who the fuck I am."

Wallace breathes out through his nose. A goose's wings flap on the water nearby, carrying it up and up. Wallace has not considered the possibility that Cole, the simplest of all his friends, the kindest and most gentle among them, might be unknowable to him. He has not considered the possibility that the ease of Cole's nature might be distorting something else, flattening it; or that it might be the result of a carefully orchestrated game, an illusion. All the parties, the deferring in conversation, the thoughtful inquiries about well-being, the baked goods, the plainness of his clothes, the flexibility of his schedule, the placid nature of his demeanor—all of it suggesting a genuine concern for others and a lack of selfish regard. How can Cole, of all people, doubt himself, who he is, when the person he presents to the world is so carefully constructed? It's only now, even, that Wallace is aware of a certain puckering at the seams, a hint of construction showing through. It's only now that he realizes that all along, Cole has perhaps been smiling with teeth to hide a grimace.

"I know that feeling," Wallace says. "I know that feeling pretty well."

"So don't say it, okay, that you know me, that you know how this will turn out, because you don't and can't."

"Okay," Wallace says. "That's fair. Okay."

"I'm just really scared. I've loved him for so long. We've been in this thing for so long. I don't know if I can begin again."

Of course Cole is afraid to lose Vincent. Of course this is the peak, the pinnacle of Cole's desires, not only for this relationship, but for the very configuration of things: a career, a loving partner, friends, lovely little parties, tennis on the weekend. What Cole wants from life is, above all else, that matters be settled before they are even raised, that everything fall into place. He expects that they'll simply finish graduate school and settle into the next phase of life just as they are now, only a little older, a little wealthier, a little better off. He has not planned for a loss, for any of the many ways that life can and will go wrong. Vincent is not just Vincent, but also a symbol, collecting with each passing day more and more significance. He is a ward, an inoculation against the uncertainty of the future.

"I hate that you feel this way. I hate that you're dealing with so much."

"No, you," Cole says. "Your dad—*fuck*, I'm going on again, I'm sorry."

"Don't worry about it. Don't worry. Really."

"It must be so much, to lose your dad, it must be awful."

"It's . . . mostly fine," Wallace admits, getting too close to the bone. He doesn't want to go back over the thing about how grief can feel diffuse and dense all at once, like a flock of birds in the sky. He doesn't want to get into it. He can taste dirt on his lips and in his mouth, granular and salty.

Cole blinks like he's looked into the sun for too long. *Mostly fine.* This is why Wallace never tells anyone anything. This is why he keeps the truth to himself, because other people don't know what to do with your shit, with the reality of other people's feelings. They don't know what to do when they've heard something that does not align with their own perception of things. There is a pause. And a silence.

"But it was your dad," Cole presses. "You don't have to say that. You don't have to be embarrassed."

"I'm not. I'm not ashamed. That's how I feel."

"I feel like you're not being honest. Like you're not really accessing things here."

Wallace sits up from the ground, more dirt in his mouth. He picks loose grass from his hair. "I'm feeling very accessed right now."

"I'm here for you. Let me be here for you."

"Cole."

"Stop pushing me away."

Wallace clenches his jaw tight, presses his lips together. He counts back from ten. The air in his nose is hot. Cole is sitting there with his pale limbs wrapped around himself, looking on with those watery eyes of his. He looks sad. Bereft. Alone. This is Wallace's penance for pushing Cole on the tennis court, fair play, wound for wound.

"Okay," he says, and, summoning up a tremulous voice, he adds: "I'm just really numb to it, you know, just really unable to process it."

"I hear that," Cole says, nodding. "I hear that, Wallace."

"And, uhm, I just, yeah, I'm going through it, working the steps of grief, you know?"

"That's so important." Cole touches his arm. "I'm so glad you aren't just internalizing things."

"Thanks," Wallace says, letting the edge of an emotion he doesn't feel rise in his voice. "It's been really helpful to have people in my life who really get me."

"We all love you, Wallace," Cole says, smiling. He pulls Wallace in for a hug. "We all want you to be happy."

Wallace rolls his eyes when Cole hugs him, but he is careful to look cheered if somewhat mournful when he pulls back. They get up from the lakeshore just as the game at the stadium is ending. There is a huge cry from beyond, as all the herons and the geese alight from the water and take to the air.

Gray water falls from their wings, and for a moment it's like rain.

4

For what feels like the first time in days, Wallace is alone—though not entirely, as his apartment still smells like Miller. It seems unfair that Miller has overwritten the smell of his apartment in only a few hours; it seems out of proportion. The scent is not overpowering; in truth it's barely there, discernible just in passing, as though radiating from the pulse points of the apartment, from the obscure corners: tangy citrus and open lake. Wallace briefly contemplates washing the gray duvet, the slate-colored sheets, getting Miller out of his bedclothes entirely. His room smells like their bodies, like their sex, like their sleep, and it is almost enough to make Wallace want to climb back into the bed and draw the blanket over himself and never leave. And it is that desire to climb back into the bed that makes him want to wash the sheets, to reset things, get even again. He rose from the bed this morning, leaving Miller sleeping there looking sweet, looking defenseless. Wallace left him there. It is a decision he regrets now, a little bitterness to chew on for the rest of the night. He pauses in the doorway of his bedroom. He can smell beer, too, leached into the air from Miller's skin and breath. That wet, sour smell with which he is intimately acquainted, though he himself does not drink.

He thinks with some resentment of the surprise people show when he tells them this fact about himself, that he does not drink. The scramble that follows, the backward shuffle into a half-hearted apology for offering him wine or beer or gin—as happened last winter when Henrik offered him gin at Simone's holiday party and Wallace told him, shyly, *No, none for me*, but Henrik said, *You passed your prelims, you're an adult now*, and Wallace said, finally, *I don't drink*. Henrik's gray eyes, the gentle tremor in his lower lip as if bunted with a newspaper, made Wallace feel guilty—so guilty he almost took the glass—but Henrik squared his shoulders and took it away. If Wallace had known then that that would be the last thing Henrik said to him, the last thing Henrik offered him, he would have taken the drink and downed it. He has no real sense for alcohol, how it ought to taste. It all tastes the same to him, though some of it burns when it goes down.

His parents used to drink. All the time. His mother, a broad, massive woman with kind eyes and a mean streak, used to drink weak beer because she was a diabetic. That's what she said, *It's because of my sugar pressure*. And she'd drink beer after beer in her chair, reclining and looking out the window, its parted curtain—scanning the world, for what, Wallace did not know. They lived on a dirt road then, in a trailer, surrounded by relatives whose houses had been built out of cheap material and set up on bricks. There had been nothing in the world for her to see, in their obscure, dark corner surrounded by relatives and pine trees, nothing to watch except the churn of wind and the passing of clouds. But she sat in her chair and watched, every day, and that was how he found her, as he arrived home from college for the summer, sweating it out in his old bedroom, passing the time as they all did, waiting for the heat of the day to break, crawling into whatever cool corner one could find.

He found her in her chair, her eyes open, her body gone stiff, gone tight. The doctor said she'd had a stroke. Something out of the blue. His mother had worked in a hotel on a golf course for ten years. But then, a while back, she had developed a tremor and for long periods of time thereafter she was locked up and couldn't move. That's what Wallace thought was happening to her. On the day he found her, her cup was still full of melting ice—the blue kind she liked from the hotel; she had a friend who brought her a new bag every couple of weeks—which was how Wallace knew she hadn't been gone long. But that was years ago now, the summer before he left for the Midwest, for graduate school and a new life. What had she been looking for, all those days she'd spent in the chair, is a question he thinks of often. But for some questions there are no answers. When asked, *Why don't you drink?* Wallace almost tells this story. But he does not. He says something else, something like, *Oh, you know.* One of those nonsense phrases meant to buffer the silence native to any exchange between people.

It is of his mother that he thinks today when he smells the beer in the air. Like a haunting. He has not thought of her in a long time. When he does, it's always the good things he remembers: how she would let him stay home from school if his stomach hurt, and how she'd spend the day with him, make him soup and let him watch cartoons; how he looked up and caught her watching him, not with pride exactly, but with fondness, with love. The rare moments when she was not shouting at him from the other room to come and tie her shoes for her, or when she wasn't telling him that he was stupid, when she wasn't bellowing in a register and at a volume that made her words indistinct and indecipherable to him, when she wasn't striking him across the mouth, or forcing him to wash under his arms and between his legs in front of her, in front of company, when she wasn't subjecting him to the innumerable dark hairs of her anger and her fear and her mistrust—then she could be, in those small moments, good to him. It is why he does not trust memory. Memory sifts. Memory lifts. Memory makes due with what it is given. Memory is not about facts. Memory is an inconsistent measurement of the pain in one's life. But he thinks of her. She falls out of the scent of beer, and he shuts his bedroom door because he cannot bear it.

There is not much time before the dinner thing anyway.

Wallace surveys the contents of the freezer. Some chicken breast, ground beef, fish, a variety of frozen vegetables, a pizza, some ice trays. The cold feels good on his face, which is still a little flushed from tennis and from the walk along the lake back to the apartment. His friends, and their friends, seldom eat meat. There are typically many different vegetable dishes at their dinners, many different casseroles of beans and pasta and cheeses and long green stalks and quinoa and peas and nuts and jams and berries and grains. Once, early in his time here, he made a dish of Swedish meatballs, like his aunts had made for gatherings. Dark

meat and onion and pepper and garlic and rich sauce made from
scratch, cinnamon and cumin and vinegar and hickory and
brown sugar, all in a Nordic-themed serving dish he'd purchased
at a thrift store. He stood on the front porch just out of the rain,
balancing the warm dish on his arms, trying to smile through his
nerves. In those days, Yngve and Cole and Lukas lived together
in a house just outside downtown, in one of the few residential
neighborhoods that remained, the way they do in some college
towns, where the barrier between the city and what used to be
the town out of which the city emerged turns hazy and porous,
and it is possible, if you stand on one street and look down it,
to see the progression of time. The shutters, the porches, the
white columns, broad windows, porch swings, lemonade on
the banisters or tea slowly steeping on wicker tables, homes that
in another time contained families, but that now contain the
mismatched furniture and chipped dishes that have come to sig-
nify their lives, they who have freshly emerged from undergrad
or grad school, their adulthood as wet as new moths' wings.
When the door swung open, it was not one of his friends, but a
girl Yngve was sort of interested in seeing at the time, tall and
brunette, from Arizona or some other dry place beneath notice.
She took one look at the meatballs and wrinkled her nose. Then
asked him if he was lost, or needed something.

Yngve explained it all later, with an arm wrapped around
Wallace's neck, laughing in his ear. "Sorry, sorry," he said. "But,
you know, she's, like, *vegan*, so . . ." Wallace tried not to look
disappointed when he collected his dish of uneaten meatballs at

the end of the night, tried not to think of the money he'd spent and the time in his kitchen, wiping sweat, toweling brown stains off his hands, trying to get it exactly right, trying to make the sauce perfect for them—and the little dish, he'd been so proud of the little dish, red with white reindeer leaping. Not Swedish or anything, but close, on a theme, he had hoped.

Since that time, Wallace has been careful to avoid bringing meat to these things. He typically brings crackers or another form of fiber because his friends are all full of shit and need cleaning out from time to time, all that cellulose from their vegetables. That is, on the few occasions when he has actually been invited to dinner with his friends. It seems to him now that they do not invite him along as much because he is in the habit of telling them no, or staying for only a little while, until the meal has just ended and they're all feeling good and talking quietly about the things they did the last time they were all together, things that do not include Wallace because he was not there or left early. It's in those moments that he experiences most acutely the feeling of his own estrangement from these people he calls his friends. Their shining eyes and wet mouths and their greasy fingers working at each other's knees, a pantomime of intimacy, a cult of happiness, a cult of friendship.

He can make a fruit salad or something. Lots of melon this time of year, and grapes are in season, particularly the green ones of which he's fond, their tart juice and squishy bodies. He'll make a fruit salad, like when they were all children, full of peaches and cantaloupe and honeydew and apple; no oranges, though, too full of seeds. A salad is easy to make.

. . .

AFTER COLE MOVED OUT to live with Vincent, Miller moved in with Yngve and Lukas, taking his place. Their house is warm and comfortably furnished. After that first year, they bought real furniture for real adults at a real store, which is to say, they bought it at IKEA and put it together one humid and shirtless afternoon. Wallace was there to offer moral support and bottles of water, watching the sweat sluice down their spines and their stomachs, collecting at the tops of their shorts, staining them. Then everyone went out back to sit in the kiddie pool, the water already lukewarm from the sun, but cool enough, and besides, it was the novelty of the act that they enjoyed so much, and that was worth something.

It's a short walk to their place from Wallace's apartment, and the bowl isn't hot this time, but slightly chilled. The early evening is pale. It's just past six thirty. He's on time. He can see them through the window as he comes around the corner, all of them lit up by the yellow kitchen lights, smiling and laughing. White string lights have been woven down the banister. He steadies himself. This will be fine. This is going to be fine.

Everyone here is his friend.

He nudges the door open with his toe, and sticks his head around the corner.

"Hello, hello," he calls, stepping inside.

"Wallace!" comes a chorus of voices from the kitchen. He toes off his shoes and leaves them at the door and makes his way through the current of warm air into the kitchen, where seven or eight people are already gathered. Cole and Vincent are washing root vegetables in the deep gray basin of the sink, bumping up against each other affectionately. Roman is sitting on the kitchen floor playing with a small rabbit. Emma comes toward Wallace with a glass of wine and wraps her arm around his neck. Lukas and Yngve chop celery and carrots at the kitchen island.

"Oh, are you making bunny stew?" Wallace asks as he sets his bowl on a nearby counter.

"Don't joke about Lila," Lukas says, pointing the knife at Wallace. There's something joking in his voice, but only barely.

"I love bunny stew," Yngve says. "Love, love, love."

Lukas gives him a look of utter betrayal and mild disgust. Wallace laughs. On the other side of the kitchen, near Cole and Vincent, there is a woman chipping ice. She is tall and solidly built, with broad shoulders and a slender neck. She's wearing a shirt with an open back, and Wallace can see freckles, rust-brown, speckling her shoulder blades. She seems immensely healthy. Her laugh is low and raspy, and she turns to Cole to say something; in profile, she is quite pretty. Her eyes are dark blue.

Emma whispers in his ear, her voice sticky and wet with wine: "That's Zoe. Yngve is trying to set Miller up."

"Oh, I think Cole mentioned something about that at tennis," Wallace says, and he tries to smile, but his cheeks are already sore and the night hasn't even begun yet.

"I think she's a rock climber or something like that?" Emma takes another long pull from her wine. Her eyes are red. She's been crying.

"Where's Thom?" Wallace asks, and it's like Emma collapses into a single, dark line. She closes in on him.

"Let's go see how those potatoes are coming, shall we?" She takes Wallace's arm by the elbow and they move through the kitchen, its bumpy tiles crackling underfoot. Roman looks up at him and gives a faint, swiftly dying smile that is neither cold nor warm.

"Roman," Wallace says.

"Wallace."

Cole turns to Wallace and hugs him tight, but he's careful not to get the cloudy water on Wallace's shirt. Cole's cologne smells vaguely like ground cardamom.

"You made it," he says.

"I did. I made it."

"I'm so glad," he says, propping his damp wrists on Wallace's shoulders.

"Wallace," Vincent says, and he reaches over to hug Wallace awkwardly around Cole. He squeezes Wallace's arm. "Good to see you."

Zoe is now at Wallace's left. They're clustered together, squeezed between Emma, who is opening another bottle of wine, and Cole and Vincent at the sink. Zoe's got the ice pick and the small mallet in hand. Her fingers look very sure of themselves. Up close, he can see that she has a wide mouth full of very expensive teeth, as he anticipated. Her eyes are set high on her head. She smiles at him.

"Zoe," she says by way of introduction. "It's nice to meet you."

"Same," he says with more warmth than he feels. "So, what do you do in town?"

It is the question they always ask people who are not in their program. What makes a person come to this place? Why this city on three lakes?

"Law school," she says.

"I see. And rock climbing, from what I hear?" Wallace says.

Zoe lines up the pick on a chunk of ice and with one smart movement cracks it open. "Definitely. My dad is a climbing instructor in Denver. So it runs in the family, I guess."

"Is that where you're from?" Wallace asks.

"No, originally, I'm from Billings. But my family moved a lot. I grew up all over, really, but Billings is home. I did my undergrad in Boston though."

"Harvard?"

Zoe's cheeks redden. She carves another section of ice. Wallace watches the gray blade of the pick descend into the heart of the ice.

"Oh. Yeah," she says, offhand.

Wallace nods.

"You?" Zoe asks.

"Auburn," he says.

"Where is that?" she asks, laughing.

"Alabama," he says.

"Oh—Crimson Tide."

"No," Wallace says. "The other one. Tigers."

"Ah," she says, nodding. Her hands are swift as she cracks the ice open into halves, then quarters. She breaks it down into cubes and ovals and crescents. It could be a party trick. Perhaps it is a party trick.

"Can I help with anything?" Wallace asks, turning to Cole and Vincent.

"No, no. Everything is all set," they all say in various ways at various times, a chorus of voices falling on him like drops of rain. The kitchen is warm and foggy, filled with the gurgle and sizzle of food cooking. "Go have a seat or something."

"Okay," he says. "All right. Where's Miller?" Zoe's shoulders open just slightly.

"Uh. That's a good question, actually," Yngve says, frowning. "He was supposed to be setting up the music, but then he sort of vanished."

"I'll check out back," Wallace says, and he steps over Roman's long legs to reach the sliding door. Roman is still cuddling the fat brown rabbit, Lila the bunny, a mascot of sorts. He would stop to pet her, but Roman has her in a protective grasp, and Wallace knows that there are limits to his frosty friendliness.

In the backyard there is grass, so it is much cooler than the front, which faces the street and the asphalt of the city. Wallace has always loved this part of the house, where Lukas keeps a tiny garden bounded by red bricks. There is also one of those upright storage units that look like the entrance to a small home. And a large oak tree near the back fence, and a fire pit, where on autumn nights they burn dry wood and drink beer and laugh as their clothes fill with the smell of smoke.

He finds Miller sitting in a chair near the edge of the yard, one of those aluminum folding chairs with tacky plastic for the seat. Overhead, the sky is lavender. Miller's drinking from a long dark bottle, staring into his phone. Texting, probably. He does not see Wallace as he approaches. Wallace stands at the edge of Miller's toes, waiting for him to notice, for the weight of his presence to shift something in the air. He holds his breath. Miller is wearing a crisp blue oxford with the sleeves rolled back, and dark blue shorts. He has always been self-conscious about his knees and the skinniness of his legs. But sailing has changed that, made him hardier, fuller, like a drawing taking shape over thin streaked lines. His hair is glossy and light.

"I can see you there," he says.

"Hello."

"I didn't know if you would come," Miller says shyly. He's nervous, probably about the girl; at first this makes Wallace want to smile at him, and then it just annoys him.

"Cole asked me to," he says.

"Is this weird? It's probably weird."

"No, I don't think it's weird at all."

"You don't? I do," Miller says, shaking his head. "I think it's terrible. I didn't ask Yngve to—"

"Oh, who cares, how boring."

"Hey, come on, don't be that way, please. I'm trying to be good."

"You aren't doing anything wrong. No one is. It's all good."

"I really hate this. I didn't even know there would be a dinner thing until I got home earlier. They sprung it on me."

"Cole told me," Wallace says. "After tennis. Or during. He said they decided after we left the table last night."

"Oh yeah?" Miller slides his leg against the inside of Wallace's legs, their bare skin skimming, touching. The warmth of it excites Wallace, brings him back to the surface of last night, when they left the table together, or separately, but wound up together. It's on Miller's mind, too, the way he's looking up with dusk filling his eyes, remembering. The tip of Miller's tongue emerges from the pink of his mouth and presses against the edge of his lips.

"Not like that," Wallace says, short of breath. "I meant— You know what I meant."

"I know," Miller says. He sits forward in the chair, brings his hand to the outside of Wallace's thigh, just over his knee. His fingers, the roughness of them, are familiar, from this morning, from last night. He jolts, almost falls down. Miller traces a thumb up the front of his knee, and he's smiling. The wind makes a soft sound in the trees, like a hushed cry. "How are you feeling?" Miller asks. "That girl in your lab, I mean. How are you?"

"Better," Wallace says. He puts his fingers in Miller's hair, which is greasy with product, but he persists, passing them back and back through its curls. "I came here thinking I'd be sulky and mad all night."

"Mad? Why mad? At me?"

"No, I don't know, maybe, yes. Mad at you. And myself, mostly. Yngve."

"But you aren't mad? That's good, right?"

"I don't know if it's good," Wallace says. "I don't know if it's good at all."

"Why wouldn't it be?"

"Because, I think, if I'm not mad, maybe that means I feel like I've won something. Like I've gotten something I wanted. But I shouldn't want it at all. You know?"

"I don't," Miller says. He puts the beer on the grass beside him and holds on to Wallace's legs with both hands. "Tell me," he says.

Wallace pulls his hands through Miller's hair down to his forehead and he presses his thumb hard there so that Miller's brows, furrowed in concentration, flatten and smooth.

"I feel relieved because I didn't want to think about you wanting someone else. But I also don't want to feel relieved. I don't want to care if you do or don't."

"But what if I want you to care?" Miller says.

"Straight boys," Wallace says, laughing, "always want what they want until they don't."

"That's not fair. We're friends."

"Which is why this is such a terrible idea," Wallace says.

"I don't think so."

There is a voice in the gathering darkness calling for them. Miller's fingers flex around him and then release him.

"I'm not done talking to you about this," Miller says.

"What's to talk about?" Wallace asks. They turn to the voice calling their names. It's Yngve. He's got his hand cupped over his eyes.

"We'll eat without you," he says. "Hurry up. And where is our music, Miller?"

Miller pushes up from the chair, and the two of them go along the grass together, not looking at each other. Wallace then feels

Miller's knuckles graze the outside of his knuckles, and for a moment the two of them are connected. The contact is over almost as it begins, and the suddenness of the dissolution heightens Wallace's sense of it: For the span of those several seconds, he felt as though molten glass were being drawn through him like liquid into a capillary. They climb the back stairs, and they are once more among their friends.

THE TABLE IS PERHAPS the one article of genuine adult furniture in the whole house. Lukas brought it down with him from his grandparents' home in northern Wisconsin. Typically the table is pressed to the far wall, where it holds the articles of their lives: dishes, laundry, newspapers, books, articles, notebooks, tools, cables, and whatever else could be discarded and forgotten. But today they've drawn the table away from the wall into the large open room off the kitchen. Lukas draped a linen tablecloth over it, disguising its bruises, its nicks, specks of robin's-egg blue from the painting of chairs. All this cartography hidden now.

Wallace sits in the middle, between Emma and Cole, across the table from Roman and Klaus. Yngve and his girlfriend, Enid, are at one end of the table with Miller and Zoe; down the other are Lukas and his boyfriend, Nathan. The table is a little cramped. Emma has parked her elbow in Wallace's side; he keeps stepping on the edge of Cole's foot. Vincent's tacked on to the end next to Cole.

"I'm first off the island, I guess," Vincent says, and there's a small murmur of laughter.

They pass the food in diagonals. Wallace takes some of the baked chicken (meat at the dinner thing, a mild thrill), some asparagus, brussels sprouts, a kind of strange mealy paste with no aroma that he presumes are the mashed potatoes. Someone passes him the wine, and he says, "No, none for me, thank you."

Roman holds the bottle, presses it forward. "No, don't be rude, now."

"Wallace doesn't drink," Emma says.

"Did you drive here? Is that it? We can surely find you a ride home."

"No," Wallace says. "I just don't drink."

Roman is very handsome—so blond that Wallace thinks he cannot be naturally so. But his eyelashes are blond, his eyebrows are blond, and his beard is mostly a white-yellow, except in places where it's gone dark red. He has dark green eyes, and a very architectural chin. To Wallace he looks not French but Icelandic. But he is French, from a small town in Normandy. His English is faultless, though accented. Klaus is stubby and dark-featured, like a minor folkloric figure. There is something perpetually strained about him, as though he is concentrating every moment of every day to make himself taller. Roman studies the early development of the heart in mice, the point at which the clump of white tissue no more animal-like than the white meat of an egg begins to jerk and to beat. He holds the hearts of tiny animals on his fingernail.

The look he gives Wallace is difficult to parse, though Wallace decides it means *annoyed*.

Down the table and back up the table goes the wine bottle, go the dishes of food. Wallace pulls the leg of the chicken out of its joint, sees the white head of the cartilage pop out. The meat itself is tender and dark. Though, at the joint, the chicken is red and a little bloody. It's undercooked, but he cuts it up anyway, all the chicken and its crispy yellow crust dissected upon his plate. Under the skin lurk pulpy, bulbous strings of fat. The corn is good. Sweet, a little oily.

"Have you been to Yosemite?" Wallace hears from up the table. It's Zoe, talking to Miller.

"No," he says.

"I do this thing with some friends almost every year—we try to go to as many national parks as we can in a summer. I love Yosemite the most, though. My parents took me and my brother there every year."

"I did Glacier a few weeks back," Yngve says. "With Enid."

"How was it?" Zoe asks with a laugh.

"Gorgeous, of course," Enid says. Enid and Zoe are not dissimilar looking, Wallace notes. Except Enid is very pale. Her hair is a dyed gray-lilac color. She has a nose piercing, and her shoulder is covered in angular dark tattoos, deep black zigzags. Not tribal, but a geometry of the self, Wallace thinks. "I kind of broke my foot, though, so it was short."

"I stayed for three days after that, though," Yngve says. Enid's lips tighten as she nods, like the gesture is costing her something. "I mean. I don't get a lot of time off, and it was kind of a big trip for me."

"Glacier's a great park," Zoe says. "I did that one too. Not this year. Last."

"I've never been to a national park," Miller says.

"Me either," Wallace says. They turn to him, as if suddenly aware that he has been listening to their conversation this whole time. He goes back to his plate. Tries to tuck himself smaller, but it is too late for that. He has squandered his opening gambit. Miller laughs.

"It can seem scary, or too big a thing," Zoe says. "I mean, *national park* doesn't really make it sound like a welcoming place. But . . . I don't know, there's just something about being in a place like that, where it's just you and nature and the cell phone service is shitty. It's like starting over."

"That's why I went climbing after my grandpa died," Yngve says. "It's you and the rock. It's you and the sky. It's you, and all that matters is, *Can I move five inches upward without dying?* It's amazing."

"I think it's like—you know how when you look back at something and you realize how stupid it was to be upset that Tiffany Blanchard didn't invite you to her slumber party? And how stupid it was that Greg Newsome didn't ask you to homecoming? Like, when you're climbing or hiking or just out there in the hills, when you see, like, the products of geological time—it's like that. It's like—" Zoe fumbles, makes slow circles with her knife, trying to find the word.

"Perspective," Emma says.

"Yes, exactly. Perspective. Thank you," Zoe says, laughing. "It's like, what am I getting upset about? Because of *torts*?"

"Don't lawyers decide if people live or die?" Miller asks, and Zoe winces.

"You know what I mean," she says. "Right?" She's looking at them, at each of them, in turn. Her eyes wander over their faces, and Wallace feels himself retract from her gaze. It is painful to watch the embarrassment come over her. She clears her throat.

"Totally," Vincent says, a beat too late. "It's like we were talking about yesterday—there's more to life than a program."

"Don't start," Cole says.

"Like, you, Wallace," Vincent says, sitting forward. The table shifts. Their glasses shake. Wallace's water ripples.

"How do you mean?" he asks, his voice drawing across the question as though to reveal a suddenly vanished rabbit.

Vincent barely pauses, says, "How you want to leave, I mean. How you want to quit. Your dad dying. Perspective, right?"

Wallace feels their gazes strike the surface of his body like pellets.

"Oh, it hardly seems the same," he says.

"Seems like it to me," Vincent replies, and then elaborates. "Wallace was saying yesterday, last night, that he hates grad school. Just hates it. Is totally miserable—poor guy—and anyway, he's like, *My dad died, and I hate it here.* Why would he stay? You know. Like, *his dad just died.* That must change things, certainly."

"Must it?" Wallace asks, and to his horror, he realizes that he isn't asking just himself. He has asked the table. His voice is a hoarse whisper. "Must it change things? What must it change?"

"Well. *Everything*," Vincent says with a wry laugh. "I mean, if my dad died, I'd be devastated."

Wallace nods. There is a hollow hissing sound from somewhere overhead. Now that they are all quiet, he can hear it perfectly. What is that, he wonders. That sound like something escaping, a leak.

"Everything must change," he says after a while, smiling, laughing—always smiling, the smiling fool, the happy clam. His eyes crinkle. The room relaxes. Roman narrows his eyes.

"Is that true? That you are thinking of going?"

Wallace thinks of three French verbs in quick succession: *partir, sortir, quitter*. He learned French in high school, where he took four years of the language. And then in college, where he studied another three years. In college, he was also friends with the North African tennis players, but he was always shy to use his French outside the classroom. Except in moments of peculiar bravery, he asked them questions about themselves, about their homes, their families, about their lives. And there was a boy, Peter, with whom he almost slept several times. Peter used to say good-bye to him with *quitter*: *Je quitte*. It is of this word that Wallace now thinks. It hangs on the edge of his tongue, but he holds it back. It is a private word. It belongs to Peter.

Wallace hums. "I mean, I wouldn't say that I *want* to leave, but I've thought about it, sure."

"Why would you do that? I mean, the prospects for . . . black people, you know?"

"What are the prospects for black people?" Wallace asks, though he knows he will be considered the aggressor for this question. Already, they're taking stock of the tension in his forearms, in his hands, in the way his eyes are narrowing. Tension gathers at the corners of his mouth.

"Well," Roman says, shrugging, "with a doctorate, you have better prospects, a better job, better outlook. Without it . . . the stats are what they are."

"Fascinating," Wallace says.

"Besides, they spent so much money on your training. It seems ungrateful to leave."

"So I should stay out of gratitude?"

"I mean, if you don't feel you can keep up, then for sure, you should go. But they brought you in knowing what your deficiencies were and—"

"My deficiencies?"

"Yes. Your deficiencies. I won't say what they are. You already know. You come from a challenging background. It is unfortunate, but it is how it is."

Wallace can only taste ashes in his mouth. He dissects a piece of a casserole and chews it thoughtfully. His deficiencies are indeed what they are. There are the gaps in his knowledge about developmental biology, which he has closed steadily over the past few years, through study and coursework. There was also, in those early years, a lack of technical expertise, which he has acquired through practice. But the deficiency to which Roman is alluding is not one of those, not one of the many ways in which people come into graduate school unprepared for its demands, wrong-footed this way and that by its odd rituals and rigors. What Roman is referring to is instead a deficiency of whiteness, a lack of some requisite sameness. This deficiency cannot be overcome. The fact is, no matter how hard he tries or how much he learns or how many skills he masters, he will always be provisional in the eyes of these people, no matter how they might be fond of him or gentle with him.

"Did I hurt your feelings?" Roman asks. "I just want to be clear. I think you should stay. You owe the department that much, don't you agree?"

"I don't have anything to say to that, Roman," Wallace says, smiling. To keep his hands from shaking, he clenches his fists until his knuckles turn to white ridges of pressure.

"Well, think about it," he says.

"I will, thanks."

Emma puts her head on Wallace's shoulder, but she won't say anything either, can't bring herself to. No one does. No one ever does. Silence is their way of getting by, because if they are silent long enough, then this moment of minor discomfort will pass for them, will fold down into the landscape of the evening as if it never happened. Only Wallace will remember it. That's the frustrating part. Wallace is the only one for whom this is a humiliation. He breathes out through the agony of it, through the pressure in his chest. Roman is whispering to Klaus, and they're laughing about something.

"Can we get that wine back down here?" Lukas asks in a tone that is both polite and pointed. Nathan is on his phone, reading the scores of the badminton competition in Singapore.

"You'll have to come get it," Yngve says, holding the bottle up and swirling it.

"Just give it to him," Enid says. "Jesus."

Lukas is already standing, coming around Wallace's side of

the table and approaching Yngve. He reaches for the bottle, but Yngve has bolted to his feet.

"You'll have to be faster," Yngve says, and Lukas loads his weight and springs for the bottle. Lukas is much shorter than Yngve. He has a compact, muscular body and the features of a cartoon character—wide eyes, large face. Yngve steps back, Lukas steps forward. It's a dance.

Nathan pushes his glasses back up his nose. He watches the two of them at the head of the table, the swing and pivot of their bodies. The wine sloshes, glugs in the bottle. There is another bottle of wine on the table. Enid watches it very carefully. There's tension in her neck. Zoe crosses her arms on the table to support herself. Her shoulders shake with laughter. Miller's eyes fall to her back just as Zoe's eyes come across her shoulder. Their gazes meet. And Wallace feels it happening, the tightening between people in common attraction.

Yngve puts his arm around Lukas, gets him by the waist, and lifts him up. "Sorry, shorty. You must be this tall to drink wine."

"Yngve," Lukas says, but he can't help himself. He's flush-faced.

"What are we, children?" Enid asks. She lifts the bottle from the table and slams it down. It does not break. "Take this one."

Yngve lets Lukas down. Lukas takes the bottle from his hand. There's no challenge in him anymore. He takes his seat, breathing hard. Nathan looks down with the same prim delicacy with which one might fold a napkin in one's lap. Wallace smells the wine, its sweet, dark scent.

Cole laughs nervously.

They are always laughing. This is it, Wallace thinks. That's how they get by. Silence and laughter, silence and laughter, switch and swing. The way one glides through this life without having to think about anything hard. He still feels the sting of embarrassment, but it has ebbed. Vincent's gaze clips the outside of his own. Wallace eats his food.

The tasteless, strained, diluted flavor of white people food, its curious texture, its ugliness. He eats his food. He grinds his teeth. His anger is cold. There's a skin stretching across it.

Roman and Vincent share a look. Cole watches them share a look. They are all looking at each other.

Wallace thinks of Peter. Of his mother. Of his father. Of Henrik. Of Dana.

"You guys played tennis today?" Vincent asks. The commonness of the question shears the skin off Wallace's anger.

"It was great," Cole says.

"We had a long talk. It was good to catch up."

"I bet, I bet," Vincent says.

"So when you were on the app last night, Vincent, were you just looking or did you really plan to fuck someone else?" Wallace asks, smiling, his teeth gleaming.

There is a stuttering pause. Cole tenses. Roman's eyes swing around to them. Vincent turns a sickly green color.

"What?" he asks. "What did you say?"

"I saw you on the app last night, and I was just wondering if . . . you know, you two were opening things up?" He looks between Cole and Vincent, as though he were asking about color swatches. He asks in a voice lighter than he feels, because in truth, at the moment, he wants to die. But it feels good, for once, to see someone else caught out.

Cole reaches down and grips Wallace's knee hard and tight, so tight it almost hurts, and that pain is nearly enough to get him through this moment. Wallace's head is pounding.

"I . . . I . . ."

"Is that true, Vincent?" Cole asks, taking up Wallace's lie, because unlike for Wallace, this truth is one that means everything to him.

"I don't . . . I wasn't . . . I . . ."

"Wow," Roman says, clapping softly. "Good for you two. It's great."

"Really great," Klaus says, nodding firmly. "It's the best decision we ever made."

"You were on there?" Cole says, letting his anger and his hurt sweep through him. He turns in his chair. "We were only talking about it. But you did it behind my back? Why?"

Wallace watches Vincent's face very carefully. That pinched, needful look of his has turned sharper and more pronounced. He has crumbs of food stuck to the underside of his lower lip. His mouth is shiny with grease. His thick brow, which juts over his small eyes like a protective cliff, has grown darker. There are some people whose shock flays them open and leaves them exposed, but Vincent is not one of these people. He has collected into himself, grown small and hard, and Wallace feels in some way both proud of him and cheated of a more discernible reaction. Yes, Wallace thinks, that's it, don't let them see you sweat, Vincent; it should be that way. But he also feels, in the baser part of himself, a snarl of anger, deprived of his reward for having turned it all back on them. It's an ugly, petty part of Wallace that delights and shivers and wishes only that Vincent were the more combustible sort.

"Holy shit," Lukas says. "Holy shit."

"Oh my god." Yngve is up from the end of the table and coming toward them, but thinks better of it, reluctant to get caught up in someone else's mess, and sits back down.

"I was just looking, Cole. I didn't mean to do anything. I was just looking."

"But why didn't you tell me? Why didn't you say something before you did it?"

"I don't know. I was scared you'd say no. I was scared I'd want you to say yes? I don't know. *Fuck*." Vincent's eyes are wet. He's on the brink of crying. Wallace feels guilty now—real guilt, gravelly and hard. He swallows. His own eyes are stinging. Cole is crying softly already, beating his leg with his hand.

"Why am I not enough?"

"It's not about you not being enough," Roman says.

Cole turns to him and says, "Shut up, Roman. I wasn't talking to you."

There is a look of surprise on Roman's face. He leans back in his chair. "You two are out here in public. I assumed you wanted input."

"Can we just have a fucking minute to be in our relationship without you wanting to stick your dick in it?"

"Someone is finally growing some spine, great for you," Roman says, clapping louder this time. "Someone is finally being a man. But a tip. If you don't want someone else fucking your boyfriend, maybe you should."

"What is he talking about, Vincent?"

"No, no, no," Vincent says, putting his face in his hands. "No, no, no. This isn't happening."

"Vincent, what is he talking about?"

"Fuck," Vincent says. "Fuck."

Klaus is dark red with anger, looking stormily at Roman, who has gone back to eating his dinner.

"Jesus fucking Christ," Miller says. Emma has gotten up to put her arms around Cole, who is staring at Vincent.

"Baby, baby," Emma says. "Baby, baby. Come on." She's rubbing Cole's back, pressing him to get up from the table and come with her, somewhere, anywhere else.

Wallace does not even try to look innocent of his role in the whole thing. Cole will likely never forgive him, but Wallace did in fact give him what he needed but could never ask for himself, and isn't that why Cole asked him to come in the first place? Yes, he reacted out of pettiness, out of a desire to see someone brought low, but in the end, hadn't something important been achieved? He looks to his left and sees Vincent sobbing into his hands, and Cole staring like an empty obelisk. Roman and Klaus speak to each other in angry French and German, words slashing at each other.

The dinner is ruined, that much is obvious, but Wallace is still eating because he is hungry. He eats the soup, even though there is too much tomato. He chews through the eggplant parm, the salads, the mashed potatoes, the pilaf, the pasta with olives, and the homemade ravioli. It feels as if some great pit in him has opened that can be filled only with food. He eats and eats, more and more servings, kale and hummus and pita chips and salty crackers. There is a variety of desserts: his fruit salad, some pecan pie, pumpkin pie, a cherry tart, lemon squares, snickerdoodles, a host of cookies. He eats them bit by bit, inch by inch, sliding them into his mouth. He is the only one eating because everyone else is speaking quietly, in twos and threes, trying to unravel what has happened.

Wallace does not look up. There was a time in second year, soon after Dana had convinced Simone that he had mixed up the purification reagents, when Wallace ate his lunch alone in the third-floor library. He would use the rickety microwave in the kitchen and then take his steaming cup of ramen down the halls, trying to keep the lid pressed tight against the sloshing hot water, and then take up residence in one of the study rooms so he could be alone with his shame. He ate while watching videos on his phone, the bright afternoon light cutting across the narrow window and lying like a golden slat on the table. He ate alone every day for a month, until one day Henrik came to find him. Wallace looked up, and there he was peering through the window in the door, watching him. Wallace jumped, knocked his cup on the floor, and Henrik's expression darkened. He got down on his knees and started to scoop the ruined noodles into the cup, and Henrik pressed the door open and said, *What are you doing in here? We have a kitchen for this.* He folded his arms across his chest, hands damp on his shirt, and he wouldn't move until Wallace collected his cup and his fork and began to walk back to the kitchen to dispose of his lunch. He didn't eat lunch at lab for a long time after that, and every day, around three in the afternoon, Henrik would take his own lunch, and he'd stop just as he left their bay and look back at Wallace. There was regret in his eyes, Wallace thinks now. Regret and something else. He wishes he had asked Henrik about that. He wishes he had asked Henrik to eat lunch with him. He wonders now if Henrik had come not to scold him, but to make some offer—of friendship, maybe—but being shy, not knowing what to do with himself, had fumbled. Or maybe it hadn't been anything.

The others have gotten up from the table. They've gone back through the archway into the kitchen. He hears them, distantly, faintly. The murmur of plans. No one speaks to him. Why would they now? He's ruined their dinner thing.

The carrots are tearing his gums. He can taste a little of his own blood. His jaws feel loose, like putty.

"What are you doing?" Miller asks, and Wallace does look up, sees Miller's face. He looks a little startled. Wallace presses his fingers to his lips, feels the warm, sticky weight of blood, not a lot, just a little. He's nicked his lips with his teeth.

"Oh," he says.

"You look terrible," Miller says. He pulls out the chair next to Wallace and has a seat.

"I feel terrible." Wallace glances through the archway out the back door. He sees the edge of someone's shirt. They're sitting under the tree out back. "I made a mess of tonight."

"You had some help."

"I knew better than to say that."

"Probably so."

Wallace groans and puts his head on the table, but instead of crying the way he wants to, he just laughs. It's not funny. It's not remotely funny. What has transpired tonight? Vincent's infidelity, nebulous though it may remain, loosely confirmed at the very least. Nathan and Enid relegated to minor figures in their relationships with Lukas and Yngve, a tragedy not entirely surprising but pitiable. Roman is a racist at best. Who knows what's going on with Emma and Thom? Zoe seems nice, but in the way that white people are nice right before they perform some new role in the secret machinery that ruins black people's lives. It seems to Wallace that there is nothing to do but laugh.

He laughs and laughs. His eyes fill with warm tears. They dampen the white tablecloth. Miller's hand is warm on the nape of Wallace's neck, a tender gesture. Wallace's laughter cinches like a wrung towel, and when it opens again, it is a wail.

"God," he says. "I fucking hate it here."

"I know."

"I fucking hate it everywhere."

"I'm sorry."

"I don't know where to go or what to do," he says, and because the words are so true, strike such a fundamental chord with who he is, he vibrates at high frequency, shivers like a tuning fork.

"It's not so bad," Miller says.

"It is."

"It'll work out."

"You don't know that."

"Don't tell me what I know," Miller says, cracking a smile. It is a deflection, and a bad one at that, which annoys Wallace. A deflection out of kindness. A kindness that seeks to encompass all futures, that asserts its constancy regardless of what might come. Miller, stroking the back of Wallace's neck and looking down at him like an amused nursery school teacher, is saying something, promising something, and all Wallace has to do is find it in himself to accept it.

"You guys never take this stuff seriously," Wallace says, and starts to push Miller's hand away from him, but he stops when Miller says quietly, "I'm sorry.

"We should be better. I should be better. I'm sorry," Miller says firmly. This is kindness too, Wallace thinks. Of a different sort. What he does not know—and maybe, just maybe, it's not important—is whether this kindness is just an extension of their friendship or something else, or if that question itself, the uncertainty, is a rebuke, an insult, a miscalculation. What is the source of kindness? What causes people to be kind to each other? "Wallace?" Miller asks after a moment. "Okay? I'm sorry."

Wallace nods, his head still against the table. Miller's thumb resumes its scratching glide across Wallace's neck.

Kindness is a debt, Wallace thinks. Kindness is something owed and something repaid. Kindness is an obligation.

The kettle goes shrill on the stove. Someone is making coffee for the group outside. The windows are open, and the world smells like summer turning to fall. There is a certain crispness.

Miller, in the darkening room, opens his mouth and then closes it. He puts his head on the table, too, and they're sitting there like two ducks with their faces in the water. It's harder for Miller, who has a long neck, but he's making it work somehow. Wallace wants to laugh at him.

The house exhales into the cool of the evening. Crickets in the garden, eating the leaves. Under the table, Wallace reaches for Miller's hand and takes it.

Voices from outside. Steps on the back stairs, coming up. Emma, slapping into the kitchen in sandals, smelling like dogwood and coconut.

"I'm so tired," she says. Her voice is warped. She's a little drunk. "But coffee won't make itself." There is the sound of her clattering about, making busy with small tasks. Miller is smiling at him, blinking slowly. Wallace could sleep forever. "Are you coming outside?"

Miller's smile is slow in coming, but he lets Wallace's hand go. Emma is in the kitchen, at the counter. The rich, dark scent of coffee joins them—she's making pour-over, less acidic and smoother than brew. The water over the grounds in the filter is hissing softly, settling in, the faint trickle of the water like rain. Wallace sits up in his chair. Emma's face goes dark.

"I guess I'll have another beer," Miller says. He gets up from the table, and Emma takes his spot, folding her legs under herself.

"Wallace, don't get mad at me—" she says. It's the slow windup. He stiffens. She's chewing on an apple slice. "What was that at dinner? It wasn't like you."

"What would be like me, Emma?" he asks low, quick. She looks a little startled by the question, by his tone, which is not neutral or kind. She resents his resentment.

"You aren't like this. This isn't who you are."

"Nobody said a thing to him when he was suddenly a demographics expert, did they?"

"That isn't the same. You might have really hurt Cole," she says.

"Hurt Cole? Me? And not his philandering boyfriend?"

"You don't know what's going on with them, Wallace. You don't get to decide how someone else's life is run, what is okay for them. That isn't your call. You should have asked him in private."

"Oh," Wallace says, nodding severely. He takes some of the apple slices for himself. He peels back their slick skins until their white flesh is bare, sees how they begin to oxidize, these naked, tender things. "Privacy. So now we understand the concept of privacy."

Emma's eyes widen at this. She gets on her knees beside him and puts her finger into his chest.

"You are so selfish," she says. "I told our friends about your loss to help you. You told everyone about Cole and Vincent's mess to hurt them. It's different."

"It seems like that should not be your call, Emma," Wallace says. The delicate skin of her throat pulses.

"Oh, so you think I'm controlling too. Wonderful. Well, you and Thom can have a fucking pity party about it. See if I care." She waves her hand at him, dismisses him. She's in his face. Their argument is quiet, contained to the air between them. Wallace glances over her shoulder, through the veil of her hair, into the kitchen.

"I never said that," he says. "I just mean—no one ever sticks up for me."

"That doesn't make it all right to go ruining people's lives."

"Sure. I'll just take it, right? I'll just take my licks," he says. Emma presses her palms to her face. She gives a full-body shudder. Wallace's stomach hurts. "Anyway, where's Thom?"

"Don't," she says.

"Where is he? What's going on? We might as well have your mess too."

"Thom didn't want to come," she says. "Does that rhyme? Thom didn't *want to come* because Thom wants to *stay home and read* because Thom *hates my friends*." There's a singsong quality to it, this story she's telling him. She pushes back from the table, gets up. Wallace follows her.

In the kitchen, the two of them look through the back door to the yard, where the others have stretched out on flannel blankets. Yngve has flicked the switch for the white string lights that hang from the tree—it's all very soft and very white out there now, under the sky, which is angled and dark. They're drinking beer from cans and bottles. More folk music, more guitar, something by Dylan, he thinks. Yngve is lying back, and Lukas has put his head on Yngve's stomach. They look silly and in love, which is something Yngve would never admit, could never bring himself to admit. Enid and Nathan sit together, filled with a sadness that they cannot articulate without fracturing their relationships, because Yngve will always choose Lukas and Lukas will always choose Yngve; they don't have to say it to know it's true. It's a trust that can exist only in silence, he realizes. They can't speak because to speak would be to dissolve it.

"I wish those two would get together already," Emma says. "It's giving me a headache."

"No kidding. But I think it's sweet."

"To be led on that way?"

"No one is leading anyone here. They're in the same place."

"If you say so," Emma says against Wallace's back, her arms around him. He does not know if it's a gesture that's meant to comfort him or comfort her, if he's meant to be pulling strength from her nearness or if she is trying to steady herself.

"Thom doesn't hate us," he says. "He can't."

"He does. I think he does. Every time we come out to one of these things, he's sulky for weeks. He doesn't talk to me. I know that when I go home, he's going to freeze me out."

"Why?"

"Because he thinks I'm always looking for a way out."

"Are you?"

"Maybe," she says, "but aren't we all? All the time?"

"Maybe," he says, and they share a laugh.

"I think that's why everyone is so on edge with you. Because you *said it*. You actually said it. You want out. You broke this illusion we all have. That it's always going to be like this, that what we have now is good."

"But it is good." Wallace takes her arms and pulls them tighter around him. She kisses his hair and then his ear. She has forgiven him. Wallace relaxes.

"I don't know if it's good. Sometimes, I think that this is all I've ever wanted. Good research. Steady. Learning all the time. Other days I'm just miserable and want to cry. We all are, I think. In our way. We're all fucking miserable in this place. But then, to actually hear it. It's like somebody said something rude during church."

"Is this church?"

"Hush, you know what I mean. I felt like, Oh no, oh no. First, I wanted to hug you. Because I've had days like that. Then I wanted to strangle you so you'd hush and not make us all think about it."

But the difference, Wallace wants to say, *is that you have the option of not thinking about it.* His misery is not novel, but it is distinct. They've all lost data, ruined experiments. There was the time in second year when Yngve's crystals failed to come out of solution and he was left with a flurried mess, all because he'd miscalculated the concentration of potassium in his buffer. Or the time Miller killed off a venerable line of bacterial cells in his lab that had been handed down from postdoc to postdoc for some twenty years because he'd taken the entire container from the -80°C freezer rather than a small aliquot and blown it all in a failed inoculation. Another time, Emma forgot to upload her latest data to the server and her laptop crashed, and there was no way to recover her qPCR runs, and she had to repeat the experiment, which took weeks. Or the time Cole dumped acid down the drain and chased it with bleach, resulting in an evacuation of the fifth floor. There were days in all their lives when things went wrong and they were forced to ask themselves if they wanted to go on. Decisions were made every day about what sort of life they wanted, and they always answered the same: *Only this, only this.* But that was the misery of trying to become something, misery that you could put up with because it was native to the act of trying. But there are other kinds of misery, the misery that comes from other people.

Is this what Dana was trying to say to him earlier? That he's not the only one who has a hard time? That he doesn't have some sort of monopoly on misery? *But it's different,* he wanted to say then and wants to say now. *It's different. Can't you see that? It's different.*

He could say this. It seems possible. But he knows what will happen. Wallace rolls his shoulders. If he makes a point of this, Emma will shake her head. She will refuse it. She will say that he's pitying himself, that he's not special. That he is not alone in his feeling of inadequacy. And this is perhaps a little true. And it's that small truth of it that makes it dangerous to him. They do not understand that for them it will get better, while for him the misery will only change shape. She will say, *Get over yourself, Wally,* and she will smile and put her arms around his shoulders, and she will love him and try her best to understand him, and he will accept this, and he will go quiet and she will sense that something has gone wrong, but he will not tell her. And it will be as if nothing has happened at all.

"All right," Wallace says.

Miller comes back with a beer and a small dish of pretzels. Emma waves it off, and Wallace shakes his head.

"I better take the coffee out," she says. "Help me."

Wallace takes a tray with several mismatched mugs bearing the logos of football and basketball teams. There is also a beautiful cherry red mug that he purchased for one of the boys during a gift exchange. Wallace received a small inflatable duck for his trouble, which made him laugh at the time as he held it up to them. Already, that seems so long ago.

It is even cooler than earlier in the backyard, and the skyline above the fence is rimmed in dark blue. The lights of the capitol building are in the distance, white beams turned gauzy, like a dream. There's a small table made up of wooden crates, and Wallace sets the cups here. Emma brings out the carafe of dark coffee and some cream and sugar. Wallace sits on the edge of the blanket. Miller takes the spot next to him, which annoys Emma, but she sits in front of Wallace, and he encircles her with his arms.

Yngve is stooped over the table, pouring coffee, when he spots Miller. He grins and straightens up to his full height.

"Okay, okay. So everyone is here now. Perfect."

Lukas and Nathan are lying together now, their hands entwined. Vincent and Cole are over near the garden, whispering quietly. Everything is hushed and perfect.

"All right, Miller, come, come." Yngve waves his hands several times, trying to get Miller to come to him, and Miller eventually relents. Wallace watches him go. Roman takes Miller's spot. Klaus is chattering in German on the phone near the tree. Yngve steers Miller in the direction of Zoe, who is wearing a terrific cardigan, slouchy, dark, a hole in the shoulder, surely too big for her.

"Wallace," Roman says, which draws Wallace's gaze up as Roman sits in Miller's spot. Wallace nods. Roman smells like gin. His eyes fall on Klaus, then back to Wallace. "I'm in big trouble there." He says it with a smile, a wink.

"It's like that, I hear," Wallace says.

"Catching too," Roman says, looking pointedly in the direction of Cole and Vincent.

"That time of the year," Wallace says.

"You surprise me," Roman says. Emma cranes her neck back to look at Roman.

"I surprise myself."

"Hush," Emma says. "Yngve is doing his best matchmaker."

Wallace tries to listen. Zoe talks with her hands. Big, sweeping gestures. She is miming some sort of climbing technique. She has her hands out, gripping stone, scaling some forbidding craggy surface. Miller nods. Mimes back. Her hands ghost down to his hips, adjust him just so, maneuver his hands. She holds his wrist steady. Yngve laughs loud, claps Miller on the back.

"I didn't know you were on the app, Wallace. I thought you'd be above that sort of thing. I've never seen you there."

"I blocked you," Wallace says without looking away from Miller and Zoe. They look like the sort of people he sees sometimes at the pier or in cafés, pushing strollers. The sort of couple the world lays itself open for. They do not seem unalike in sensibility. Miller has folded his arm across his chest. He props his chin up with his knuckles.

"That hurts," Roman says.

"I doubt that."

"It's true. It doesn't hurt much. But it does sting. We are friends, aren't we?"

"Is that what you use the app for, Roman? Friendship?"

"Sometimes," he says. "What do you use it for? Weight Watchers?"

Wallace turns to Roman, gives him the attention he is so desperate for.

"What do you want, Roman?"

"I have a theory," he says. "I have a theory that you lied. That you're not the one on the app."

"Shut up," Emma says to Roman. "It's getting good now."

Wallace follows her eyes back to Miller and Zoe, but the two of them are still just talking. Yngve's hand is resting on Miller's shoulder, and Yngve has turned around to stare at Lukas and Nathan, who are lying down. There's nothing about the moment that corresponds to anything getting good, or being different from the moment it was before, and so Wallace is confused, annoyed. He pinches Emma's hip. She lets out a sharp hiss of pain.

"Use your eyes, stupid. Look."

Wallace does look.

"I think you're covering for someone," Roman says.

Wallace looks and looks, and there it is: Yngve's face. It was hidden from Wallace at first, but when he shifts his weight, his annoyance is clear. He is staring in mild fury at Nathan and Lukas, his jaw working from side to side. His hand is gripping Miller so tight that Miller reaches for his wrist. "Hey, hey,

Yngve, bud, hey, you gotta let me go," Miller says. Yngve looks startled, finds his way back to himself.

"I think it's Cole," Roman says finally. "I think you're covering for Cole." He all but breathes it into Wallace's ear, his breath wet and warm. Wallace turns to him, and there they are, face-to-face, nose-to-nose. He can see the array of whiskers in Roman's beard, the subtle gradient of reds. The smooth surface of his cheeks. He is, up close, almost innocent. Roman's nostrils flare just suddenly, and Wallace is transfixed by the play of light in his eyes. There's mischief and something else. Wallace remembers, with a shiver, just moments before, the wet flick of Roman's tongue against his ear.

"What game is this?" he asks Roman.

"No game," he says. Then, to Emma, "How is Thom?" Emma flinches, takes a long drink from her coffee. She's sobering up.

"He's lovely. Writing that essay on Tolstoy, you know." The tree's limbs are moving again, wind in the leaves. Wallace looks up, the flash of a white stomach, a bird overhead, darting away, first low and then high, and over the fence.

"Tolstoy? I prefer Zola," Roman says, smiling.

Emma nods tightly. She's drinking from a Packers mug. Miller glances back. Their eyes meet, and Wallace looks away. Roman is watching him.

"Fascinating," Roman says.

"Get your eyes checked," Wallace says with far more cool than he deserves.

"The better to see you with," Roman says, smiling broadly.

"Excuse me," he says. "Emma, hey, I have to get up."

"Why?" Emma asks, now that she's settled in and gotten comfortable.

"Bathroom," he says gently, as gently as he can. And he slides away and pushes himself up. Roman is still watching him as he climbs the back steps and enters the house. He can feel the weight of his gaze, the pressure of it.

Wallace manages to make it to the bathroom, where he vomits. All of the food from dinner comes up. It's a mess in the bowl. His stomach heaves until he feels hot and flushed again. His head is on fire, and every breath makes another part of him ache. He hates Roman. He hates him so much he could kill him with his bare hands.

HE'S SITTING ON THE EDGE of the tub, sucking on an ice cube he scooped from the metal bowl in the kitchen, when he hears a gentle tap at the door. He assumes it's Emma, so he doesn't say anything. She'll either get the hint or come in. He circles the ice around his lips and on his tongue. He's trying to get himself to cool off. There is another tap, more insistent this time, and then Miller's voice: "Wallace, you still in there?"

"Oh, I'm sorry, do you need it?" he asks.

Miller opens the door and comes in. He sits on the toilet lid. "What happened out there? I looked up and you were gone."

"Nothing, just feeling kind of funny, so I came in."

Miller puts a hand to his head and frowns. "Are you sick? Do you have a fever?"

"No. On both counts."

"You feel warm, though."

"It's summer," Wallace says. He sucks on the ice cube, and Miller watches intently.

"Do you want to lie down? It's cooler in my room. I have a fan going."

The thought of being apart from the rest of them, being alone in a cool, dark place, sounds perfect.

"Yes," he says, and Miller rests a hand at the base of his neck.

"Okay," Miller says. "Let's go."

They go up the stairs, in the dark house, and they take a left at the top. Miller's room is long and angular. There is a circular window through which he can see the lakeshore at some great distance. There are maps and postcards on the walls, and books in a cramped case under the windowsill, where there are pillows and a thick flannel blanket. The bed is large and comfortable, with a big quilt. The room smells like Miller—oranges and salt. His bike is propped against the closet. The floor creaks under their feet.

"Here you go," he says, pointing to the bed. This room is much cooler. There is a fan in the other window, drawing the air in. He goes to turn on a light, but Wallace shakes his head.

"No, that's fine. Please leave it."

Wallace climbs onto the bed and lies on his back, staring at the ceiling, which seems too low for Miller.

"Do you want me go?"

"You would miss the party," Wallace says.

"I want to stay."

"What about the ice girl?"

"Ice girl?"

"You know—she was chipping ice earlier. She came for you. You shouldn't disappoint her."

"Zoe, you mean? Oh, she's fine."

"She thought you were funny. I saw."

Miller is standing at the door with it closed, playing with the noisy little knob. "I don't know what you want me to say about that."

"Nothing," Wallace says. This fight is already taking what little energy he has left. He puts Miller's pillow over his face. It smells so good, so like him.

"I want to stay."

"Then stay. It's your house."

Miller gets into the bed next to him and lies on his side. He puts a hand on Wallace's stomach, which makes Wallace insecure. He wants to push Miller's hand away from him, to be alone, to be perfectly alone. Miller comes closer, rests his face in the crook of Wallace's shoulder. He throws a leg over Wallace's leg. Like when they were in Wallace's bed.

"Someone could come up here," Wallace says.

"I know."

"You didn't want people finding out."

"What's to find out? Yngve and Lukas do this all the time."

"But we aren't them. We weren't like this before."

"How were we like?"

"I don't know, meaner? You picked on me a lot."

"I didn't. You picked on me. You were always scowling in the hallways. I thought you hated me for a long time."

"How could anyone hate you?" Wallace asks. "You're so likable."

"I try to be."

Outside, someone's car is having a hard time getting going. And someone else's children are running in the street. These are the last days of summer, the last days when day will be longer than night. It seems like such a waste to spend it inside with someone who is maybe sick, maybe not.

"You're going to miss the party," Wallace says.

"I don't mind. It's over, anyway." Miller's voice is warm on his skin, and Wallace relents. It would be too much to give it up, to be alone in the dark, now that he has been with Miller in the dark. What he fears, though, and it's a cold, grinding, glittering fear rising in him, is that now he'll never be able to face the dark alone again. That he'll always want this, seek this, once it's lost to him.

Miller is rubbing his stomach in a gesture that feels familial to some long-vanished part of himself. Wallace watches the edge of a white curtain flutter. Yngve is outside and below them, laughing.

"I think Roman suspects something. He said something strange," Wallace says.

"Let him."

"It doesn't bother you?"

"No. Not as much as I thought it would."

"Oh."

"Does it bother you?" Miller says, and there's so much tentative anticipation in his voice that Wallace wants to cry. "You said those things before. That you'd rather be alone."

"I think I would rather be alone," Wallace says at the edge of a long thought, "but it doesn't bother me to be with you."

"Good," Miller says, laughing because he can't help himself. "Good."

"You are funny-looking though, so there's that."

"That's true. You once said I looked like a small child put in a big man's body."

"Did I?"

"Yes, when we first met at the bonfire. You said it right to my face."

"No wonder you thought I hated you."

"No wonder."

"I didn't mean it."

"I got that, later, but I got it."

They turn to each other. It's different from the time in Wallace's apartment, from last night, when they turned to each other in desire, out of not knowing what else to do with themselves or their bodies, when the outcome seemed so uncertain. They turn to each other now of their own volition, and it's so easy. Wallace puts his face against Miller's chest, and Miller puts a hand on his thigh. They're just lying there.

"But you would rather be alone," Miller says. "You don't want the hassle, I guess."

"I would rather be alone. Or, I'd rather be the sort of person who'd rather be alone. It's hard to want to be with other people because they just vanish on you, or they die."

"I don't think I'm dying anytime soon."

"You could. It could happen anytime. I could die."

"You are so morbid. You're so, so morbid. I don't think I knew that before."

"My dad died fast."

"I'm sorry, I know, I'm sorry."

"People die before you know them. And then you get stuck wondering, what if, what if."

"My mom . . . well, I told you already."

"I'm sorry," Wallace says, kissing Miller's throat, where it is bristly and firm with cartilage and muscle.

"But I'm saying, I don't plan on dying. I plan on sticking around."

"That makes one of us," Wallace says. "You heard that shit at dinner."

"I hope you stay. But I hope you leave, if that's what you want. You can't stay for anyone but yourself."

"It's strange. They say, study science and you'll always have a job. And it seems so easy. But they don't tell you that there's all this other stuff attached that will make you hate your life."

"Do you hate it that much?"

"Yes, sometimes, you know—we all do, I guess, was what Emma was saying earlier."

"Me too, yeah. But I love it more than I hate it."

"But fuckers like Roman," Wallace says, growling under his breath. "They make it unbearable."

"I still can't believe he said that to you."

"No one said anything to him; no one did anything."

"I wanted to, but then, I guess, I chickened out."

Wallace pauses, stills in Miller's arms. There will always be this moment. There will always be good white people who love him and want the best for him but who are more afraid of other white people than of letting him down. It is easier for them to let it happen and to triage the wound later than to introduce an element of the unknown into the situation. No matter how good they are, no matter how loving, they will always be complicit, a danger, a wound waiting to happen. There is no amount of loving that will ever bring Miller closer to him in this respect. There is no amount of desire. There will always remain a small space between them, a space where people like Roman will take root and say ugly, hateful things to him. It's the place in every white person's heart where their racism lives and flourishes, not some vast open plain but a small crack, which is all it takes.

Wallace presses his tongue flat.

"Good white people," he says.

"I'm sorry."

"It's fine." The air is getting colder, darker. The sun is gone. Wind in the trees. They're breaking wood outside, cracking it open. They're building a fire. Its orange glow issues up in the night, and occasionally, there are embers that pass by the window like stars, or fireflies.

"Wallace?"

"Yes?"

"Will you tell me about yourself?"

"Why?"

"I just want to know. I want to know about you."

"What's there to know?"

"Please," Miller says, pressing. "Please."

Wallace considers this, the act of asking, the intent behind it. Such a strange request. How long has it been since someone attempted to know him? There is Brigit, of course, the person to whom he has said the most and also, perhaps, the least of it. And Emma, who has tried to know him in her way. But there are so few others, because the moment he arrived he decided to shed his other life like a skin. That is the really wonderful thing about living in a place to which you are not connected. It cannot lay a claim on who you were before you arrived there, and all anyone knows of you is what you tell them. It was possible to become a different version of himself in the Midwest, a version without a family and without a past, made up entirely as he saw fit.

It's never been put to him so directly, a request to tell something of himself, so complete a history. Miller is losing his nerve. Wallace can feel it in the way his breath is becoming ragged. All he has to do is wait him out, give it time to become another question, something easier, more bearable. Something less complete, an impartial accounting, even, of the events that have brought him here.

He could say something about taking a Greyhound up. He could say something about the Gulf of Mexico or the mountains of North Alabama. He could say something about the fields filled with white cotton or the beans picked that turned your hands purple or blue. There are so many minor details he could conjure, incomplete reflections of something larger and more awful. But that is not the question that Miller asked him. That is not what Wallace has been asked to disclose.

The whole of his history feels dark and cold and far away, but it's in him, settled down, like blood drying. Miller's eyes are open. He isn't retreating.

"Tell me," he says. "Tell me."

His voice is insistent, but gentle, the way you ask questions of people when you know it's rude. What is he going to say, or do? What can he say or do? It seems impossible at this point to avoid it.

"I don't even know where to start," he says.

"Anywhere. Start anywhere." Miller is shocked by his good luck. He was bluffing, gambling.

Their friends' voices on the other side of the glass drift up to them. More laughter. They're telling stories.

"You already know it," he says.

"I don't."

"You know I'm from Alabama."

"I know that."

"That's it, really."

"No, it's not. It's not it."

"Why do you need to know?"

"Because I want to know you."

"Knowing about my past won't make you know me. I'm who you think I am. I'm not mysterious. I'm not full of secrets. I'm me, and who I was then wasn't me."

Miller sighs. Wallace sighs. This isn't getting them anywhere.

"You are so determined to be unknowable."

"We're always unknowable."

"I'm not," Miller says. "I'd tell you anything about me."

"Because you're good."

"You're good."

"I'm not."

"You are."

"I'm not, and that's just how it is."

"You are good," Miller says. He kisses Wallace, and rolls on top of him, and kisses him again. "You are so good."

Each time he says it, Wallace feels as though he floats a little farther away, sinks a little deeper into himself until he's butted up against the cold flat surface of his past. It's there under him, undulating like a sea beneath ice. Miller is kissing his shoulder and his neck and his mouth, kissing him because when they're kissing, they're not talking, not arguing, kissing because it's easier than this disagreement that threatens to split them. Wallace puts his hands under Miller's shirt, pushes the buttons apart, and rubs his fingers over his stomach.

Miller lies flat against him, rests his head on Wallace's chest. They aren't going to have sex this way. That much is obvious to Wallace. He's been pinned. Miller's breathing evens out after a few minutes. He's drifting off to sleep, and the weight and warmth of his body is making Wallace drowsy too. They're on the cusp of dropping fully into sleep when Wallace hears a loud crack outside, and a sea of embers issues up by the window; for a moment he thinks of lightning and thunder, those twin forces that shape a southern summer, where the weather is wild and full of strange magic.

Wallace gasps, jerks under Miller, who reaches for him in the dark, and for a moment, neither of them says or does anything. They breathe, and then Wallace says, "I'll tell you."

It stormed all the time—thunder and lightning and wind so hard it shook the trees and sometimes twisted them clean out of the dirt. There was so much rain one summer that we couldn't keep anything in the ground, and there were strange patches of tomatoes and cabbage growing in the briars because the seeds had been swept across the sand by the rain. That's what comes to me first, the scent of the damp earth, the heat clinging close to the ground, and the gray mist rising after a heavy storm. The clouds were purple-black and gray, softening when the weather broke, and you could tell which way the storm had come from because the trees were still split wide and there was a path through the woods as if some huge animal had come slinking through them. And on the hill, looking down into the ravine, all that water on the leaves glinted like little stars, little trapped earthbound galaxies flaring into life. Soon the ants came, and they latched on to whatever had drowned in the rain, and they took it off piece by piece; once, there was a rat that had been drowned near the corner of the house, its white and gray fur all matted, and the ants were thronging in and out of its mouth like air, like breath made of small dark bodies. Another time, there were birds that had been thrown from their nests, skin translucent and blue like fresh ice from a vending machine, their pink mouths flung wide. Delicate little clothes of skin and feather, bones so light that in another life they might have floated away into the sky, riding on currents of warm air, but now splashed in mud and being disassembled by ants, so many of them that they too were a skin, writhing and dark beneath the shadow of the bushes, almost obscured except, at the moment of passing, when the eye drops down and sees them, and in the body, a star-tled, horrifying jolt, that something there is dying and dead already. That's how it was with storms, coming on suddenly and then vanishing, leaving behind dead things wreathed in dark ants and in mist coming out of the trees like ghosts. During the storms themselves, my grandparents turned out all the lights and we sat in the house sweating and breathing in the dark, trying not to move except for our fingers twisting and pulling at the threads in the carpets. Grit slid between our fingers, sticking there when we squirmed and tried to be still. Flies, fat and dark, moving around us, buzzing close to our ears, and we, turning to each other, slapping at each other, trying to kill the flies, but missing, them swinging just out of reach, beyond us, but close by, so that we could feel them sliding around us, moving close to our eyes and then away again. My grandparents sat in their chairs, eyes pointing out through the window into the gray veil of rain rushing down from the sky, turning white and frothy as it spilled down the banisters and met in great torrents those floody waters from the fields and the yard. There was the joining of many waters out there, eddying up the birdbath and pushing hard and steady against the shrubs. When it was over, there would be plums and berries scattered across the lawn, and birds would come swooping, snatching them up and taking them to nests that had been plundered of their contents by the wind. With the storm howling, pushing hard on our windows, we sat and listened both to the groaning outside, the great tumult of the world beyond, and to the hum of our grandparents, who told us stories or sang spirituals. They told us of the Bible and how the flood had come upon the land and drowned all the wicked, and how we'd be next if we didn't stay still and quiet. They told us how the world was coming to an end soon, that Jesus was coming back and was testing us. The house stank of our sweat and piss and the bathroom always smelled like shit because we kept the used toilet paper in a little tin can next to the toilet. And in that house, fetid and stinking and sweating, I learned all about the ways that a person can do God great ill. Lying, as in the story of the man who had lied his whole life and in the end had been bashed in the head by his wife with a hammer, but before the hammer had come he had been visited in his sleep by demons, licking, lapping his feet with their horned tongues, and in the end he hadn't even felt it, the clank of the hammer going into his skull through to the other side, because he'd been lying his whole life, because he'd been using and lying and telling falsehoods, bearing false witness against those in his life, and against his wife, that poor woman, wrung clean out of her mind by his lies so that she didn't know what was coming or going and in the end had reached for the hammer to ease something in herself. You could also harm God by reaching out in the dark for something that was unholy—the shape of another man, for example, as was my case. You get to wanting it all the time, my grandfather said, get to needing it so much you can't do anything or keep a job or a house or a family, and you go out there and you get AIDS and then it's over, that's it, you die. I didn't need the lights on to know that he was talking about me, talking to me, across the space between us, interspersed with blue lightning streaking the sky, no I didn't need anything to confirm for me; I knew even then that I was going to hell, that I couldn't make sense of the space in me that was supposed to be where God slept but in me was just a cavity like a tooth waiting to turn to rot, my soul a blackness, a wound gone sour. If you talked while God was doing his work, you were making space for the devil. If you opened a window while God was doing his work, you were inviting the devil. If you used any electricity at all while God was working, you were making a route for the devil to enter your body. Storms were the only consistent church in my life, the only time I couldn't sleep in from sermons or turn a blind eye to God. You can ignore a pastor's words; it is easy not to hear them. But when you see lightning flash or hear thunder crack open the sky, there is no denying God's fury, his power to break the world with very little effort. And when your grandparents rock in their chairs and sing the songs that their grandparents sang that their grandparents sang that their grandparents sang, there is no denying the power of ghosts, those who are always among us, moving through air and earth, resting their fingers upon this or that, collecting what is there, depositing what they have no need for. There were storms every day—thunder and lightning—and I learned to make myself so still I thought I might slide out of my body, thought I might then and there die, cease to be, fold back into the next life as if it were a comfortable bed, so perfectly parallel had I drawn this life to the next. Even then I was spotting and waiting, watching the world pass me by in repeated patterns, the impression of lightning on the window, its shadow thrown long behind it. Once, there was a red weathervane in the yard, and lightning hit it, charring the paint, and beneath it there was the shape of a rooster, a huge black rooster that was made of metal but had been painted, and so all my life I had thought it red, and that in lightning it was burnt pure and clean, it had reverted, turned back to something else, something new. There was a boy then, a boy I liked who lived around the dirt road from me, who lived in a trailer. He was tall and dark and strong, and once, I let him take me into the woods, let him climb on top of me, let him spill himself inside me, and I went home, bleeding and ugly and dirty, and climbed into the green bin that we kept in the tub because our tub didn't work, and I tried to bathe, tried to clean myself up, and there were little birds' nests in the windowsill, and sometimes the babies fell through the mesh and broke their necks in the tub, and I was washing that day, trying to rub at the bruises between my thighs, where he had pinned me open with his knees, trying to make it go away, to become my skin again and not bruised, not marked, not streaked in shit and blood and cum, and trying to reclaim myself, the feeling of wholeness again before I had been breached, before I had let him breach me, before I had let him shatter the membrane that kept the world out. No, another way, another way. There was a man who slept in my house. He was not my brother. He was not my father. He was not my uncle. He was not my friend. He was tall and black and his face was like death's face, and I woke in the night and there it was, hanging over me, a grimacing thing from the other side, hanging low over me, and he took me into his mouth, and I wanted to cry and wanted to shout but I didn't because I couldn't, and he kept coming back, kept climbing into my bed, except for the last time when my mother caught him and threw him out and then she turned to me and slapped me and called me faggot called me sissy called me everything except son, said everything except I'm sorry that happened to you, but then she had no language for such a thing, no language for apologies, for cruelty, because she had been made that way, because my brother's father was not my father, because my brother's father had done that to her, caught her on the way home from school one day, in the kudzu, had dragged her down, pulled her down with him and climbed on top of her like a common beast. This is the story I know. This is the only version I know. That I have. From her. She told me that he raped her. She told me that she hadn't wanted children. And her mother, my grandmother, told me that my mother had wanted it. That she had deserved it. That she got what she had coming. So it's not surprising that on the day she threw him from my bed, she slapped me and told me that it was my fault. That I shouldn't have been acting that way, that I was a child and should know better, but also that cruelty comes this way, visits us, and that in our family we are powerless to do anything except open the door and welcome it. And my father, on that same sunny day, turned to me and grinned with his front teeth missing, already decaying on the inside, already breaking down, and said that he hoped I had had a good time, that he hoped that man, now walking down the road, his wiry shoulders swinging, had done something good to me, for me, that he didn't care so much that I wanted men. And I stood there squirming on the porch, feeling bruised and beaten, tall for nine, itching all over. I wanted to get out of my skin. I wanted to forget how, in the night, the man from the couch had slid back the wool blanket and had come close to me, smelling like oil, smelling like the pond, like the creek, like fish before you skin them, and how he, so smooth down there, had touched me, put his fingers inside me. And I had lain there, sweating, staring out the window into the night, where there were trees swaying, and I kept thinking how like dinosaurs they looked. And then he wet his fingers some more and put more inside me, and the bed was creaking while he made room for himself, and then, the first, ugly heat of being split open, and I wanted to die, every moment of it, I wanted to die, could feel myself going further and further away from myself, shrinking and shrinking and shrinking, sinking like a stone, heavier all the time, downward through some vast inner ocean. And his face, that smirking skull's face, over mine, swinging into my body, more beast than man, and then it was over. And I was on the porch, just squirming, just writhing, trying to slip out of my skin like those fish do sometimes, when you're cleaning them and they are smooth and perfect beneath the scales, as perfect and unfledged as a baby's skin. How at night I was no longer unfledged, no longer pure, no longer untouched, but sullied. Later, when I went around the road to see the boy I liked, to touch his arms when he asked, to press my lips to his neck and to his stomach, and to let him fuck my mouth, I thought of all the times they had let that man into my room, my mother out of apathy and my father out of a sick pride, and how this young man now, in my mouth in the woods, on my knees, the leaves rippling in the breeze that smelled like honeysuckle, his skin tasting like soap, how I was down there, letting him go at me from the back, gripping the branches, gripping the vines, green, whiplike, how I had brought this about, how this desire I felt was the blooming of something planted in me, and how God couldn't take it away. I prayed a lot then, layering the words over each other as if they could form a lattice that would protect me. When I let him come on my thighs, and when I let him push me down and punch me and kick me and break me, I kept praying, thinking that the pain I felt would absolve me, that the fire I felt in my guts would abate, would cleanse me. And overhead, trees dappled in sunlight. You can't know how beautiful the sun is there, how it touches everything and soaks it through, succulent, like water, like moisture. Light beading on the skin, dew, glistening. So much light, an ocean of it, a sea of light spread across everything. He kicked and kicked and kicked, and I went home to wash it all off, the briars and the bruises and the places where he'd dented me, broken me, made me somehow uglier, and when I rubbed the salve on my skin, I kept thinking, kept hoping God would make me whole again. I wanted what I wanted, but I wanted not to want what I wanted. I didn't know much about God and the devil except what you shouldn't do to invite one or the other, but I knew that I wanted to be full of one, and if it couldn't be the one I wanted, then I would take the other. That if

God wanted nothing to do with me, then I'd take the devil. I'd take him on my knees where I'd taken the men, let him pull me down in a bed of kudzu and fuck me, so long as I wasn't empty anymore. I'd keep a tiny God inside me, and one day I might lie down and let the ants take me. When I left it behind me, when I got up the money to go to school and get away, I sealed it all behind me, because when you go to another place you don't have to carry the past with you. You can lay it down. You can leave it for the ants. There comes a time when you have to stop being who you were, when you have to let the past stay where it is, frozen and impossible. You have to let it go if you're going to keep moving, if you're going to survive, because the past doesn't need a future. It has no use for what comes next. The past is greedy, always swallowing you up, always taking. If you don't hold it back, if you don't dam it up, it will spread and take and drown. The past is not a receding horizon. Rather, it advances one moment at a time, marching steadily forward until it has claimed everything and we become again who we were; we become ghosts when the past catches us. I can't live as long as my past does. It's one or the other.

6

When Wallace wakes alone in Miller's bed a little before midnight, all he can say is, "Fair enough." Miller's room is dark except for the indistinct blue haze coming from a tangled cluster of string lights on the floor. There's a dense clump of hurt below his belly, pressing against his back. His bladder. The sleep has been partial and rough. His face is swollen from pressing into the pillow. He can smell Miller's sweat. The room is cool from the fan in the window. The voices on the lawn are gone. There are no voices in the hall. A fine crack rings the upper edge of the wall, near the close, white, angled ceiling. There is a skylight there, a trapezoid of deeper black, a few caught leaves flattened to its corners. *These old houses*—the words spring to mind like a bit of old music, a line dredged up from the holiday party at Simone's house the previous year, Henrik's last year.

He and Henrik had been sent down into the basement to retrieve chairs. Simone stood at the top of the stairs, watching the two of them move into and out of the pool of light at the base, stacking the chairs. Henrik had been drinking gin already, and his lips were red. His eyes were a little pink. Wallace could smell the piney scent on him. At one point they both stepped out of the light into the shadow at the same moment and reached for the same chair, and their hands brushed low over its base. Henrik grunted, and Wallace drew back stiffly. Henrik lifted the chair in one smooth move and he motioned with his chin to the far wall, deeper into the shadow under the stairs, where there was a faint, barely discernible crack running through the concrete. *These old houses*, he said. *They've got shitty foundations.* Which at the time had not made sense to Wallace, because how did a thing with a shitty foundation get to be old? He thought about it as they climbed the stairs together over and over, carrying two chairs at a time, and each time the stairs creaked or threatened to give way under their weight; he thought about it until it became a kind of song. *These old houses.* Henrik's last party. Henrik's last year. *These old houses.*

Wallace gets up to piss. He draws Miller's flannel around his shoulders. They get cold, these old houses, Wallace thinks. On the landing, he presses close to the railing and waits. The front hall is dark. The kitchen is dark. But the silence is not perfect. He can make out the soft scratch of the edge of whispers. Not the words, but the impression of sound pressing against the air. He is not alone. It makes sense, after all, that Miller would still be in the house. And Yngve. People live here. Their lives go on. He has not been left entirely alone. The incompleteness of his abandonment makes him want to laugh a little, but he also feels the curious, inverted sweep of vertigo. The shame of having given away too much of himself, and to Miller of all people. The reflexive desire to seek cover, to hide, flashes through him. There was a time—running up to Friday, even—when giving so much of himself away would have been a fatal mistake. He would have had to live the rest of his time in graduate school fearing reprisal, fearing having it sprung on him at odd turns, strange moments, always having to peer around the corner just to make sure. There was a time when Wallace would have trusted this suspicious streak in his nature, would have trusted it to keep him safe, but he had done a stupid thing, has done a stupid thing, in telling Miller all of this about himself, and so all he has is hope, and he has never been a person who can depend on hope.

The bathroom is clean, full of wicker and white, like a bathroom in some beach town. He pisses with the blanket wrapped around his shoulders, smelling like Miller, and he watches the water in the bowl turn yellow. The stink of urine, too much coffee, the smell of ammonia. He rinses his hands, pulls the blanket back around him, and then he descends the stairs.

In the air: musk and burning pine. Thin blue vapor. At the edge of the doorway, he sees them sitting on the kitchen floor. The piercing red glow of an electronic cigarette. The back door cracked. Miller's and Yngve's long legs stretched out past each other. Miller with his back against the low cabinets. Yngve with his back against the wall. They pass the vape pen back and forth, each taking his time, the one not smoking looking out the door into the night, where the blankets are still strewn across the grass, getting damp. Yngve and Miller, they look like brothers this way, except that Yngve's face is angular, sharp, and his body's got a boxy quality, like he was cut from a piece of thick leather. Miller is softer, that stupid curl in his hair, the baby fat of his cheeks and his jaw. They're talking about the boats, but what about them Wallace cannot tell, either because he lacks the knowledge or because they are quiet, or maybe it's both. But he's desperate to know, gripping the edge of the door so tight his nails ache. He needs to know what they are talking about because he is afraid—the rising chill at the nape of his neck, the heat of blood in his nose—that they are talking about him. His senses sharpen. The smell of grease from dinner. The tinny drip of water into the basin sink. The hiss of the resin as it burns, as the plant matter in the vape pen congeals. He can smell the heat. He can taste it on the tip of his tongue. And he watches the slow, dark motion of their mouths, their eyes turning toward each other, glinting, and Wallace takes that fatal step forward, the floor underneath him groans, and there, just before Yngve turns to him, Wallace watches a ripple of muscle up his neck, a sign that surely his head *will* turn, and on Miller's face, a momentary beat at the hollow of his throat. In that moment, Wallace sees it all, the whole world, deepened and shaded, can feel them, can hear them, knows even before they do what action, what motion will come next, and he steadies himself. Prepares himself for it.

"Wallace," Yngve says brightly. "Come smoke with us."

"He doesn't smoke," Miller says with some stiffness, not quite formal, not distant, but tight. Wallace crosses the kitchen, collects a glass from the cupboard.

"I'll sit with you," he says. He fills the glass near-full, and this reminds him of the previous night, when he filled the glass and made Miller drink from it. His face grows hot at the memory. The inappropriateness of it. The subtle way they have been drawn into re-creating it, except that when he looks to Miller he sees no recognition on his face. The moment passes, which is at once a relief and a disappointment. Wallace sits next to Yngve. Yngve draws the blanket around himself; their elbows and shoulders touch. He is cool from sitting near the open door. Miller sucks off the end of the gray vape. His eyes close. Yngve snaps quick and hard.

"Come on, come on," he says, motioning back toward himself. Wallace can smell the vapor on him and the beer. Something else too, darker liquor, maybe. Yngve is sour from sweat. Miller is wearing a yellow sweater with exposed stitching. Wallace watches the blunted ends of Miller's fingers, their thick knuckles. Yngve crosses his legs. A white sickle-shaped scar across his knee, faint railroad track scar. Wallace reaches down, presses his thumb to it, can feel the tension in Miller's gaze as surely as if it were a thread caught to his hand. Yngve gives a little involuntary shiver under Wallace's thumb. Miller gives the vape back to Yngve. The coarse blond hair of Yngve's leg. He traces the scar; Yngve shivers again.

"How did this happen?" Wallace asks.

"I've had that for years," Yngve says. "I got it right before I came to grad school. It was from soccer, all those years. Junky joints." A silver shred of vapor from the corner of his mouth. He rests the back of his head against the wall. "They went in and cleaned it out for me."

Wallace is still stroking the scar when he looks up, spots Miller staring at him. Wallace takes his hand away. Yngve passes the vape to Miller.

"Does it hurt?"

"No," Yngve says. "It doesn't. *Before*, that's when it hurt like hell. But now, nothing." Yngve presses his palm flat to his knee, and Wallace watches as he gives it a squeeze as if to emphasize his point. Wallace drinks.

"Some night tonight," Miller says.

"Some night," Yngve says. It's Wallace's turn to shiver.

"Is that what you were talking about before? When I came in?"

"No," Yngve says quickly, but then he laughs. "Yeah, I guess we were."

"I didn't know all that about Cole and Vincent," Miller says.

"Me either, but maybe we should have guessed."

"I mean, they fight, but not like this," Miller says, frowning. "But I guess you can't know what other people are doing. Or feeling."

Yngve nudges Wallace's side, and Wallace cannot tell if it is because Yngve is saying that Wallace is the one who started it all or if he is saying that he suspects something is going on between the two of them, Wallace and Miller. Either implication leaves Wallace feeling cold and afraid. So he shrugs, and Yngve laughs again. It's not a mocking sort of laughter, glinting and ferocious. Nor is it entirely insinuating, winking. After a few moments, Wallace realizes that Yngve is just laughing at Miller.

Yngve says, "Listen to him over here. Real wise guy."

"Shut it," Miller snaps back, but there's a crooked grin on his face.

"Do you think they'll split up?" Wallace asks, out of guilt more than anything. "Do you really think they'll break up over it?"

"No, it was dumb," Miller says. "I'm sure they'll be fine. They went home together."

"They did? When?" Wallace asks. "God. Fuck. I wish I'd gotten to say something before they left."

"You said enough," Yngve says, still smiling. He puts his arm around Wallace's neck and pulls him close. "Little Wally got himself into enough for one night, I think."

Miller hums in assent, and Wallace feels a quick pulse of hurt. But they are right, he knows. Nothing he could have said would have made them feel better. And yet he went off with Miller instead of cleaning up after himself. He let himself be drawn away and comforted. But was it comfort? Talking to Miller, feeling a little worse with every word he said? That's the strange thing about it, he thinks. That he started that story in order to feel better or to feel clearer, started it because it seemed a thing within his grasp and Miller had asked him to and it felt good to give Miller something he wanted. But Wallace does not feel better for having told Miller all that. He does not feel happier or comforted. Perhaps it was right after all, he thinks. A kind of justice.

"When did they leave? When did everyone go?"

"A little while ago. You were asleep."

"You two did vanish, that's true," Yngve says.

"I got sick," Wallace says.

Yngve does not look at Wallace. He looks at Miller.

"Is that so?"

"And I owed him for last night. Helping me."

"You two are so chummy these days," Yngve says.

"I hate him," Wallace says. Yngve pinches the side of Wallace's neck.

"Don't lie. You don't have to lie. We're friends. We're all friends here."

"Is Lukas here?"

"Yes, upstairs," Yngve says, but then, catching himself, he says, "Oh, no. He's with Nate." There is something in his voice, not sadness because it would be too easy to call it sadness, or regret. There is something about the way he says it, the way he turns back, as if he convinced himself that Lukas is upstairs asleep, safe and sound, as if by some trivial bit of magic he made himself believe that. Some act of sleight of hand, and now, facing the truth, the voice turns soft, tinged at its edges, like turning your palms up, caught. Yngve's eyes are red-rimmed, glossy, blue-gray like river stones.

No wonder the house is so quiet.

Wallace offers some water to Yngve, who smiles and takes the glass. A look of annoyance flashes across Miller's face, but then it's gone, as if he's thinking how trivial, how childish, let him drink. Yngve drinks as if he's under a clock.

"Well," he says. "I'm going up to bed."

"Okay," Miller says. "Sleep tight."

Yngve says something in Swedish, kisses Wallace's cheek, and then is gone. They listen to Yngve going up the stairs, his weight coming in even intervals, plodding up and up, growing fainter and fainter until it is indistinguishable from the mass of the house itself. Miller nods to the space beside him, and Wallace slides over to sit next to him. Miller takes some of the blanket, the way Yngve did.

Wallace puts his leg across Miller's, and Miller puts a hand on Wallace's knee.

"You left me," Wallace says.

"I left a note."

"Did you?"

"No," Miller says, laughing.

"I didn't look, anyway."

"Did you sleep well?" Miller asks. "Are you feeling better?"

"I did. I am," Wallace says, though he's getting nervous again. "I thought I had scared you off."

"No," Miller says. "You couldn't scare me off."

"I don't know if that's true. It's okay if you're freaked out or whatever. It's a lot, I know."

"I'm not," Miller says. He's fumbling with the edge of the blanket, not looking at Wallace. His neck is red, his cheeks are red. The boyishness, the part of him that's always hesitating, faltering, is so evident now. Wallace kisses his shoulder.

"Okay," Wallace says. "That's good. I'm glad. It's just that you didn't say anything after." He's putting himself out there, laying his uneasiness at Miller's feet to acknowledge or ignore. He could take Miller at his word, believe him, that the silence is nothing at all. He won't push. He will let it go. He will be easy. He will be calm.

Miller does not respond. He's back to looking outside into the dark. It's hard to see anything out there, only the faint outlines of shapes and figures. He is flexing his hand again, the knuckles thick and hard. The tension runs up his arm to his shoulder, where Wallace can feel it throbbing. It isn't an angry silence. It isn't like that at all. But there is something in it, a gathering of something hard and unyielding, a knotting sensation.

Has he done this? Has Wallace caused this? He should have been firm in his resistance to remain silent on the matter of his past and his history. He should have kept his mouth closed.

"Well, I guess I better get going," Wallace says, lightness in his voice. Miller's hand finds his under the blanket.

"No, you should stay. It's already late."

"My walk isn't that long," Wallace says. "I've already put you out."

"You haven't."

"I have—and I don't want to. I don't want to be a hassle."

"I wish you would stay," Miller says firmly. "I want you to."

"You're being nice. You don't have to be. It's fine."

"I'm not," Miller says. "I'm being selfish. I want you to stay." Miller is looking at him now. Whatever the silence might mean, there is such sincerity in his voice and his gaze that Wallace relents. Miller kisses him.

"Okay," Wallace says. "I'll stay." Miller takes his hand, and Wallace enjoys the lovely weight of his fingers, their warmth, their texture. He puts his head against Miller's shoulder. He wants to sleep, could sleep.

"If you're tired, we can go upstairs."

"This is fine."

"Are you sure? You don't have to stay down here because of me."

"Didn't you just say to stay?"

"I did, but—"

"Okay, then," Wallace says, cutting him off. Miller laughs at him. The nervousness abates, and so does the nausea, the churning sense of being gossiped about. You have to learn to trust people, to believe that they mean you no harm, Wallace thinks.

"I'm sorry," Miller says after a few moments. "For before, for not knowing what to say."

"It's okay," Wallace says. He's already forgiven whatever harm the silence did. He's already over it. He will survive.

"I'm sorry all that happened to you, that I made you tell me."

"You didn't do anything wrong. Besides, I guess I've been walking around waiting for someone to ask."

"Have you?"

"Maybe so," Wallace says. "Maybe we all are? I don't know."

"When I told you that stuff about my mom last night—I didn't know about your parents, about what he did. I feel pretty stupid," Miller says.

"Oh," Wallace says. "That's what this is about. You feeling stupid. I see."

"Jesus. That isn't what I meant at all, Wallace. That isn't what I meant. What a thing to say."

"It seemed like that's what you meant," Wallace says because he cannot stop himself and because he is familiar with this version of things between them. The scolding, halting nature of their relationship is a comfort to him in this moment. Miller clenches his jaw and breathes heavily out his nose. Wallace sees a cluster of tiny blackheads at the corner of his nose.

"What do you want from me?" Miller asks.

"Nothing. I don't want anything from you."

"Okay, right, all right, then," Miller says, nodding stiffly. He puts his head flat back against the low counter. He closes his eyes. "You are exhausting. You are completely exhausting."

"Then I should go home."

"If you want me to tell you to go home, I'm not going to do that. If you want to go, go. Stop trying to make excuses."

"You just called me exhausting."

"Because you *are*," Miller says. His eyes are squeezed tight. Wallace presses his thumb to the wrinkled surface of Miller's eyelids. He's warm. Damp from the cool air coming in through the open door, but he's warm. His chest is broad. Wallace's hand slips down to his throat. The low, steady rhythm of Miller's pulse. Wallace should know better. He knows that. Picking fights over petty things, over invisible things.

"If I'm so exhausting, then why don't you kick me out?" he says as he straddles Miller's lap. He lets his weight rock back against the tops of Miller's thighs. "If I'm so exhausting, then just tell me to beat it." Wallace presses his thumb into the smooth, firm cartilage below Miller's Adam's apple. The silvery surfaces of Miller's eyes pass along the creases of his lids, which have now slit open as if released by the pressure of Wallace at his throat. Like a tiny machine. Like a toy. Press one place and see another pop open. Miller wets his lips. His face comes close to Wallace, but Wallace pushes him back, flattens his palm against his throat, so that Miller encounters the resistance of Wallace's body. The more Miller pushes, the tighter Wallace's hand cinches around his throat. They're caught this way, separated by sharp, angular distances. Miller grunts under him. Wallace feels him swallow.

Miller relaxes. The tension in his body goes slack, and for just an instant Wallace fears he's done something horribly stupid. He lets go, and in that instant, a span of time like the head of a pin, Miller snatches his wrists and drags Wallace's hands down to his stomach to bring the two of them as close as possible. Wallace blinks and suddenly there they are together, faces close enough that their noses touch, their lips touch, their cheeks touch. They're so close that Wallace feels he can see the red crescents of the insides of Miller's eyelids, so close he can hear the blood rushing in Miller's body, so close he might mistake that rushing blood for his own.

"Cheap," Wallace says, but he can't get his wrists loose. Miller's got him cinched up tight. Wallace struggles a little harder, but Miller will not let him go. He pulls back and away, but he goes nowhere. Miller is stronger than he is. It isn't fear that Wallace feels, exactly, in this moment. It doesn't have that wild, gamy taste. There's something else, regret, in its place.

Miller watches him from beneath his heavy eyelids. "Ask for what you want," he says.

"Fuck you."

"Be a good boy."

Good boy.

"I was never good."

"Me either," Miller says.

"Yeah, right," Wallace says, but then Miller's expression goes a little sad and Wallace remembers what Miller told him. About his mother, who had died, and how things had not always been easy and good between them. "Oh. I'm sorry. I didn't mean that."

"Sure you did. Of course you did."

"We were just talking."

"Just talking," Miller says a little meanly. "That's what we're doing. Who knew?"

There's a little more give to Miller's hold on him, so Wallace takes his chance and gets himself free. His wrists burn from the tension of Miller's hands, from the structure of his grasp. On the undersides of Wallace's arms, where he's palest, he can see the dark red afterimage of Miller's palms. He slips from Miller's lap back to the floor. Miller has closed his eyes again. It's as if the past few minutes never happened.

Wallace wonders if this means that he should leave. He presses his thumb down against the back of Miller's hand, where it rests on the floor. He digs at the skin with his thumbnail, and Miller jolts again, jerks back to life. It's like before, with Yngve. What is this part of him, Wallace wonders, that makes him provoke people this way? What is it in him?

Ask for what you want, Miller said. It makes sense to Wallace now. It's his way of asking. He can't just say what he wants. Because he doesn't know what he wants.

"Wallace. Don't start with me," Miller says. "You won't like it."

"I'm not," Wallace says, but he's already humming inside. He can barely contain the warm, rushing sensation inside him. "I'm not starting anything." This feels essential somehow, that he say this to Miller, though he suspects that he is. He puts his lips against Miller's neck, and breathes. He feels Miller swallow. The heat of his skin. The rhythm of the muscles rising and falling. The softness of his hair against Wallace's nose. The fur of some tender animal. The skin pimples under his breath. The shiver of life. He sinks his teeth against Miller's neck and shuts his eyes against the white jolt of being shoved back and pinned against the floor. Miller is sitting on top of him. His hands are pinned above his head, in which swims his brain, a yolky mess. This too feels necessary. Miller leans low over him.

"I told you not to start with me," Miller says, but his voice is shaky, uncertain. Something catches in it. Wallace's head aches, pulsates. "I told you."

"I didn't," Wallace says. Miller is straining against himself, fighting something. Wallace has never witnessed this part of him, though now that he's close enough he thinks he may have caught glimpses of it. There was that time in their first year, when Wallace had accidentally let the door to the ice machine snap shut just as Miller was reaching in to fill his bucket. It had been a true accident, a minor miracle of bad timing and misread intentions. Wallace was scooping out some ice, door propped on his hip, when Miller came jogging up and said something to him just as he was looking away, and Wallace had let the door swing shut and it almost cut Miller's hand off. Miller stood there stunned, staring down at his hand as if it had been cleaved clean off. Wallace was terrified. Then, slowly, their eyes met, and Wallace saw that Miller had every intention of punching right through his face. He watched the fingers curl. He watched the fist rise with slow solemnity, like a head bowing in prayer. But then something changed. Instead of him, Miller threw his punch at the slanted door of the ice machine and let out a curse. *Goddammit, Wallace*, he said. Then he kicked the machine. *You are so fucking selfish*. Another time, one lunchtime in second year, they

were sitting in twos on a maze of stone walls—Miller and
Yngve, Cole and Wallace, Lukas and Emma—when Miller
and Yngve started to fight about something. It looked like a
playful skirmish, but then, after some moment of pride bruised,
Miller suddenly pushed Yngve, hard, and Yngve went flailing
back off the wall onto the concrete below. For a moment Miller
sat there looking at him, his posture rigid, head high, as if he
were proud. And then, quick as anything, he jumped down after
Yngve, and the rest of them came running after. Yngve was all
right. He went home with a concussion that day. And Lukas
stayed with him. Wallace wondered if that may have been the
start of things between those two. Now, in the kitchen, Wallace
is not surprised to find himself pinned by Miller. He's not
shocked. This is something he's been after, isn't it? Why else goad
him? Wallace lifts his knee until it's against Miller's chest.

"Why are you pressing me, Wallace?"

"I don't know," Wallace says. "So you'll tell me to leave, I
guess."

"I won't," Miller says.

"Not even after all that?"

"It barely hurt. You're a baby."

This stings Wallace's pride, a pride he did not know he
possessed until this very moment. With some embarrassment
he realizes that he thought himself capable of dealing Miller
harm. Didn't he hurt Miller by telling him all that stuff about
himself? Isn't that why he did this here, to bring Miller's anger
upon him? Because he thought himself capable of doing harm, of

taking something from Miller? And to be told now that he was nothing more than a baby.

"Tell me about *your* damage," Wallace says.

"You don't need to know my damage."

"I think you want me to know," Wallace says. "That's what this is all about, isn't it? You want me to know about it."

He shifts under Miller. His back hurts. His head hurts. The world is still uneven, jagged. Like bits of a mirror fit unevenly together. Miller is kaleidoscopic in gray and black and silver, his face a shadowy hall of mirrors, a riot of shapes.

"I hurt someone, Wallace. Really fucking bad," Miller says.

Wallace breathes through the dull shock of the words.

"My parents sent me away, after. Some kind of camp, I guess it was. But that kid—his heart stopped. That's what people said, back home, anyway. His heart stopped three times in the ambulance."

"Wait, Miller . . . Why?"

"I don't know—it's like that, I think. With trauma, arrhythmias. His brain bled where I hit him. He had deficits for a long time."

"No," Wallace says. "I meant—that's not what I meant."

Miller retreats. Wallace follows. Miller stands. Wallace stands. He takes Miller's elbow, tries to get him to turn.

"Why did you do that to him?"

Miller's eyes are sad and downcast. He turns from Wallace. Knocks into the glass. Cold water on their feet. On the floor. The glass cracks, but doesn't break.

"Shit," Miller says. Wallace breathes. The wind pulls back through the trees. The air is cold and dark. "Shut that, will you?"

Wallace nods. He slides the door shut as Miller picks up the glass. The room is suddenly, with the door closed, quiet.

"Is that your answer?" Wallace asks.

"I don't have one," he says, resting against the counter. "I don't have an answer, Wallace. He was this kid from home. He followed me and my friends around. It wasn't like it is here. I'm not like Yngve. Or Lukas or Emma. I'm not from *this*." He gestures broadly, taking in the house and the yard and their neighbors who sleep soundly, deeply, encompassing the capitol and the square and the lakes and the trees and the whole bright world. "Anyway, his dad was an engineer at the plant where my dad worked, and all this kid could talk about was going to Purdue. *Early decision*." Miller's face is knit tight. Closed, like he's seeing it all again. "He was just this little pissant kid, Wallace. He was just so sure."

"You attacked someone because they were *sure*?"

"No," Miller says, shaking his head. "No, it wasn't that. But it was, I guess. It comes down to that. He was sure. All I had waiting for me was some job making brake shoes like my old man. And this kid is just walking around like, *I'm going to Purdue. I'm going to be an engineer!* And *I* went around mad because nobody out there wanted me. Nothing I wanted wanted me back."

"I understand that," Wallace says.

"Do you? One day, we steal some cigarettes, right? And we're out behind the old grocery store, smoking and talking shit. Usual stuff. This kid, five feet, no inches, leans over, and he just plucks the butt right out of my mouth." Miller smiles as the memory surfaces, like he can taste the perfect, gritty flavor of his rage. He breathes deeply. "And he says, *I'm really gonna miss you guys*. Talking about missing us while smoking *my* cigarette. I'm like, *This kid*. This kid has got it coming. So I get even."

Wallace feels a little dizzy. He wonders if he hurt his head. Miller, having given himself over to the story now, looks content. He wets his teeth and then his lips. There is the hint of a smirk on his face, as if he is enjoying himself, or he is inhabiting the version of himself who enjoyed hurting someone. Get even sounds like the rallying cry of weak people who have no other way to bargain with the world. What does that mean, Wallace wonders. There was no hurt done to Miller in this story. What score is he trying to even? Miller turns to him and his face shifts. His eyes widen slightly. Wallace feels a momentary chime of panic, that he's been caught out, and that Miller can read his mind, knows what Wallace thinks of him. No, Wallace thinks. Miller is afraid. That's what this is. He is afraid that he is bad and that no one wants him back.

"You wanted to get even," Wallace says quietly.

"I just wanted him to feel like I felt. What else was I supposed to do?" Miller's voice breaks as he says it. This is not from some long-ago memory, something reluctantly remembered. It's been there near the surface this whole time. *What else was I supposed to do? Anything else*, Wallace wants to say. *You didn't have to hurt that boy*. But Miller is not asking him to justify it. Not really. He wants someone to be on his side.

"It was impossible," Wallace says. "You were in an impossible place." What an ugly thing this is.

Miller turns to him then, fully. He draws Wallace close and puts his face against Wallace's neck.

"I didn't want to," Miller says. "I didn't want to do that. I try to be good. I try to be good. I try to be good."

"You are good," Wallace says, mildly alarmed at himself.

Miller laughs coolly. "I don't know, Wallace. What I just told you makes me sound like a really bad person."

"There are no bad people," Wallace says with a shrug. "People do bad things. But after a while they're just people again."

"So I guess that means you've forgiven your parents?" Miller says, and a sharp streak of hurt flashes behind Wallace's eyes. "I thought not." He pauses. "There are bad people. I kept thinking about that kid's face when you told me about what happened to you. I could feel his bones breaking. And my bones breaking. And I just kept going. Because I was mad. How sick is that?"

"You were trying to escape your life," Wallace says.

"By tearing a hole in someone else's."

Wallace lets it lie. Whatever Miller wants from him, it isn't this.

Miller takes his hand. "Let's go to bed," he says. Wallace nods and follows him up the stairs. There is so much trouble in the world. There are people suffering everywhere, at every moment. Who is happy, truly happy, ever? What is a person to do with it all? Except to try to slide laterally out of one's life into whatever gray space waits for them.

Miller's room is as they left it. He shuts the door, and Wallace climbs back onto the bed. Miller gets into bed with him, and they slide under the quilt. Soon it will be fall, too cold for just a quilt, but by then Wallace might be hundreds of miles away. He might be somewhere warm. He might be anywhere at all. And Miller will still be here, in this room, changing over his clothes and his bed for winter. The contrast makes Wallace uneasy— how unrooted he is in this place, how tenuous a grasp it has on him. Miller wraps his arms around him, and for a moment, at least, Wallace feels anchored, moored.

"I hope you don't hate me," Miller says. "Isn't that stupid? To tell you what I am and then say, *Please don't hate me*?"

"I don't hate you," Wallace says.

"Okay. I'm glad."

Wallace turns to him, and they kiss again, more deeply this time. When Miller moves inside him, Wallace closes his eyes so that he doesn't have to see Miller looking at him. He does not trust himself with this uncertain feeling gaining momentum. Miller asks him to roll onto his stomach, and Wallace does, and he's relieved not to have to close his eyes so tight. Miller kisses his shoulders, his back. It's tender. But it's still fucking, and it still hurts, which, in this moment, is a blessing because it gives Wallace something to feel anchored in. When Miller finishes, he goes across the hall and comes back with a warm towel. Wallace cleans himself, but Miller looks away from him shyly, still unable to face the necessary discomfort of fucking a man. Wallace laughs, and Miller looks up sharply.

"What's so funny?"

"Nothing," Wallace says, and gets back under the quilt. "I was just laughing."

"At me?"

"No, at myself, I guess. It's funny. I didn't have sex for a long time, and now it's just a thing."

"Was it good?"

"Yes," Wallace says. "It was fine."

"Fine," Miller says, narrowing his eyes. Wallace kisses him.

"Don't hurt yourself," he says. "Don't think so much."

"Did you?"

"Did I what?" Wallace asks, and Miller looks down at him meaningfully. "Oh, it's fine."

"Are you sure?"

"Yes," Wallace says, and it is fine because he doesn't think he could get hard even if he wanted to. It isn't anything to do with Miller or not wanting him, he realizes. But he feels disconnected now, suddenly, from the part of him that is necessary for fucking or coming. "I'm tired."

"Me too," Miller says.

They lie there for a long time, just breathing next to each other. It is like the night before, Wallace thinks. Except now they are in Miller's bed instead of Wallace's, except now they're in this part of town rather than downtown, except for all the rest of it; it's like the night before except somehow shifted, the world at angles to itself, an oblique reflection across some strange line of symmetry. Wallace feels a childish sense of glee at this revelation, a small bit of happiness at having discerned it. But there is no place to tell it, nowhere he can set it down and present it to Miller.

When Miller falls asleep, Wallace pulls his arms apart and slides from the bed. He puts on his clothes as quietly as he can. He moves about the dark room, collecting his shoes and his shirt and his sweater. It's cold, and the world outside is gray with coming morning. When he is dressed, he slips into the dark hall and down the stairs. He leaves the bowl he brought. It's not worth it. And he goes out onto the street, making sure the door is shut firmly behind him.

It's getting to be four or five now. There are a couple of cars. The sky is lightening. Wallace stomps in his shoes and wraps his arms around himself. The street slopes upward. There are the familiar houses, their identical facades in minor variations, cream and hunter green and navy blue. Their doors shut firmly. Here and there a porch with wooden furniture on it, or a couch with ugly upholstery. Scraggly city grass. The odd tree. Cars parked neatly against the sides of houses. Up the street he goes, his steps echoing softly. The air is cool and damp. He's sore and feels like he's all scratched up inside. Ahead of him the top of the capitol is visible, beyond it the gray bulk of the lake. He's almost home.

Did Miller really almost kill someone? Bring his cracking bones down on someone because he didn't know what to do with himself? Anger could be like that, moving from person to person like an illness or a plague. The way Wallace himself was cruel at dinner, lobbing that grenade at Vincent because of what had been said to him. Or the way that telling Miller about Alabama prompted Miller to tell him about Indiana, the two of them passing cruelty back and forth like a joint. Perhaps friendship is really nothing but controlled cruelty. Maybe that's all they're doing, lacerating each other and expecting kindness back. Or maybe it's just Wallace, lacking friends, lacking an understanding of how friendship works.

But he understands cruelty. He understands violence, even if friendship is beyond him. Just as he can feel the coming weather, he can discern from shifting tides the shape of violence on the horizon. It is his native element, his mother tongue—he knows how people can maim each other. He sensed it in the bed with Miller, drifting off to sleep—that if he stayed, something terrible would happen. Perhaps not in that moment, or even the next day. But soon enough something awful was coming their way. Why stay, then? Why, if he could feel it in the ache of his belly, in the pressure collecting behind his eyes?

Wallace reaches the top of the hill, where the street flattens out and becomes a side street adjoining the capitol. There are cafés and bakeries here, though they are not open. He walks briskly past a little patio, where people sleep in soggy blankets on painted benches. The scent of urine and old food rotting hangs in the air. How easily he might have become one of them; how simple it would have been for him to be homeless here, or down in Alabama. This too is a kind of life, a way in which things can go wrong for a person.

When Wallace finally reaches his apartment, he realizes he has left his phone at Miller's house. This is a complication, but not a serious one. Tomorrow is Monday. He will see Miller in the biosciences building where they work. He will ask him to bring the phone on Tuesday or another day—a simple favor, just two friends helping each other. Clean, efficient, nothing like the prying open of one's life, the splitting of the past like an egg.

Wallace runs a hot bath and climbs into his tub, which is deep and white. He can barely stand the heat of the water, which is blue and up to his chest in the tub. The bathroom is quiet and too bright. If he were not afraid to sit in the tub in the dark, he would turn out the lights, but that might cause him to fall asleep, and he would not like that, to drown in his tub alone. Who would find him? A neighbor? His landlord? When the scent of his rotting body made its way outside and down the hall? When someone complained? Or would Miller come for him?

Wallace presses his knees together. The water ripples. He sinks lower into its scalding heat. He's turning the color of clay, his skin reddening, stinging as if burning from the water. He soaps himself up and then rinses himself clear, and the water is gray with soap and dead skin and filth. He still smells like smoke, from the fire, and perhaps from Miller's story of the time when he, smoking, punched a boy until he bled. Wallace dunks his face in the water, clears the smoke from his eyes. Slides deeper, until the water is level with his chin. His legs are floating. He would drown in an instant.

SOMETIME AROUND MIDMORNING, Wallace is awakened by a persistent knocking on his door. He pulls himself out of bed, where he has been drowsing on and off for hours. He is wearing a green sweater and blue cotton shorts. The apartment is blisteringly bright even with the shades drawn. Wallace opens the door and there is Miller, standing in front of him, his hair wet from the shower, his skin scrubbed and red and fresh. There is something raw about him.

"You left," he says. "You left. After all that shit I said, you left."

"I know. I'm sorry. I just didn't want to be a hassle."

"Even after I said you weren't, even after I said I wanted you to stay. You left. You *left*, Wallace."

Wallace is already tired. Are they going to chase after each other this way? Across town, from bed to bed? He rests against the door. Miller holds out his phone.

"You left this behind."

"Thank you. I was going to ask you for it tomorrow."

"Tomorrow?" Miller asks. There is hurt in his voice, and annoyance. Wallace sighs.

"When I saw you at work. It's not a problem. You didn't have to bring it."

"You left," Miller repeats. He's wearing some sort of cropped top beneath a cardigan. Gym clothes. His stomach is clenching and releasing. He's out of breath. Sweat on his skin. He ran all the way here, Wallace realizes. Something in him softens.

"Do you want to come in?"

Miller kisses him hard on the mouth, takes two steps forward, shuts the door behind him. His mouth tastes fresh like toothpaste, of course. His lips are warm and close, insistent. Wallace lets himself be kissed and pressed to the wall. They knock the broom over with a loud clack on the floor.

"I didn't know if you'd even want to talk to me again," Miller says. "When did that become so important to me? I don't know."

Wallace wants to laugh at that, or feel insulted by it, but he can't. Miller is so earnest, so sincere in his doubt that to make fun of it would be ugly. Instead, he gingerly extricates himself from Miller. He takes a seat on the couch near the window, and folds his legs under himself. Miller begins to fuss with the bar stool, shifting it around.

"Well, thank you for bringing my phone," he says. "I appreciate it."

"We're having brunch," Miller says quickly. "Some of us, I mean. You're welcome to join."

Wallace is already on his way to rejecting the offer when Miller says, "I'd like it if you came."

Small favors, Wallace thinks. Small, clearly defined favors. He wets his lips.

"Okay," he says.

"Good," Miller says. "Good."

THEY GO TO BRUNCH TOGETHER. It's one of the places on the square, where there is seating outdoors behind green partitions. They sit at a broad table, just the two of them at first. Miller kneads Wallace's knee anxiously under the table. Wallace stares down into his coffee. The world is too bright, too saturated. He would prefer to sleep, to be asleep. The traffic on the square is slow. Families on tours of the capitol, their thick Midwestern accents sailing through the air. Farther away he hears shards of music, buskers warming up for the day. The sun is hot on his neck. His sweater has a duck on it.

Soon, their friends appear. Miller's hand drops from his knee. Lukas and Yngve and Thom and Cole and Vincent and Emma. They move to one of the long tables. Wallace can still smell the booze on their skin. They are all wearing dark shades. Cole and Vincent are holding hands on top of the table. Things must have put themselves back together over there. Wallace is relieved. Emma puts her head on his shoulder. Vincent's shades reflect Wallace's gaze.

"I'm starving," Yngve says. "Lukas, what are you getting?"

"Crêpes, I think," Lukas says, studying the menu carefully. He is fastidious in pronouncing the word, as he often is with such things. Cole kisses Vincent's cheek and then his hair. Vincent is staring through Wallace. Or rather, the surface of Vincent's sunglasses is pointed in Wallace's general direction. Where the eyes beneath are pointed is a mystery. The waiter brings their drinks. Cappuccino for Emma, double espresso for Thom, mimosas for Cole and Vincent, who are clearly feeling celebratory, and refills of plain coffee for Lukas and Yngve. Miller isn't drinking. His cardigan has a hole in the shoulder.

They all end up ordering crêpes, as if unable to resist the power of suggestion. Wallace isn't hungry, but orders anyway.

"So I hear I missed a crazy party last night," Thom says. "What happened?" His eyes are gleaming. He spent the night reading Tolstoy, he says, assembling an argument about some obscure text. Wallace would rather talk about that than the party, anything other than the party.

"Nothing, nothing," Cole says, smiling. "It wasn't that bad."

"Yeah," Vincent says, but there is no smile on his face or in his voice. He looks out into the street. Wallace drinks from his coffee.

"That's not what I heard," Thom says, grinning. He bumps against the table, rocking it slightly. "I heard it was a shitshow."

"It wasn't that serious," Lukas says. "Yngve, sugar?" Lukas hands Yngve several sugar packets. Yngve takes them, tears them open, and dumps the contents into his cup. Thom is starting to look a little defeated by this. He turns to Emma.

"Babe? I thought you said it was crazy."

Emma lifts her head from Wallace's shoulder and shrugs. "It's not really worth rehashing. I told you." Things have not quite put themselves back together between these two, Wallace notes.

Thom has made a critical miscalculation, assuming that whatever Emma alluded to had been something the others would feel comfortable discussing. He probably thought she was talking about someone getting too drunk or saying something slightly off-color or starting some sort of silly contest. He did not assume that the craziness Emma mentioned had been anything worse. Thom's shoulders slump, and Wallace feels pity for him. It's always this way. He's always on the outside of things. But then Wallace remembers that Emma and Thom are fighting and his pity shrinks, recedes. He has his own shit, after all.

"I can't believe the weekend is over," Cole says. "Can you guys?"

"No," Lukas says. "I have to go to lab today and get things ready for tomorrow. It's going to be a long week."

"Same," Yngve says, nodding. "Protein preps."

"Genomic shearing."

"The worst," Emma says, lolling back against Wallace's shoulder.

"I just have to passage my cells," Cole says. "It's . . . well, you know."

"Is that light-sensitive?"

"Yep," Cole says. "And I have to do it in the cold room. For hours."

"Better pack a parka," Lukas says.

"How long are you working?" Vincent asks, and Cole turns to him with a look of apology already forming.

"Oh, babe. Not that long. Probably till five."

Vincent's lips stretch into a thin line. Wallace does not need to see his eyes to know that they are filled with disappointment, that whatever fragile truce they've formed is already in danger of rupturing. Wallace wants to kick Cole under the table, to pay attention, but it isn't his place. The sun is high overhead now. Their food comes out, all crispy and brown and soft. Wallace's crêpes are plain, with just powdered sugar and strawberries on the side. The tartness of the berries and the sweetness of the sugar are nice, soothing something in him. He chews evenly, slowly, eyes on his own plate. He dissects his food with a careful hand into edible segments. It's the only way to keep it down.

Miller watches him from across the table. Yngve and Lukas are talking, fighting quietly.

"You didn't say you weren't coming back," Yngve says. "You said you were going to take Nathan home and come back."

"I was tired, Yngve. Besides, what happened to Enid? Wasn't she supposed to stay over?"

"She had to take Zoe home."

"Well, that was nice of her."

"You didn't answer my texts."

"I was asleep."

"Fine."

"All right."

"I didn't know you weren't coming home, that's all. I waited up. Miller and I used your vape."

Lukas shrugs, and Miller laughs to diffuse the tension. Yngve and Lukas are never really fighting. It's just scratching the surface. Lukas's hair is bright in the summer sun, and he's so freckled that he looks tan. He is coppery all over. Miller nudges Lukas with his elbow.

"You're quiet," Emma says to Wallace, which startles him.

"Oh, just eating," he says.

"Are you all right?"

"M-hm." He gives her a smile, but she sees right through it. She puts her hand on his leg.

"Are you?" she asks again, and her voice lowers so that only he can hear her. What is he supposed to say to that? That he is fine but not, here but not, wishing he were in his apartment?

"I'm just tired," he says.

"When did you go home?" Vincent asks him, and from the directness of his gaze, even through the sunglasses, Wallace knows he's been caught out for something.

"This morning," he says before he can think of something else. "I walked home."

"Yeah, because we were all outside, and you just vanished," Vincent says. "Which is funny, considering how all of . . . last night happened because of you."

Wallace licks the sugar from the corner of his mouth and takes a steadying breath. "Was that because of me? I thought it had something to do with you and Cole."

"Oh, no, it was you, Wallace."

"Vincent," Cole says.

"You opened your big mouth and then you decided—hell, I don't know what you decided, but suddenly, you're gone. Why is that, Wallace?"

"I wasn't trying to start anything," Wallace says. "I'm sorry it happened the way it did, but I wasn't trying to start anything."

"But weren't you?" Vincent's voice stabs through him. "Weren't you trying to start something because you're miserable? Because you're angry? Because you don't know what you want? Isn't that it?"

"No," Wallace says, but it's a small sound.

"I think you need to mind your own business, Wallace. You're going to ruin someone's life one day."

"That's not fair," Miller says. "Don't do that."

"Why, Miller? He intruded where he wasn't wanted."

"Babe," Cole says. His face is flushed. He is giving Wallace a look of apology, but Wallace only shakes his head. He has this coming, after all. He's got it all coming.

"It's not fair to blame Wallace. We're friends. We sometimes fuck up, but come on," Yngve says.

"It's all right, Yngve. I don't mind," Wallace says, shrugging. "Vincent is obviously very angry at me. It's fine."

"It's fine," Vincent says. "You know, Wallace, just because you don't have someone doesn't mean that the rest of us also have to suffer."

"That's true," Wallace says. "You're right."

"Vincent," Emma says. "Maybe calm down."

"No, Emma. It needs to be said. He doesn't get it. He doesn't get how people's relationships aren't toys for him to play with. That he doesn't get to fuck it all up for other people. This is real life, Wallace. Do you understand that? It's real life."

Wallace nods slowly, carefully, making sure that the gesture is immaculate, perfect, a faultless contrition. He can do this. It is a skill in life, serving this function, to be contrite, to pay obeisance.

"I'm sorry," he says. "I'm sorry for causing you so much trouble. For hurting you. I didn't think."

"You didn't think," Vincent snarls. "You didn't think that it would have consequences. That other people wouldn't suffer. It's not a game. It's my life. It's Cole's life. Next time, think of others."

"I will. I'm sorry," Wallace says quietly, his voice hot, like asphalt congealing. Miller and Cole share a look of horror, of shock. Emma is making soothing sounds, rubbing his knee. Vincent goes back to his mimosa.

"Wallace," Cole begins, but Wallace looks up at him and smiles.

"It's okay, Cole. It's fine."

The others at the table settle into tingling quiet, which eventually is broken up by the clatter of their forks and knives. It is a re-creation of last night's dinner, how after Roman humiliated him, they all went back to eating, sitting in polite refusal to acknowledge the blow dealt to Wallace. He is not sad. He is not overcome with grief or sorrow at this. He has prepared himself for it, after all. It is a blow Wallace has been anticipating since last night; he is only surprised that it took this long to land. He wipes his mouth with his napkin, cuts another segment of crêpe, and he eats.

The taste is bland, but he chews anyway. Miller looks at him anxiously, as if Wallace might vanish at any moment. Wallace drinks his coffee.

"Emma, what are you doing for the rest of the day?" Wallace asks.

"Oh, I'll nap, probably," she says, laughing. "Maybe I'll read."

"Me too," Wallace says. "I got that book Thom mentioned. I like it so far, I guess."

"Do you?" she says wryly. "Don't let Thom hear; he'll never stop suggesting things to you."

"I'd like nothing more," Wallace says. Thom is too busy wolfing down his crêpes and bacon to pay much attention to them. He is a nervous eater. That is, when anxious, he eats with a single-minded ferocity. Wallace can relate. His appetite swells when he's nervous. "What are you reading?"

"I'm on a strict Judy Blume diet," Emma says. "Classics, you know."

They share a bittersweet laugh. Emma's eyes are red. She is angry again on his behalf, but she, like the rest of them, remains silent.

"What are you two whispering about over there?" Yngve asks. "The rest of us could use a laugh too."

"We're talking about books," she says suggestively. "Big books."

Yngve's expression grows more curious, and he says in a loud whisper, "I love big books."

Emma is not sure what to make of this. Wallace laughs. Lukas says, by way of explanation, "He's not lying, actually. He loves the Russians. And Muir, for some reason."

Emma frowns. Thom looks up with renewed interest.

"Russians? I'm writing a critical analysis on Russian literature," he says. "All the infidelity." The word makes Cole and Vincent flinch. Wallace watches it happen, the slow play of their features, the gathering of tension and cessation of movement on their faces. "The Russians, you know, and their morality. Very strict."

Yngve nods, but because of what he knows of the situation, he squirms uncomfortably.

"Yes, dear, very nice," Emma says. "Very strict, yes."

"Some think that Tolstoy—"

"Are we going sailing today?" Miller asks Yngve.

"Do you want to? We can."

"I'd like to go sailing," Emma says.

"Me too," says Lukas.

"Do you want to come, Wallace? We can get a big boat," Yngve says. The thought of spending the day on the water beneath the sun, all that churning makes him want to vomit. What he wants is to crawl into the cool darkness of his bedroom and sleep for an eternity or more.

"No, no, it's fine. I think I'll stick close to home."

There is a look of disappointment on Miller's face, but Wallace cannot rise to it. He cannot bring himself to spend more time outside in the world. He wants to sink down and down, hide himself.

"That's too bad," Yngve says. "We'd have a lot of fun with you along."

"You have to," Emma says, pulling on his arm. He gives her a look that he hopes is apologetic and pathetic enough. He's had enough of people and enough of the world. He's had it. He's full up. He can't bear it a moment longer. He can't go on this way, with them.

"I can't," he says. "I better get going." It's just like Friday. The days are repeating themselves. He kisses Emma's cheek.

"I'll go too," Miller says.

Wallace wants to scream. He does not know if he can stand to relive the entire weekend. He does not know how he will survive this folding back of time upon itself. But he does not scream. He tamps it down.

"But we're sailing," Yngve says, trying to extract the promise before Miller is gone from the table.

"We're sailing. At three, maybe."

"Okay, I'll call ahead for the boat."

"Perfect. Thank you, Yngve."

"Of course," Yngve says, waving him off. Wallace is already

leaving the table, and Miller lopes up beside him. When they turn the corner, away from their friends, Miller reaches for his hand. Wallace lets him take it.

"Are you okay?" he asks.

"I'm fine," Wallace says. "But I'm tired and want to go home. I want to be alone, if that's okay."

"It's okay," Miller says. "I'm sorry about what Vincent said."

"I had it coming," Wallace says, looking down the street ahead of them. Miller squeezes his hand in a gesture that Wallace assumes is meant to comfort him, to bring some sort of reassurance. What is Miller trying to assure him of with this gesture? What is he trying to smooth or fix?

"You didn't," Miller says. "You didn't deserve that."

"Who ever deserves anything?" Wallace asks.

"Come on."

"No," Wallace says. "It's fine."

"It's not."

"I cannot have this conversation a single time more, Miller." Wallace stops abruptly. He takes his hand away. "I can't. I'm not angry. I'm not mad. But I cannot have this conversation again."

"Wallace."

"No, Miller. I can't." It is perhaps the truest thing he has said all morning. The refusal to go forward, to repeat the pattern, to let himself be folded up into this language that robs the world of all its honesty. He does not want to get swallowed up by it again, by this way of looking at things without looking at them, by this oblique shadow-speak. Just because you say you're sorry, or you say that someone doesn't deserve something, does not erase the facts of what has or has not happened, or who has or has not acted. Wallace is tired.

"Can't what?" Miller asks. "What can't you do? You don't want to talk to me? Fine. You don't want to be around me, fine. Go. Okay. Fine."

"That is not what I meant."

"What did you mean, then?"

That he wants to be alone. That he does not want to speak to anyone. That he does not want to be around anyone. That the world has worn him down. That he would like nothing more than to slip out of his life and into the next. That he is terrified, afraid. That he wants to lie down here and never move again. What he means is that he does not know what he wants, only that it is not this, the way forward paved with words they've already said and things they've already done. What he wants is to break it all open and try again.

"I don't know," he says, and then, "I just want to be alone in my apartment. I just want to sleep."

"Fine," Miller says. "Okay."

Miller digs in the pockets of his cardigan. He extracts a pack of cigarettes and lights one, takes a long drag and exhales. He runs a hand through his hair.

"Fuck," he says. "Fuck."

"I'm not mad," Wallace says.

"I know. It's fine. I'm just fucked up over this."

"Over what?"

"I don't know, Wallace. Over you, over me, over the shit with

Cole and Vincent. I don't even want to go sailing. I just said that because of the drama."

"I know. I figured. I mean, I'm sorry."

"But I'll go sailing," he said, taking another drag. "I'll go fucking sailing with Yngve and the others."

"I can't go, Miller."

"I know you can't. Will I see you later?" His voice is soft, low.

Wallace touches the edge of Miller's cardigan, slides his hand inside its coarse knit, to the place where his skin is bare. "I don't know, Miller. Maybe."

"I need more than a maybe, Wallace," he says, blowing smoke from the corner of his mouth. "I need something. A yes. A no. But more than a maybe."

"Why do you want to see me anyway?"

"The weekend's not over," he says, smiling, but it's that shy smile from before, the one that started all the trouble in the first place. Wallace looks away.

"Call me," he says. "We'll see."

"I'll take it," Miller says, and he draws Wallace in for a hug. He smells like smoke and ashes, and also like oranges. Wallace wraps his arms around Miller's waist, and he doesn't make to leave. For all his talk of wanting to be alone, having been brought close to another person, he realizes that what he would like more than anything else is to be held. But he can't bring himself to ask for that now, and knowing himself, he'd only change his mind later, would regret it the moment he got what he wanted.

"Well, I better go," he says.

"So you say," Miller says. Wallace laughs, and then steps backward out of Miller's arms.

"See you," he says.

"See you around."

Wallace goes down the street, and every so often he looks back. Miller is there smoking each time, watching him. There are more people now. The sun is out. It's bright. It's hot. Eventually, it is impossible to discern Miller from all the other people crossing the street or walking toward and away from the capitol. Eventually, they are all just people going about their lives, shopping and eating, laughing and arguing, doing what people in the world do. This too is real life, he thinks. Not merely the accumulation of tasks, things to be done and sorted, but also the bumping up against other lives, everyone in the world insignificant when taken and observed together.

He stops on the corner and supports himself against the building there, closing his eyes. The world spins, shifts underfoot. The week is ahead of him, waiting, with all its demands, its structure, and soon enough another academic year will begin. If he advances toward it, marching ever closer, will it swallow him, till the sound of his weight traversing is absorbed into its bulk, his life no more discernible from the outside than the lives of others on the street are to him?

He would like to sleep for a long time, but there is lab, the nematodes, and so while he might go home, he knows that he must leave again. He pushes off from the building, gathers his strength, and points himself toward home—a little rest, he thinks, he's earned that much.

A bird has flown into a window and lies dying on its back, Wallace discovers when he arrives at the biosciences building. The day is still cloudless, and the sky is an almost iridescent blue, the way it can be in late summer. The sight of the bird startles him. He has retained a fear of birds since childhood. This is one of those vague Midwestern birds, gray with a white belly. Its head is nearly crushed down inside its body, and its long dark legs are like twigs from certain bushes. Occasionally, its wings spasm open. A thread of dark ants already stretches from a nearby bench to the bird, and Wallace knows, without thinking too hard, what will happen next.

This reemergence of death in this immaculate city of the North—the suddenness of it jolts him almost as much as the bird itself. He cannot remember the last time he actually saw something die, not counting the worms he burns at the end of the titanium wire. How long has it been since he came across such a clear and present illustration of the order of things, of life ending, moving on? Long enough to have grown comfortable with death happening elsewhere, off in the margins. Or perhaps he's making too much of it, imbuing the moment with more significance than it warrants, in the wake of all he told Miller about Alabama.

How did his father look at the hour of his death? Or later, at the funeral? Was he buried on a day like this? No, it must have been warmer, surely, in Alabama, at the height of the heat, the crying cicadas. Wallace breathes, turns. He hops up the steps and enters the building. Enough, he thinks.

The familiar rattle of the machines greets him, and he relaxes. It's dry and cool indoors; he feels the humid tent of his sweater begin to dry. He takes the elevator to the third floor, lets his fingers glide along the wooden railing as he walks past the balcony. Down below, a field of purple tiles depicting the molecular structures of various sugars and biomolecules. There is an error down there somewhere, a carbon with five bonds—a Texas carbon, they call it, after the points on the star on the flag of Texas. Someone pointed it out to him during orientation, and he strained to see it, squinting while the others merely laughed and shrugged. They didn't need to see to get the joke. Someone had to explain it to him later: because five bonds on a carbon is impossible. He smiled, nodded. Of course: A carbon can make four bonds, not more. He knew this. He had learned it in chemistry.

He majored in chemistry at a small undergraduate institution in Alabama. His undergraduate research was in organic adduct reactions, trying to understand how and why molecules merge, become other molecules, within the specific context of environmental chemistry. His adviser, a tall, wiry man with a long, sloping step and a mild tremor, was a respected if minor researcher in the field of acid rain. His work described a process, the slow accumulation of particles in the air that when combined become toxic or acidic, washing out of the sky into rivers and cities, destroying buildings and homes. Wallace's job in those days was to watch as his professor mixed various solutions in a slender capillary tube and stuck it in a machine to measure its spectra.

It was beyond Wallace to understand such things then, but he was good at memorization, and he took detailed notes. He was interested enough in science, enough to know that it was his way out of the South for good. That day during orientation, when the tour guide told them about the Texas carbon, Wallace blinked slowly, dumbly. He had never heard of such a thing. The drawings from which he had learned chemistry had left no room for jokes or humor. It had never occurred to him that there could be five bonds on a carbon, even sarcastically. He had learned chemistry the way one learns French in school: too properly, too much by rote and routine, by memorizing all the rules, which of course is no way to learn a language that one intends to use.

The lab door is already open, and Wallace drops his bags at his desk. An email waits for him—from Simone. He doesn't have to answer it. He doesn't have to read it. But he does, doesn't he? It's only a matter of time. Besides, if he doesn't answer this one, it will be followed by another and another and another, a hail of emails falling down on him like knives until eventually he must.

Beyond the window, the birds are gone. He bites the corner of his lip, opens the email, skims it. Among the responses to his last progress report, flagged in red, two lines leap out at him: *Let's talk. I'm worried.*

Wallace immediately closes the email. His gut tightens. He

squeezes his eyes closed. Simone's face blooms in the dark of his mind, her intelligent blue eyes gazing at him, impassive, knowing. What will she say in that immaculate office of hers, with its delicate pieces of Danish carvings and line drawings? What does it mean, worried? Wallace has had enough of other people's worry, enough of their concern. It's been following him around since Friday like a persistent, hacking cough.

"Hey, Wallace," someone says from his left. It's Katie, coming along his bench with a look of fierce determination on her face. "I wanted to check in with you about these results. What's the status?"

"Oh, Katie," he says. "I'm on damage control. Trying to recover the strain as best I can, you know." He hates the wavering uncertainty in his voice, the tremulousness of it. He shrugs.

"Okay, but where are we, I guess, in the big picture?"

"I'm sorry, I don't understand the question," he says with a sense of sharpening dread. Katie's patience is dwindling already, her small features narrowing. She presses a hip to the bench and folds her arms.

"You were going to do some staining experiments, right?" Wallace nods. "Okay, so what I'm asking is, where do you see those fitting into this project? I'm trying to wrap up some stuff for this paper, and I'm just realizing I actually don't know what the hell you're even doing."

"The staining is supposed to recapitulate the previous results," he says after a moment, slowly, thinking his way through it as best he can, trying to remember why he had even begun this in the first place. "From your work last year. We needed to re-peat it, so I was doing that . . . repeating it."

"And that has taken a month."

"Yes, Katie. It's taken a month."

"I just feel like I could do it myself, faster, instead of waiting around."

"Well, yes, you could, but it's my project."

"But it's not your name, Wallace, on the paper, is it? It's not your thesis."

"My name is on the paper."

"As third author."

"Yeah, well, it's still my name. It's still my work."

"But you don't really . . . you aren't really . . ." Katie isn't ex-actly frowning at him. She isn't exactly glaring at him. Wallace knows she is trying merely to get to the heart of something that is confusing to her, that she cannot understand. It's the look of someone sifting through their thoughts, turning things over. What she wants to say, he can tell, is that he isn't working hard enough, that his dedication is lacking in some way. She is trying, in her own way, to say this as gently and kindly as possible.

"It's my work," he says. "It's my work, Katie. And I'm doing my best. And if that isn't fast enough for you, then I'm sorry."

"Right, that's fine, but you can't just take your time when other people's work is on the line, Wallace."

"I'm not taking my time. I'm doing my work," he says. "I'm doing what I can."

"Well, I think sometimes you have to step aside when your

best isn't enough. Like, objectively, if you aren't cutting it, then it's selfish to stay in the way."

"Am I in your way, Katie? Is that how you feel?"

Katie does not say anything to him. She does not look at him. She is leaning fully against the bench now and has crossed her feet. There is a repetitive banging in the other part of the lab, the rattle of glassware. Water running. Wallace feels cold. His fingers are stiff.

If he is in Katie's way, then he will step aside. If he is in Katie's way, then he will give her what she wants. But she knows as well as he does that the fact that she can perform the experiment better and faster does not mean she has time to do his work in addition to her own. There was a reason the larger project had been divided this way, Wallace taking on the technical work while Katie performed the more rigorous line of experimentation: because she could not do it all. There comes a time when you have to acknowledge your limitations, that the capacity to do something is not a mandate to do it. She is frustrated by this. It's all over her face, the irritation. She sighs.

"Let's just get this shit done—I'm tired of waiting," she says, turning. "Get it done, Wallace."

"All right," he says. Her words sting. His head hurts. The lab is piercingly bright. What to do? He scarcely has time to think before Simone emerges from the small break room. When she sees him, she turns and approaches him.

"Wallace," she says, voice raspy and inexplicably southern, "do you have a moment?"

"Sure," he says. "Sure."

"Perfect," she says, smiling now. "Let's go to my office."

Simone's office is on a corner. It has a view of the bridge in the distance and a row of small but robust trees. There is a juniper bush too, and from this height the tennis courts and even a sliver of lake are visible. The office itself is open and white. There are books and papers scattered over her desk, but it feels tidy, neatly arranged, everything sorted into its particular order. Simone is tall. She has a fondness for crisp lines. Her hair is a stylish bob, and her glasses are prim, like those of a librarian in a cartoon. She pulls a chair aside for Wallace, and she takes one opposite him, crossing her legs.

"So, Wallace," she says, opening her arms a little. "I hear it's been rough."

He takes his time answering that opening gambit. If he agrees too quickly, she will thrust it into his chest. If he deflects it entirely, she will call his bluff, conjure up covert intel from Dana and Katie and others in the lab, or from peers or professors, an unseen army of spies observing his every move. She's wearing a look of sympathetic grace, waiting.

"It's been a time," he says, smiling, trying to match her breezy concern.

"Tell me all about it. I'm sorry I've been gone." Where has she been? Copenhagen, or London. She has an apartment in Paris with her husband, Jean-Michel, who is American but French by birth. There are long parts of the year when Simone is absent from his life. She travels often, giving seminars and talks both on her research—the research of the lab—and on the nature of science itself. She is a bit of an evangelist in this way, and Wallace can certainly understand why. She is good at making you feel like the center of the world, like your concerns, no matter how trivial, are worthy of consideration. The problem, however, is that the same gravity is given to your flaws, no matter how minor. Except for Dana, he thinks, who seems immune to the flip side of Simone's attention.

"It's just been pretty messy, I think. My experiments—"

"Yes, your stocks were contaminated."

"Right. And I lost the summer's data."

"Well, that's unfortunate," she says, frowning. "I'm so sorry to hear that it's been hard for you."

"It's okay," he says reflexively. She puts her hands around her knees and nods slowly several times.

"I got an email from Dana last night, and it raised the hair on my neck, I must say, Wallace."

"Oh?" he asks. "What kind of email?"

"Please do not do that, Wallace. Please do not pretend that you don't know what the email was about."

"I see," he says. "I see. Okay."

Simone frowns, flexes her jaw. She continues, "I just worry that the two of you are butting heads and it's creating a toxic environment."

"I understand why you have that impression," Wallace says. "That's not my intention."

"I cannot have a misogynist in my lab, Wallace," she says sharply, directly, looking into his eyes, which makes him want to cry, suddenly. The wave of stinging tears comes to the brink of his eyelids, but it holds steady. He breathes deeply, slowly.

"I am not a misogynist," he says. "I am not."

"Dana's email was . . . I have never read something so horrible in my life, Wallace. And I thought, that can't be right."

A flicker of hope, a minor reprieve. Wallace nods.

"But I have to take this very seriously. I have to think about what is right for you and for Dana and for the lab. I'm retiring soon, as you know, and I can't have this kind of dysfunction." She holds her hands up, separates them, as if to say on one hand she wants him to stay, and on the other hand, well.

Wallace feels a chasm opening up beneath him. He could say what Dana said to him. He could say that she is racist, homophobic. He could say any of the things he has wanted to say since he came here, about how they treat him, about how they look at him, about what it feels like when the only people who look like him are the janitors, and they regard him with suspicion. He could say one million things, but he knows that none would matter. None of it would mean anything to her, to any of them, because she and they are not interested in how he feels except as it affects them.

"I see," he says again, blankly.

"I don't want to ask you to leave the lab, Wallace. But I do really want to encourage you to think about what you want."

"What I want?"

"Yes, Wallace. Think about this really hard. Is this what you want? To be a scientist? To spend your life in academia? I must be honest; I really, truly must be honest. I like you. I do. But when I look at you, I don't think you want this. Not like Katie. Not like Brigit. Not like Dana. You don't want it."

"I do," he says. "I do want it. I want to be here."

"Do you want to be here or do you . . . do you just not want to be somewhere else?"

Wallace looks down at his hands, which are cupped in his lap. His lips and throat are dry. He thinks of that bird again, lying on its back, eaten by ants, eaten as it dies, as it lies dying. His shorts are blue cotton, faded from too many washes. He digs a finger into his knee. What does he want, after all?

"I don't know," he says.

"I thought not. Why don't you take some time to think about it?"

"All right," he says. "Okay."

"Okay?" She puts a hand on his shoulder. He isn't crying or anything like that, but he feels blasted a bit, shaken. The world is shifting again, as if realigning itself to some new axis. Her touch is firm and warm. She runs her hand down his arm and up again. It's meant to be a comforting gesture, he supposes.

"Is that all?" he asks.

"That's all," she says, and she smiles again, showing her imperfect teeth, the discoloration that comes with age and coffee and life lived, if only briefly, outside this charmed circle.

AT THE LAKE'S EDGE, he can hear the train coming. Wallace always stops, wherever he is in the city, to listen to the sound of the train passing. It's a lonesome cry, like the baying of dogs in the woods, a sound to which he is especially attuned. There was a time when, very young and very impressionable, he believed his grandfather's stories about spectral dogs that would come and spirit him away if he dawdled when playing out in the trees. The sound of any dog howling or yipping in the distance would send a chill through him, and he'd run straight ahead, no matter if he were going away from or toward home, because he knew, sure enough, that he'd arrive on either side of the woods and be safe with his aunts on one end or his grandparents on the other. But on days when his courage did not fail him, he would stand perfectly still among the shifting pines, put his shoulders back, and howl into the clear blue sky. Something in him was wild and wanting to be free, to be loose, and he howled at the top of his lungs, his little voice flattening, then fraying at the edges, until there was no more air in his chest and he was hollow.

After a few moments, the train passes.

Wallace is on the lakeshore path again, though this time he's turned right and walked past the boathouse, where the boys are out oiling their boats again. Their swim trunks hang low on their hips, and their skin is tan and clear and slick with sweat. Together they are the picture of health. Occasionally one of them snaps a towel, leaving a streak across another boy's back. There are fat ducks sleeping at the ends of the docks. Wallace walks past a dorm. He sees people dancing on a balcony, enjoying the weekend. A big white flag with the university's mascot is hanging down the front of their house, and men are throwing a Frisbee on the little lawn. Wallace watches one of the men, tall and pale, reach back and fling the yellow disc from a grotesque position. It flutters at first, then settles into a clean arc that takes it over the heads of people sitting on a floral upholstered couch on the lawn, until another man, squat and dark, leaps up and snatches it from the air. Watching them, Wallace feels a kind of peace.

The noise inside him quiets. He feels as though he can think clearly now. He's standing in the yellow gravel of the trail with his back to the lake. There are bicyclists swooping by, dark with motion. The bramble is filled with staccato animal calls, and out on the water there are people sailing. His friends might be out there, he realizes. That was their plan for the day, after all, to spend the last bright hours of the weekend on the lake together.

He imagines Yngve and Miller piloting a small, compact boat out to the center, where they'll drift for a while, letting the others take small sips of whiskey or beer, letting them get drowsy and hot and drunk. The peace Wallace feels deepens as he imagines this scene, circling its completeness, Emma in the back of the boat, legs crossed, hair wild with wind. Thom reading or trying to read, getting seasick, flimsy and delicate. And Miller, looking out over the water, always looking out into the distance. Yngve would be sitting with Lukas tucked up against him, the two of them conjoined. And a wind, smooth and clear, warm with summer heat pressing down on them, nudging their boat farther and farther out, perhaps to the distant shore, where they might get out and have dinner in the rich part of town. And then their coming home, stumbling upon the pier, bronzed and raw, chapped from the sun and the wind, the air cooling as it does this time of year. Where will they go then—somewhere on the square, maybe? Or to Yngve and Miller's, to drink more and smoke? They will scarcely think of him, Wallace knows, except for Miller. They will not consider his absence conspicuous, but he only has himself to blame. He should have said something at brunch.

How easily he might be among them had he not severed the connection and said he was going home, knowing full well that he wouldn't be, that he would be going to lab the moment he left them, walking all the way there, stopping only to collect his bag. How easy it would have been to be with his friends if he hadn't taken pains to ensure that he couldn't. This, too, he has predicted, though, hasn't he? The moment he hugged Miller goodbye on the corner, he knew he would regret leaving; still, he thinks, better to be here now, regretting not being there, than to be there and regret not being here. Better to imagine his friends happy than to see their unhappiness up close. And unhappy they certainly would be—that has been the lesson this weekend, hasn't it? The misery of other people, the persistence of unhappiness, is perhaps all that connects them. Only the prospect of greater unhappiness keeps them within the circumscribed world of graduate school.

Wallace takes a seat on a bench under a couple of trees on a sandy patch adjacent to the running trail near the lake. He tucks his legs under him. The metal slats are hot, but pleasantly so. The view of the water is stunning. Blue and gray bands of water all the way out to the dark figure of the peninsula, which juts, sphinxlike, into the lake. Boats in the distance. The low, mossy branches of the tree overhead provide shade. Some clouds coming in out there, yes, darkening. There will be rain, he knows, and then the great cooling. Fall is so close he can almost taste it in the air.

He is seized by the urge to call his brother. They have not spoken since those frenzied weeks when his brother called him every day to communicate to him the facts and figures of his father's death. The first prognosis, which had been good, his voice light and full of hope. The dwindling prospects, the tumor refusing to stop growing, the insignificant victories, a successfully installed feeding tube running through his father's body, then the collection of water in the lungs, the swelling, the failing of the organs, one by one, each organ getting its own phone call—first kidneys, then liver, then finally the heart. His brother's voice was like those old boyhood prayers they used to say before they went to bed, nonsense words to Wallace even then, and yet somehow necessary to get through it. Wallace knew early on how it would go, that the hope in his brother's voice was a matter of self-deception, and yet when the end came, he found that he was surprised, despite what he knew, because his brother had somehow convinced even a small part of him to hope too, to believe too, that things might turn around.

The desire to call his brother, then, is another urge toward self-deception, about the end of something, the dwindling hours of his life here in this city by this lake. He could call his brother down in Georgia, where he works as a carpenter for the state, call him and tell him the facts. It would be easy. And his brother might have some hope for him too, a belief in the goodness of things, in the capacity of the world to turn around and change its mind. Wallace takes out his phone and stares down at it. He could do it. He could make himself less alone just by calling.

"How stupid," he says to himself. "How stupid, Wallace." He puts the phone away, gets off the bench, and takes the lakeshore path back to the pier, where the people are already gathering for the evening. It's only late afternoon, but here they are, snagging the famous multicolored tables. This is the site of the city's greatest confluence of university students and what Wallace and his friends call real people; that is, locals who are not affiliated with the university. It amazes him to think how quickly he has forgotten how to move among such people, who seem rough and ugly when they look at him, all bloated faces and missing teeth. They move through the world with a kind of clumsy ease, as if they don't care how the next day will unfold because it holds so few possibilities for them. These are not people who spend their lives contemplating the minute shifts in their fortunes; they are like the happy, well-fed fish that grow in fisheries, hatched and grown to adulthood in tiny, controlled spaces. And then farmed for food.

Wallace climbs the gray steps from the lake's edge onto the platform and looks around. He is close to his apartment. It would be nothing to go back there now, but he doesn't like the idea of it. He's too wound up to stay at home. The library is nearby. He could go there and read for a few hours, spend time in a quiet, cool corner, watching the water. A boy and a girl run by him, holding hands. They're seven or eight, he thinks, small and white and fast. They're laughing, their little blond heads bobbing as they go. Their parents bring up the rear, an attractive

middle-aged man—Wallace has seen him on the app, he thinks—
and a woman with a tight, mean face, dark hair, green eyes, lots
of freckles, skin like an aging banana peel.

On the lower level of the platform a band is setting up, pudgy
white college kids in dark sweatshirts and ratty jeans. The equip-
ment looks expensive. There are a couple of black people, scattered throughout the tables, though not together, separate. One
of them, a young woman with long braids and skin so smooth
and dark that he gasps when his eyes light upon her, turns to him
and smiles. There is a flicker of recognition, an easing of some
tension inside him. She is with a group of white girls, all of them
wearing sundresses in bright floral colors. The black girl is wearing yellow. She is the prettiest among them, but they are all talking over her, around her, and at a group of white boys standing
on a platform below them, in casual khaki shorts and sweatshirts.
One of the boys has his leg up on the platform where the girls are
standing, his fingers tucked inside his belt loop, nodding aggressively. The black girl smooths her dress, flips her braids over her
shoulder, and laughs, though there is boredom on her face.

Wallace feels sorry for her, but then also for himself, because
this has been his life since he came to this place, alone among
white people. He's sweating again. It's collecting on his forehead.
The lake is lapping softly, its turquoise and gray water soothing.
Little brown birds hop among the folded tables, pecking at loose
bits of food. He could grab a table maybe, sit for a while. That
might be nice, just to be in a place. He could ask Brigit to come,
spend an hour or two by the lake. The prospect of seeing Brigit,
who might be on her way to lab and therefore nearby, lifts his

spirits. He feels equal to that task, texts her quickly before he loses his nerve. She is close by, she says, and could swing by for a little while. It's a plan, he says, and looks around for an empty table for the two of them.

THEY END UP taking a table far away from the band. This is by design. The music is always too loud and not very good, as if the volume is meant to compensate for the lack of actual music being played. Brigit is wearing soft clothes, her hair in a loose braid down her back. They're sharing a bag of salty popcorn. Wallace is drinking water. She has a light ale in a plastic cup. They've got their feet up on a third chair, their arms twined loosely together.

"How's your weekend been?" she asks.

"Fine, good, you know," he says, thinking of how they saw each other yesterday and how even then he was not being entirely honest with her about his feelings. "It's been okay."

She watches him from the corner of her eye, but does not say anything. She rolls a piece of popcorn around between her fingers. The lake is growing darker as the sun sinks. The air is getting cool and still. The boats are coming in, though many remain out there in the growing darkness. The lights of the shore are blooming. Wallace holds his cup to his lips, biting its plastic rim.

"My dad died," he says, and he feels Brigit gasp and flinch and turn to him. "Before you freak out, though, it was weeks ago, I'm fine, I'm fine."

"God, Wally, oh my god," she says.

"I'm sorry I didn't say anything. I'm sorry."

"Don't apologize to me. No. Are you okay? Oh my god."

He is about to say that he is fine, that he is okay, but he doesn't. Brigit is staring at him, expecting an answer, and he knows that he could give her one, the one that would make this easy, make it simple for them to move past this moment. But he does not want to do that. He doesn't want to give her that answer. He wants to say something about the thing with his dad and Alabama and Miller and Dana and Simone. He wants to say that he's just barely hanging on, that within he's raw and sad and spinning down and down and down. But how does he begin to say that, to manifest it in this world, which resists all the hardness of life? It's too real, what he wants to say. There are no parameters. When someone is shocked in this way, you don't shock them more. You make them feel better.

"Yep," he says, nodding, choking the word out. "Yep."

"What does that even mean, Wally? 'Yep'? What does that mean?"

"It just—it's hard. It's been hard," he says, though he isn't sure if the hardness pertains to his father, to the strangeness of that grief, or to everything else that has gone wrong—what has been hard? Specificity. Particularity. Ascertain. Navigate. What to say? How to speak. "But I'm alive." There is a wet ache in his voice. "I'm alive."

Brigit hugs him tightly. She presses her face against his sweaty hair and she just holds him tight to her. She too has reached the edge of her vocabulary for such things. She has no way to comfort him for the things that he has no way of expressing, and so they are coming as close as they can to getting at it. He can hear her heart beating hard. She smells sweet and a little like the pop-corn they've been eating. Her body is soft and warm. There are seagulls over them, circling, riding the air currents, which makes Wallace uneasy.

"Anyway, now you know. I'm sorry I didn't say anything before."

"My god, Wallace. When was the funeral?"

"Oh, weeks ago."

"You didn't go."

"No, it was too far, wasn't worth it."

Brigit lets this remark go without further comment, for which Wallace is grateful. She starts to eat more popcorn. He drinks his water, which is growing lukewarm. The band is start-ing, something lonesome, off-key, and drowning in reverb.

Having told her about his dad, he doesn't feel the need to tell her anything else. It feels sufficient, in a way, a part tell-ing the whole.

They slide lower in their chairs, which squeak a little as their thighs slip over the metal. They laugh at the sound, comical in the moment. Their laughter swells beyond its context, till it's dis-proportionate, till they're not laughing but crying hot tears. Wallace lets loose the ugly hiccupping moan of a small child or someone who has forgotten himself. Up it comes, all the tears, the frustration, the difficulty. He's convulsing, shivering, tears and snot and coughing, crying, putting his palms flat to his eyes, his shoulders bouncing, hot, so hot, and wet. And Brigit is weeping on his shoulder, a staccato sound like animals in the underbrush, that clattering, rickety cry.

That time in Alabama, after the man left his house, Wallace cried. His father stooped and grabbed him around the waist, and he asked him, *What are you crying for, what are you crying for?* The reason had seemed obvious to Wallace, but the more his father asked him, the more Wallace questioned why he was crying, until after a while he stopped. His father had done some magic trick, converted certainty to doubt with no more effort than it took to ask, *What are you crying for?* Why had he done that? Why?

But here, with Brigit, the reason sharpens, its clarity terrifying. He is crying because he cannot recognize himself, because the way forward is obscured for him, because there is nothing he can do or say that will bring him happiness. He is crying because he is lodged between this life and the next, and for the first time he does not know whether it is better to stay or go. Wallace cries and cries, until eventually he is hollow and empty and there's nothing left to cry about, until he feels like he's being rung like a bell.

THEY ARE FEELING a little waterlogged by the time it's all over, and also feeling kind of ashamed of themselves, self-indulgent. There is something very American about this, Brigit says—that anything that feels good must come with shame.

"It's because we're all Protestants," she continues.

"Didn't you go to Catholic school all your life?" he asks, and she laughs at him.

"Yes, but my point stands."

They go inside to get ice cream. Wallace requests a waffle

bowl with vanilla, for which Brigit mocks him. Brigit herself requests chocolate on a cone, which Wallace doesn't think is any more adventurous than vanilla. The hall is decorated with a mural of some kind, depicting the charitable actions of some white man from a long time ago; he's giving out candy to small, strangely demonic-looking children, and the whole scene is both bucolic and horrifying. There are many people loitering, eating ice cream, talking, eating brats. The music from the outside is louder here; the band has moved on to some very earnest rock covers.

Off to the side, a man is eating something from a cardboard bowl. He has the sort of lean face in which the muscles of his jaws are visible as they work. Wallace watches the muscles slide and shift beneath the man's skin, which is olive colored. There is also the thickening of muscle in his neck as he swallows, the food passing down and down through his throat and into the darkness of his body. This is an ordinary act, so commonplace as to seem invisible, but when any such act is considered, there is a wild strangeness to it. Consider how the eyelid slides down over the eyeball and back, the world cast into an instant of darkness with every blink. Consider the act of breathing, which comes regularly and without effort—and yet the great surge of air that must enter and exit our body is an almost violent event, tissues pushed and compressed and slid apart and opened and closed, so much blood all over the whole business of it. Ordinary acts take on strange shadows when viewed up close.

Wallace wants him too, but the act of wanting is distinct from sexual imagination. He can comprehend this simultaneously at two levels, what it is to want—though he only ever engages the first, the most superficial, the glance, the gaze, the ascertainment of object, fetish, token. Below this, of course, is the act itself, articulated through innumerable possibilities. Fucking and sucking and chewing and pinching and grinding and sliding and hitching and thrusting and rolling and tasting and licking and biting; there's being held, there's being whispered to, being pushed down, being thrown up against the wall and kept there. So much of it geographical, physiological, so much specificity to it. There is sex in the mind, which follows from the identification of objects of sexual potential. Indeed, the sexual potential is but the shadow of sexual possibility projected forward; we know we want someone when we encounter them because of what could come if we just reach out and say it: *Hey, look at me.*

But when Wallace looks at such people, people he wants, he always feels so much worse afterward. Being so aware of their bodies makes him aware of his own body, and he becomes aware of the way his body is both a thing on the earth and a vehicle for his entire life's history. His body is both a tangible self and his depression, his anxiety, his wellness, his illness, his disordered eating, the fear of blood pouring out of him. It is both itself and not itself, image and afterimage. He feels unhappy when he looks at someone beautiful or desirable because he feels the gulf between himself and the other, their body and his body. An accounting of his body's failures slides down the back of his eyes, and he sees how far from grace he's been made and planted.

It's not even that he wants to be them—though queer desire

has this feature baked in, so better to say it's not *just* that he wants to be them. He wants to be not himself. He wants to be not depressed. He wants to be not anxious. He wants to be well. He wants to be good.

There are ways to wrangle a body's dimensions, but these dimensions correspond solely to the physical space it occupies. How to wrangle the body that is unreal? How to wrangle the histories of our bodies, which are inseparable from the bodies themselves and are always growing? How to change or shape that part of us? Wallace is unwell. Parts of him are falling off. It's maudlin, he knows, but it's also true. When he sees a good body going around in the world, he finds he's unable to look away from both it and himself. The truly awful thing about beauty is that it reminds us of our limits. Beauty is a kind of unrelenting cruelty. It takes the truth, hones it to a terrifying keenness, and uses it to slice us to the bone.

A good body is a monstrous thing; it stalks and hunts us in the smallest parts of ourselves. It extracts from us painful truths. When Wallace sees a good body, what he feels is thirst, or else an ache, which is the sensation of beauty forcing its way inside.

The thing about Miller's body is that it isn't a beautiful body, not like this man's, and so Wallace is able to interface with it as a sexual object. It isn't beyond him. There is something definitively human about Miller's body, its weight, its length, its odd angles, its pockets of fat and flesh. The places where it goes suddenly soft or hard, where it is unexpectedly supple or strong or taut. Miller's body is accessible, understandable in all the ways that it is flawed. It is legible to Wallace. The man eating dumps out the rest of his food and leaves. Their ice cream is ready, and Brigit passes him his bowl and they go out into the evening air.

It has gotten much darker, the water almost invisible. The clouds from earlier are overhead, thick and purple. A moist wind is blowing. Wallace can tell even at this distance that there's rain coming fast, thunder on the horizon. It will rain, certainly.

Their table is occupied when they return to it, so they find another, unfortunately close to the band, where the tables have been left conspicuously unoccupied. Hundreds of people are gathered now on the pier and at the tables, thronging the area. It's maybe the last good weekend of weather for such things. Soon, they'll have to shut it down. Just a few weeks left before the end.

They're at a yellow table. Brigit has both her feet up on a chair, and she is thoughtfully licking her ice cream. Wallace is eating slowly. His stomach is still uneasy, tight, quivering. There are wasps swinging through the night, attracted by the stickiness of beer left on the table and by their ice cream. He frowns at them, as if that will drive them away. Brigit laughs.

"Can you believe tomorrow is Monday?" she asks, groaning, throwing her head back and giving it a shake. "I cannot believe this."

"It happens every week. It's like some sort of trend or something."

"You are not a funny person."

"I'm aware. We all have our faults. And our gifts."

"You are unkind," she says, dryly, but with no menace. "I heard you had a talk with Katie."

"Who you told you that?"

"Katie."

"Oh, I might have figured," he says.

"If you want . . . well, you know."

"I know," he says. "I know, thank you. But there's nothing for it but to do it, I guess."

"Okay," Brigit says, but she is not convinced. There is worry knitting her brow. Wallace wonders just what it is that Katie said, how she might have put it. "She was not thrilled you left today, by the way."

"I know, she seemed pissed. But she always seems pissed."

"That's true. She does. It's just because she's graduating, though—soon she'll be gone and all will be well."

"And then you," Wallace says quietly. "Then it's your turn."

"And then it's *your* turn!" Brigit chirps, which makes Wallace shrink, quieten. The ice cream is cold and perfect. The vanilla is an empty flavor. He draws the spoon around his lips, letting them numb. The paper wrapping for the waffle bowl is soggy now. Brigit, sensing that she has crossed some line between them, shoots him a look of apology. But for what is she apologizing? What is the point of apologizing to him at this point?

"Simone—" he begins, pressing his tongue to the back of his teeth, looking out over the water. "Simone wants me to think about what I want. If I really want to stay here. To stay in graduate school."

"Oh god," Brigit says, rolling her eyes. "What a pretentious cunt."

"Brigit," he says.

"She is. What kind of question is that?"

"A very serious one. There was shit with Dana yesterday. It's not worth rehashing, but Simone is on my case."

Brigit grows more serious. "Is she thinking about kicking you out?"

Wallace does not answer. He spoons more ice cream into his mouth, savors its perfect coldness. Brigit squeezes his arm.

"Well, is she?"

"She wants me to think very carefully about what I want," he says. "And that's fair. I get it."

"I don't," she says. "I don't get it at all."

"Don't pretend, Brigit. You know it's been rough."

"It's rough for everyone."

"Not you."

"That's not true," she says. "It's been hard for me too. It's been really fucking difficult."

"Has it?" Wallace asks, and he can tell that the question hurts her feelings. There's a look of shock, surprise shifting into indignation.

"You can be so selfish sometimes, Wallace. Yes, it's been hard for me. Do you think I enjoy being in a place full of white people working myself stupid every hour of every day? Did you know that Simone asked me for Japanese recipes?"

"You aren't Japanese," Wallace says, trying to be funny, but Brigit makes a disgusted sound under her breath.

"And then—nothing I do is good enough, Wally. I could literally cure cancer and Simone would look at me like, *Of course, that's what your people do.* I'm not a person here, Wallace. I am not Brigit. I'm the Asian girl. I'm just a face to them. And sometimes not even that."

"I'm sorry," he says. "I'm really sorry." He hates this, the reflexive way that he responds to her. *I'm sorry* has so little use, is of such little worth, that to offer it seems almost an insult. He wants to swallow the words back, choke them down. In her eyes, as she absorbs the empty words, he sees the hard flat surface that separates even them, the closest among the group. They're pressed up against either side of it, but cannot break through, cannot get to what is real. "Brigit."

"No, it's fine."

"Brigit."

"Wallace," she says.

Both of them are tense. The ice cream slides down her fingers, and she lifts her hand to lick it clear. There are tears at the corners of her eyes. He has underestimated her suffering.

"If you leave," Brigit says, studying her ice-cream cone. "If you leave, I won't know what to do with myself, and that's the truth. But if staying is so awful for you, I want you to do that."

"I don't want to leave you," he says, "and I don't want to be a failure."

"But you won't be," she says. "You won't be a failure just because you leave. Especially if it makes you happy."

"What about you?"

"I'll have to get along without you," she says, and she laughs again. "But I'll be happy for you."

"Let's just run away together," he says, perhaps more seriously than he would like to admit. "Let's just go away and never look back."

"That would be a dream," she says, then, shaking her head, "but the thing about dreams is, you gotta wake up, Wally."

"Don't I know it," he says, but the thought of a life with Brigit, simple and easy, predicated only on the notion of what would bring them happiness, seems irresistible. They could live in her tiny house on the East Side, with its garden, making jams and sauces and reading on lazy, sunny afternoons. They could live entirely among themselves, apart from everything and everyone.

They finish their ice cream and stand up, stiff and achy. Brigit hugs him firmly one last time, and he almost refuses to let her go.

"Stay," he says. "Please."

"Oh, Wally," she says, and kisses his cheek. "You will be fine. Be safe, okay?" He walks her to the platform and waves good-bye to her. He watches her go, her white sweater moving away in the darkness. The other people are of little consequence to him. They do not matter. They do not matter. They do not matter.

WALLACE IS COMING UP the street to his apartment, tired and slow-headed. The sun has left him feeling warm and drowsy. He would like to draw a bath and sit in it for a long time, just dozing. He suddenly wishes he could teleport, but the walk is mercifully short. He walks along the tree-lined street, in the light of the white globe lamps. This time last night, he was across town with Miller. Just twenty-four hours ago—one rotation of the world, one displacement across space and time.

There is a theory that every moment of our lives is happening all the time, simultaneously. He thinks again of that line from *To the Lighthouse*: And all the lives we ever lived. Every moment. Both the night before, with Miller, and all those moments along the line of his life that have brought him to this moment; the man in the dark, his skeleton's face coming toward Wallace, suspended there forever, and the sensation of being torn open, permanently, forever; that boy that Miller mauled, his blood gushing hot while Miller punched him again and again—all of it at the same time, coming down the line.

The sheer weight of it makes him pause. He presses his hand to the brick of his building, and vomits in the alley. A couple of thick boys coming down the sidewalk stop and look at him.

"Are you okay?" they ask in their flat Midwestern voices. "Buddy, you okay?"

Wallace waves them off, and they, needing no excuse, go on with their evening. In the street, people call out for their friends. People stand in line at the bar down the street, some of them smoking. The air smells like rain and cigarettes, beer and piss. Wallace wipes the corner of his mouth. His eyes are hot.

In his apartment, he slides back down into the tub again, like earlier. The water isn't going to melt the skin off his bones this time, but it's warm enough. He presses his head against the tile, lets the water level rise. His insides are on fire, churning. The tile is yellow, and the bright light has been blunted by a blue scarf he's draped over the vanity at the risk of starting a fire, but he doesn't plan on staying in the tub that long. What is Miller doing at this moment? He said he would call, but he hasn't.

He is probably at home with Yngve and Lukas, maybe Emma and Thom, or Cole and Vincent, maybe all of them together. Wallace splashes the water on his face, rubbing at his eyes, trying to get above this feeling of uncertainty. It might have gone differently had he stayed in Miller's bed this morning, might have gone another way.

But it's pointless to think that now, to want things to be different from the way they are. When has that ever worked for him? When has that ever been his power, to shift the world based on his wants or needs? The world leaves him behind, streaks out ahead of him; he is not accustomed to being satisfied with the state of things. He rests his head against the side of the tub now, staring down at the brown rug and its bits of loose hair.

After a while, Wallace gets out of the water and stands in front of the mirror. He touches his stomach, which hangs down toward his thighs, and he brushes the other hand across the nub of his flaccid penis. He grips himself and tries to imagine a sexual scenario while staring at his own body. He tries to will himself erect, tries to find some spark or ember of desire buried deep inside him, but nothing will come, nothing will move within him. Something necessary has died, or is unwilling to engage. He cannot bring himself off, cannot get himself hard enough to jerk off. It's a fleeting desire, and it's dead before too long. He wraps a towel around himself and goes into his bedroom, where it is dark and cool.

The fan is going. He puts his head under the pillow and tries to sleep, tries to count backward from some enormous number, but he fails. Sleep will not meet him.

He reaches for his phone, scrolls through it until he finds Miller's number. It's not too late, he thinks. He dials and waits. The tone goes on and on and on. No answer. Nothing. He waits. Dials again. Nothing. Wallace lies on his back and stretches his arms out. He dials again, watching his shadow on the opposite wall. No answer, just silence opening up on the other end after the voicemail. He hangs up. Dials again, this time pressing the button with more firmness, as if this will draw an answer from Miller. Nothing.

Didn't Wallace say earlier that he couldn't bear the thought of a single moment repeating itself? And here he is, dialing over and over again, compulsively, like a crazy person, repeating himself so that Miller might come and repeat the morning with him, hoping that as each second knocks into the other, Miller will pick up and say, *Yes, I will come over; I will come see you.* But there is only silence, and more silence. Where is he? What could he be doing? A wild fluttering rises inside Wallace.

He goes into the kitchen and makes coffee. In the living room, he lies on the floor and drinks, slow and steady, the hot black coffee. He is staring at his phone, its glow comforting in the dark. He is reading an article online by some obscure poet from Kansas about a new queer art, a new poetics of the body—and understanding very little of it—when the article vanishes and is replaced by a call screen. His phone vibrates. Yngve's name comes up.

"Hello?" he answers.

"Hello," Miller says. "Wallace, hi."

"Miller?" Wallace asks, and there is happiness in his voice, surprise. "Hey, how's it going?"

"It's fine, hey, I dropped my phone in the lake. Sorry I didn't call earlier. Are you at home?"

"Sure, yes," Wallace says. There is noise in the background, loud music, people talking, shouting.

"Great, hey, I'll be by in a little bit, okay?" he asks.

"Okay," Wallace says.

"Perfect, okay, great, okay, see you then," Miller says, and then his voice is gone, along with the noise. He is drunk, Wallace realizes. Drunk and out with the others, at some bar or the pier. Who knows? But he is coming, or he plans to come, and that is something to which Wallace can affix some hope. He rests the cup against his face and tries to breathe. He is not nervous to see Miller. Too much has happened between them for that to be the case. But there is something else now, not urgency exactly, but a kind of wildness.

He sets the cup on the table and tries to find something to do with himself, with his hands. He's sitting on the edge of his bed, waiting. Outside in the alley people are shouting again, as on Friday, the first time he was here with Miller. There is a knock on the door, and it takes everything in Wallace not to sprint from his bed. He opens the door and there is Miller, looking down at him drunkenly. He's still in his clothes from this morning, the cropped gray shirt, the cardigan, smelling like beer and the lake, tanned all over from the sun. His cheeks are chapped and red.

"Wallace," he says in a voice that is raw and a little raspy. "How are you?"

"Good," Wallace says. They've shut the door now.

"Wallace, Wallace," Miller says, singing almost.

"How are you?" Wallace asks.

"Great, super, wonderful." He drums his fingers on his stomach. "We went sailing. You should have come."

"I was busy."

"Oh, were you?" Miller asks, squinting. "Were you busy?"

"I was," Wallace says, nodding, needlessly earnest. Miller hums and then bites his thumbnail.

"You know. You know. You know," Miller begins. His eyes are bloodshot, his knuckles red, bruised. Wallace looks more closely, and what he took for windburn is actually something else, scrapes and scratches. His body is thrumming with heat.

"What happened to you?"

Miller seems to think about it, smiles slowly. His lips too are cracked, slit, swollen.

"Nothing," he says, drawing the word out. "Nothing happened to me."

"Did you get into an accident?"

"No. No. No," Miller says, wagging his finger, and then biting his nails again. There is dried blood beneath them. "Not an accident."

"Well what happened?"

Miller laughs, shakes his head. He reaches out and grips Wallace's shoulder. Fear floods Wallace and he pulls away, but Miller will not let him go, will not unclench. His grasp is absolute. He digs his fingers into Wallace's shoulder, and it hurts. Miller is still laughing, but this time his eyes are closed. He draws Wallace close to him. The heat is black and close. He puts his mouth on Wallace's, and Wallace can taste the beer, the ash, the blood, the iron, too warm on his tongue. He tries to wrench loose, but Miller is stronger than he is. He turns Wallace around, loops an arm around his neck, not choking him, but close, holding him up flat to Miller's chest and stomach.

"I got into a fight," Miller whispers. "I got into a fight at a bar. You know?"

"Know what?"

"You know—are you afraid of me now?"

"No," Wallace says, "I'm not." Miller holds his arm tight to Wallace's throat now, and air is harder to come by.

He puts his face next to Wallace's ear and laughs, that low, dark laugh, and he says, almost too quiet to hear, "Do you know that story about the wolf, Wallace?"

8

The heat of Miller's breath against his skin makes Wallace uncomfortable in the dark of his apartment. So does the weight pressing against his throat, making him feel as if he's suspended at a great height from thin, flexible cables. The hardened skin of Miller's knuckles is tucked up under Wallace's chin, where he's clamped his wrist to keep Wallace in the choke hold. He isn't choking Wallace exactly, just pressing, but because he is taller and stronger, even the casual tension in his arm carries intent. Wallace, unbalanced by the suddenness of the moment, shuts his eyes for just a second to regroup, to find his center. He lets his arms dangle, lets his body go still.

"Do you remember it?" Miller asks. "The story, I mean, about the wolf and the pigs?"

"Do you mean 'The Three Little Pigs'?" Wallace asks. "Is that the one you mean?"

"Yes," Miller says, laughing. "That's the one."

"What about it?" Wallace asks. "What about that story?"

Miller presses his cheek to Wallace's, more hitch and scrape, skin over skin. Whiskey or something else, booze on his breath. He's holding Wallace against him, cradling his body almost. It would be tender if it weren't also a choke hold. Wallace might let himself give in to such an embrace, if it didn't also contain the threat of violence—not that Miller is threatening him exactly, but Wallace has been put in choke holds before, by people stronger and bigger than he, people who have meant him real harm.

"You let me in," Miller says. "I knocked on your door in the middle of the night and you let me in. I could be a wolf."

"Are you?" Wallace asks.

"I don't know. I could be."

"What happened to you, Miller? Why are you all bruised up like this?"

"I got into a fight at a bar. And then I came here."

"What did you fight about?"

Miller clucks his tongue. Wallace can feel Miller's chin pressing down on the top of his head.

"That isn't an answer," Wallace says, feeling himself relax because the gesture has shifted, transformed into something less threatening. But he's still not free to move as he pleases, which he figures should concern him more than it does at the moment.

"I didn't give one," Miller says.

"Why not?"

"Who cares?" Miller asks, sighing. "Who gives a damn? I'm here now." He sounds so tired, so absurdly tired. Then why the question about the wolf, about the pigs? Why go through the trouble of it? Wallace puts his hands against Miller's arms, rubs them slowly, tenderly.

"I care," Wallace says, knowing he sounds too earnest. "I'd like to know what happened to you—if you're okay, I mean."

"Would you?"

"Yes."

There is no answer. Wallace waits for something, anything, but there is only the quiet of their breathing.

"You didn't seem like you cared," Miller says at last. "You didn't seem like you gave a damn one way or the other."

"What does that even mean, Miller? What are you talking about?"

"Earlier, after brunch. And last night I guess, too, when you left. I told you all that shit about me, and you left in the middle of the night. Even before that, before dinner, you told me you weren't interested. I should have listened. Why didn't I listen?"

"What does that have to do with anything? Or the sorry shape you're in now?"

"What a question," Miller says, soft shock in his voice. He laughs. "What a fucking question." He drops his arms from Wallace's shoulders, pushes gently at his back to make space between them. Wallace steps forward reluctantly and then turns. He is stung by this, a bruise darkening somewhere inside him. He feels in that moment that to even ask what Miller means by this is to prove some point about himself that he can't comprehend yet. The light from the alley washes Miller in a dirty blue shade. His eyes are not discernible except by the glossiness of their whites. His features are distorted, by shadow or anger or both. He is frightening, though his teeth are gleaming.

"What did I do to you?"

"You fucked with my head," Miller says. "You got in my head and now I'm all fucked up about it. I never tell that stuff to anyone. I never let anyone know that part of me. But I told you. And you left."

"I'm sorry," Wallace says. "I felt like something terrible was going to happen if I stayed."

"Something terrible," Miller repeats, his voice leaping up in volume and pitch, sharpening, breaking. "You thought I was going to do something terrible to you? What the fuck was I going to do to you, Wallace?"

"No, that's not it," Wallace says. "No, I just felt like something awful was coming our way. I don't know. I'm sorry."

"You're sorry," Miller says. "You're always sorry, aren't you, Wallace? Other people have problems too, you know. Other people are afraid too."

"What are you afraid of?" Wallace asks before he can stop himself. The question slips out of him like a small, swift bird.

Miller's broad jaw is working over something that Wallace can't see, grinding it up. The tendons flex and bend. There's a hardness to his face.

"The same shit everyone is afraid of, Wallace. Being left. Being tossed aside. Not being good enough. Being a fucking monster. Do you know how I felt when you left?"

"No, tell me," Wallace says.

"I felt like the wolf in that story. I felt like I'd just killed someone. When I woke up and you were gone, I thought, Shit, Miller, you're really something, man, you're really fucking something, aren't you?"

"I didn't mean for you to feel that way," Wallace says.

"No, you never mean it, do you? Like with Cole and Vincent,

or that girl in your lab. You never mean it, but here you always are, somehow. *Your* feelings, *your* feelings. No one else's. Not mine, anyway." Miller sucks air through his teeth and shrugs. "Not my feelings."

"That's not true," Wallace says, though now he wonders if it might be. Miller folds his arms across his chest, gives Wallace a look somewhere between amused and annoyed.

"So I go to a bar tonight," Miller says. "I go to a bar and I'm drinking with Yngve and Lukas, and we get to talking. But I can't pay attention to what they're saying. I'm still thinking about this morning. I'm still thinking about what happened when I woke up and you were gone, and I'm thinking about how this guy I like, a fucking guy, no shit, how I like him and now all of a sudden I'm not good enough. I'm trash. He just used me and left. This guy I thought I knew. I told him things about myself that I don't tell anyone, and he tells me things he doesn't tell anyone, and I thought, stupidly, I thought it means something, but, well, you know the rest, don't you?"

Wallace does not say anything. He's looking down into the space between them. He can't make himself acknowledge Miller. When they parted earlier, things were tense but fine, certainly. He did not imagine, it's true, that Miller might be harboring such frustration or anger toward him. He took their pleasant good-bye as a sign that things were fine, all right, between them. But as Miller said, he has been thinking of only himself, of his own feelings of inadequacy, of being damaged goods. He has not stopped to consider that Miller, having just revealed his history of violence, might be feeling vulnerable himself. He did not stop to think about how Miller might feel when he awoke in the morning and found himself alone, for the second time. It is true, Wallace thinks, that he is guilty of myopia, and the knowledge of that fact weighs him down.

"But how did you get into this fight?" he asks. "Why did you get into a fight, Miller? That's not my fault."

"You're right," Miller says, nodding. "You're right, Wallace, it's not. Some guy bumped into me, and I said, *Watch it*, and he called me a faggot. Can you believe that?" Another laugh, short and dark. "He called me a faggot, so I had to set him straight. Because I'm not a faggot, Wallace. I'm not." Each time he says the word *faggot*, it's like he's spitting it, throwing a punch to Wallace's gut. The word pushes down through him.

"You're not," Wallace says, nodding. "You've made that clear."

"Good," he says. "I'm glad."

"Why did you come here, then? Just to yell at me? Did you just come here to call me a selfish faggot? Do you want to hit me too?" Wallace looks up then, widens his eyes, his mouth parting just slightly, in the way he practiced back in Alabama, seeking the attention and the violence of men in the woods. He opens up his shoulders, steps forward. "Do you want to hit me too? Did you come here to fuck me up? Is that it?"

A thick vein in Miller's neck throbs, writhing like a little worm beneath the skin. Wallace can see it in the plane of light illuminating his shoulder and throat, the collar of his sweater wrenched open. He sets his teeth on edge, Miller does, and takes a long, ragged inhale. His nostrils flare.

"Don't tempt me," he says. "Don't tempt me, Wallace."

"Do it, then," Wallace says. "Do it if you want."

Miller's hand lashes out so quickly that Wallace can barely follow its motion. He grips Wallace's throat, the roughness of his palm hot on his skin. His fingers dig in, not drawing blood, but squeezing, pressing. Miller's face is an impassive mask, distant.

"You don't want this," he chews out. "You don't want it, Wallace."

Wallace reaches out and presses his palm to Miller's cock through his jeans, squeezes it, feels it filling with blood.

"Seems like you do," Wallace says, and Miller squeezes harder, lifts Wallace's chin up.

"Fuck you, Wallace," he says. "Fuck you." But then he crushes his mouth down onto Wallace's, hauls him up close and bites his lip so hard it draws blood. Wallace drowns in the immediacy of it, feels himself let go and sink down through the sensation of weightlessness, dizzy with it. Miller whirls him around and whips down Wallace's shorts, jabs his fingers into him, and it hurts so much that Wallace wants to cry, but he doesn't. He just breathes through the awful heat of it, the invasive, rough exploration of Miller's fingers. Miller pushes the back of Wallace's head down, shoving his face against the slick, cool countertop. The initial impact is hard and intense, and the world slides briefly into black and then back out, turns gray at its edges.

Miller's fingers in him are thick, coarse, and hard, their blunted ends pushing, threatening to split him open. There is an intense heat radiating down the side of his face and neck, a scent like sweat and skin and soap and beer. His eyes sting. Miller slides his fingers out of Wallace, and Wallace takes a shuddering breath, suddenly cold. The scrape of shoes backward across the floor. Wallace pulls his shorts up, but he doesn't turn; he's still lying against the counter, his body heavy, too heavy for him to move.

"I didn't mean that," Miller says. "I didn't mean it." His voice is jagged and cold, like wet gravel against the side of a house. "I didn't mean it."

Wallace can taste blood in his mouth. Where he's been dug out is still throbbing with heat, like a wound. He draws himself upright—a sharp pain cuts through him, and he doubles over, has to grip the counter to stay up on his feet.

"Goddamn, goddamn," he says.

"Wallace," Miller says, and he reaches out, touches Wallace's hip, but Wallace jerks back from him, to the side, so they're facing each other. Wallace holds on to the back of one of the chairs. Miller is in shadow, leaning toward him.

"It's fine, I'm fine," he says. All that courage is fleeing him, leaving nothing but its embers, inadequate to the task, to anything at all except facing Miller this way.

"I'm sorry," Miller says. "I'm sorry. I don't know why I did that. I don't know."

"Because you're a wolf," Wallace says, nostrils flaring, trying to laugh but failing, landing on a kind of hitching sob. "Because you're a fucking wolf." He watches Miller's stomach suck in and out, the way it kind of ripples when he breathes. Miller flexes his fist, and something corresponding in Wallace convulses. Was that the hand that had been inside him, then?

"Wallace," Miller says, but he doesn't have anything to say, that's obvious. What is there to say after that, after such a violation? He should leave, Wallace thinks. One of them should leave now. But neither of them moves to leave, seems to be able to go. In the alley there is a horrible scraping sound as someone from the bar on the corner drags a trash can across the pavement. The noise swells and swells in the apartment until it overtakes the two of them. They're watching each other this entire time, Miller's eyes settled on Wallace, Wallace's on Miller. They are exchanging looks, gazes, trying to read the silence of the other person as some people claim to be able to sense the energy in a room by its configuration of furniture. What, then, does Miller see in the set of Wallace's jaw, the wetness in his eyes, the tension in his throat, where he is already bruising, the way he shifts his weight restlessly because he cannot be comfortable in his own skin now? What does Miller make of him, Wallace wonders. Can Miller see his hurt the way Wallace can see his? Seeing pain requires a correlate if you are selfish. Does Miller have a correlate for Wallace's pain as it is now, arranged and waiting for a conduit into the outside world?

Cruelty, Wallace thinks, is really just the conduit of pain. It conveys pain from one place to another—from the place of highest concentration to the place of lowest concentration, in the same way heat flows. It is a delivery system, as in the way that certain viruses convey illness, disease, irreparable harm. They're all infected with pain, hurting each other.

Wallace licks the warm blood from the corner of his mouth. Miller takes a step toward him. Wallace forces himself to stay still, which surprises Miller. They're suddenly too close. Wallace can smell the scent of sex in the air now, the inside of himself, coming from Miller.

"I provoked you," Wallace says.

"No, you didn't," Miller says. "You didn't. I fucked up here. You didn't."

"I provoked you, and you reacted. It's fine."

"You didn't, Wallace. Please stop saying that."

"I provoked you, that's all," Wallace says, his voice coming out of his body but seeming to originate somewhere just behind and to the left of him. He realizes that the world is still hazy and gray to him, rippling at its edges, shifting like a flag in the wind. His balance is compromised. "I provoked you, and you reacted."

"You didn't provoke me, Wallace." Miller grasps his shoulder and Wallace flinches, his head turning down. "Please, Wallace. I'm sorry."

Wallace presses his mouth shut because he knows that he will simply repeat himself. He feels like one of those toys that utter a catchphrase when pressed: *I provoked you, and you reacted. It's fine.* He has said he is fine so much this weekend that he no longer knows what it means. What would it mean to be fine at this moment? Particularly after having brought it on himself. He had brought it on himself, hadn't he?

Miller looks very sorry. His eyes are sad, no longer hooded or shaded or full of mystery. They are clear to Wallace now, and shining with regret. Miller came here angry, bristling, on the edge of himself, but now he is soft, boyish, contrite. He is empty of his rage. Miller wraps his arms around Wallace, and Wallace lets him. He restrains that part of himself that wants to flinch and recoil, presses that part of himself flat and smooths it until he is perfectly still and pliant. Miller kisses his mouth and says again that he is sorry, so sorry for being this way, for hurting him. He kisses Wallace again and again on the mouth, and Wallace lets him, kisses him back, closes his eyes. He runs his fingers down Miller's hair, smooths it, kisses the bridge of his nose and his cheeks. Miller says again and again that he is sorry, kisses Wallace's throat and shoulder and collarbone, kisses him and pulls at his clothes, and they are undressing on the floor, sinking into each other.

When Miller enters him this time, Wallace breathes through the agony, through his discomfort. He remakes his face into a mask of pleasure. He sighs when Miller touches him, moans when Miller slides in and out of him, writhes when Miller kisses him again. But beneath the surface of his pleasure there is a vast, roiling rage.

Is this all his life is meant to be, the accumulation of other people's pain? Their assorted tragedies? Wallace digs his fingernails as hard as possible into Miller's back, sinks them as deeply as he can; he rakes them down to Miller's hips, leaving long, dark gashes. Miller lets out a sharp cry of pain and then he looks down into Wallace's eyes. What does he see there, Wallace wonders. What gazes up out of the lapping black sea of his anger? What strange dark stones make themselves known to him? Miller tries to kiss him, and Wallace bites at his lip, presses his knees as tight as he can to Miller's sides.

Miller is encouraged by this, shoves himself roughly into Wallace, and Wallace only bites harder, digs harder, like he's scaling some great mountain, as if his life depended on it.

"Fuck you," Miller says, lip swelling. "Fuck you, Wallace."

"Fuck you, Miller," Wallace says, and he darts up, sinks his teeth into Miller's shoulder, which is tan and hot from the sun, even hours later. Bites him like a savage. Miller shoves him down, and his head thwacks hard against the floor, and they begin to punch and fight and kick and roll and throw each other against whatever they can.

Miller is tossed rough against the side of the counter, but then lashes out his long white leg and pushes Wallace away, back against the couch. Wallace, breathing hot through his nose, blood throbbing hard in his head, throws a punch down into Miller's thigh, bruising it. Miller reaches for him then, grips his wrist, and pins him down on the dirty floor. Wallace watches the ceiling fan turn and turn overhead. Miller is panting over him, sweating. It's so hot everywhere. Sweat drops from the end of Miller's nose onto Wallace's chest. And then another drop. A small puddle growing on Wallace's skin, salt water, a sea blooming in the brown desert of his body. Miller is trying to catch his breath. Wallace spits up at him, and Miller pulls away, which lets Wallace wrench his wrist free. He punches Miller's chest. He punches it again. Again and again, in the same spot, over and over, and Miller lets him. He absorbs it. Wallace punches and punches, his hand growing hot and then numb from the impact, hard and soft alike, no longer doing any damage, just acting on muscle memory. Miller wraps his arms around him, pulls him in close. No more punching. No more.

IN WALLACE'S BED, they lie down. Miller is on his side, favoring the nasty bruises on his chest and his back. Wallace is lying on his belly. The fan is going, drawing humid air in from the outside. They are not asleep, but they are silent, lying there like stones.

Wallace's arm is still numb from the punching and the tossing and the struggling. His fingers are swollen and thick. Too much recoil. Too much collision with a solid body. In all the numbness and the swelling, there is the shardlike pain of something else. He hopes it isn't broken. When he tries to move his fingers, it's like rotating a blade beneath the skin. But he can move them, at least. There is hope.

Miller's weight on the bed is close by. He can feel Miller's eyes on him, watching him. Wallace is staring into the space beneath his pillow where he's folded his arm.

"Wallace," Miller says.

"What?"

"Are we going to talk about this?"

"I'd rather not," Wallace says. "I'd rather just lie here."

"Do you want me to go?"

"No—" Wallace says, starts to say, but then stops. "I don't want you to go." But what he means to say is that he does not want Miller to stay or to go, that there is a flat, cold indifference in him, inflected by his nature to please. At heart he wants only to please people. Miller relaxes, unclenches. They're still naked, their skin slick with sweat and gritty from the floor.

"I'm sorry I hurt you," Miller says. "I'm sorry I was so rough, so ugly to you."

The words land, and it's like small bits of water striking a windowpane. Each word a little impact, a soft hollow sound, empty. What do they mean, these words? What is their significance? What is Miller apologizing for at this point? Haven't they already hurt each other? Haven't they already resolved it with their bodies? Wallace coughs, then laughs, then coughs.

"Don't bother," he says. "It's okay."

"I don't feel okay," Miller says. "I feel like I fucked up here pretty bad. I feel pretty fucking awful, Wallace."

"Oh?" Wallace asks. "Is that true?"

"Wallace."

"I think that you feel guilty because you think you hurt me, and maybe you did. But I hurt you too, obviously. So what's there to be sorry about?"

"That's not the point, Wallace. That doesn't make it better. So what if you hurt me? I shouldn't have hurt you first. I shouldn't have done that to you."

"I imagine you shouldn't have. But you did."

Miller lets out a hard sigh, and his breath brushes up against Wallace's cheek.

"But you did," Wallace continues. "What I'm saying is, I guess, it doesn't matter to me. What you did. It doesn't matter. None of it does."

"Of course it matters," Miller says hotly. "What do you mean? What are you talking about?"

Wallace rolls gingerly onto his back and puts the pillow across his chest. Miller comes up close beside him, and the bed squeaks awkwardly under their shifting weight. There are shadows thrown across the ceiling from the outside and from the other room, where the light in the bathroom is cutting an angular path through to Wallace's bedroom. He stares at the place where the walls meet, and the light flattens, yellow turning diffuse, until it fuses with the color of the ceiling paint. Wallace puts his tongue to the back of his teeth. It is raw and sore. He can feel its meaty pulp against his gums. His vision is still fluttering on its periphery.

"When I went to middle school, my dad moved out of our house," he says. "He moved up the road into this other house my brother's dad had built. It used to be an art gallery or something. A house first, then an art gallery, then a house again. Anyway, my dad moved into it, and he lived there. I wasn't allowed to visit. He said he didn't want to see us anymore. I asked him why. And he said it didn't matter why; it just was. He didn't want to see us. Me. Anymore."

Wallace is circling the rim of this old bitterness, can hear his dad's voice rising up out of the past, that raspy laugh. He shook his head and smiled at Wallace, put his hand on Wallace's shoulder. They were almost equal height then, his fingers bony and knobby. He simply said, *I don't want you here.* And that was it. Wallace was not granted an explanation for the break, for the severing of their family that left him in the house with his mother and his brother—he learned then that some things have no reason, that no matter how he feels, he isn't entitled to an answer from the world.

His eyes are stinging again. He puts his thumb to the bridge of his nose. The tears are collecting along his eyelashes, their warm salt welling, but they're holding for now. He can feel the sadness like fiberglass, like cotton stuffed into the cavity behind his face, in his hollow cheekbones.

"And now he's dead, and I don't know why he didn't want me around. I almost never saw him after that. He stayed just five minutes up the road, but it's like he vanished from my life entirely, just evaporated. Gone. I don't know why. I'll never know why. And he was right, you know; it didn't matter why. There was nothing I could have done to change his mind. There was nothing anyone could have done. It doesn't matter why he did it, just that he did. And the world went on. It always does. The world doesn't care about you or me or any of this. The world just keeps on going."

"Wallace—"

"No, Miller. It's like I said before, at your house. It doesn't matter. I'm angry all the time, and it doesn't matter. People expect me to react. To do something. And I can't. Because I keep thinking about that—how no matter what I do, it can't change the thing I'd like it to change. I can't rewind things. I can't erase them. I can't take it back. It doesn't matter. You did it. It's a part of us now. It's part of our history. You can't pick it up and throw it back like a fish you caught. You can't replace it like a broken window. It's just there. It's permanent."

"I don't understand," Miller says. "I don't get what you mean.

Just because it happened doesn't mean we can't talk about it. I think it means the opposite, right? We have to talk about it."

Wallace shakes his head, the act of which makes him dizzy. He puts the pillow across his face and sighs into it, letting his breath collect in the fabric. He wants to scream. He does not know how to communicate it to Miller, this sensation he has, the pointlessness of these words filling the air. His throat is hot and dry. He'd like to hold his head underwater and drink for an eternity.

"I think that's the difference between us," Wallace says. "You want to talk about it. And I don't see the point."

"I can't pretend it didn't happen."

Wallace smiles, slowly, beneath the pillow. "But that's it, Miller. I don't need to talk about it to know it happened."

"Then why aren't you angrier with me? Why aren't you pissed with me? Please, something, do something."

"We already had that fight," Wallace says. "I'm bored by it now. I'm over it."

"You're not. I'd rather you be honest with me."

"I am being honest with you."

"This doesn't feel like honesty, Wallace. It doesn't feel real."

Wallace draws the pillow back from his face and sits up. It hurts to move, but he does it. He presses himself through it until he's sitting up and looking down at Miller.

"You think that, if I hurt you sufficiently, you will feel sufficient guilt to get you through this. Because you feel like a monster. But I don't owe that to you," Wallace says. "I don't owe you any more pain than I've already dealt you. It's selfish of you."

"It's not," Miller says, but he stops himself. He lies flat on his back and puts his arm across his eyes. Wallace lies next to him, their shoulders touching. It's this minor point of contact that Wallace focuses on as he drifts off to sleep, the world softening and receding until it feels as though he's drifting on a sea made of soft leaves. The sound of Miller's breathing comes in and out, in and out; to Wallace it seems oddly familiar, like wind moving through the kudzu.

WHEN THEY WAKE UP, they are stiff and bruised and covered in dried blood. They climb from Wallace's bed in the gray middle of the night, the part that turns irrevocably toward morning, and they get into Wallace's shower together. Wallace leans against the far wall, and Miller fiddles with the faucet until he gets the temperature and pressure right. The water hits his chest, and then after some adjusting it gets all over both of them. The water is hot, turning to steam in the shower, and Wallace closes his eyes, letting it sluice down his body and his face. Miller slides around so that he is behind Wallace, being taller, and he braces his arms against the wall to keep himself upright. The shower is decently sized for one, but for two it's complicated.

The hot water feels good on Wallace's face and shoulders. He collects it in his palms and splashes it over his eyes and mouth. The water in this city is hard, so it is treated aggressively with chemicals. It tastes alkaline and smells strongly of something like chlorine, though Wallace isn't sure of the exact chemistry. Miller puts his arms around Wallace's shoulders again, sinks against his back. Their wet skin sticks together a bit. The light from the vanity is gauzy yellow as it spills over the shower curtain. Wallace can feel, through the wall of water and steam, the press of Miller's lips against his neck again, tracing the place where the bruises are growing as if he could push them back down forever with an act of tenderness.

The alcohol is still in Miller, coming out of his skin, especially now that they're sweating in the shower. Wallace turns to him. The water is soaking into his hair and striking Miller's throat, turning it red on impact. Miller laughs and looks down at him. He has to bend his knees a little. He's too tall.

"This is not as easy as I thought it would be," he says.

"It never is."

"I guess that's true," Miller says. Wallace puts his fingers flat to Miller's stomach. Miller shakes his head, and water flies everywhere, striking the curtain. They are as clean as they are going to get this way, so Wallace shuts off the water and they get out. There's only one bath towel, so Wallace dries himself first and then hands it to Miller. Wallace sits on the counter watching Miller pass the towel over his long limbs, his body somehow more impressive now in this room that seems too small to contain him. Now that Miller has washed off the grime and blood, Wallace can more appreciate the dark purpling where his fist landed earlier, and also the gash that is already healing along Miller's cheek where the guy at the bar must have punched him. He's got a split and swollen lip. And there's an oblong-shaped bruise along his spine. It's ugly, Wallace thinks, and like the photo negative of something else, the imprint of the thing still unsaid between them. Miller is looking at him, wrapping the towel around his waist, and there's something like a smile on his lips, but it loses its shape almost immediately, turning sadder, or at least more inward, darker.

The bathroom is humid. Miller sets his weight against the counter, bracing his fingers on either side of the sink basin. His reflection is occluded by the mist on the mirror. Wallace lets his bare skin stick to the glass.

It's cold and wet, despite the warm air in the room.

At some slim dark hour, one of the last of night, Miller and Wallace wake in his bed again.

"I'm hungry," Miller says.

"All right. Let's feed the wolf," Wallace says. Miller growls, though there's no threat left in it.

In the kitchen, they take familiar postures. Miller sits on one of the high chairs, his elbows on the counter. Wallace stands behind the counter, surveying the ingredients in his refrigerator. The food he rejected on Saturday now holds new potential, because he is not cooking for many people and does not have to chart the landscape of their preferences. It is late, so he has only the topology of hunger to consider, the abatement of emptiness. Miller was likely raised up on the same kinds of food as Wallace—meat and vegetables, starch, lots of oil and grease, the kind of food their friends look down upon because it lacks elegance or restraint. But here in the cool darkness of his kitchen, he can make whatever he wants for the two of them, does not have to consider how others' palates might diverge. Wallace props his knuckles on his hip and taps his toes against the floor, thinking, looking into the cold, bright interior of his fridge.

"You know, the other night," he begins. "Friday, I mean, I thought about making dinner for you."

"You did? Why?" Miller asks, and though Wallace is not looking at him, he can tell that there is a smile growing.

"Because you said you were hungry. And Yngve was giving you such a hard time. You looked so pitiful. I thought, *I could make him something.* But then I thought better of it." Wallace takes some fish from the freezer. He takes eggs from the fridge and flour from the shelf in the cupboard. He crouches and removes from the low pantry some vegetable oil, its container slippery and filmy with grease.

"Why didn't you offer?" Miller asks, and Wallace shrugs as he rises from the floor and puts the oil next to the other ingredients on the counter.

"I don't know—I guess I was afraid of you finding out how much I liked you. It seemed kind of . . ." Wallace's voice tapers into silence, and he takes a large, deep skillet from beneath the stove. He runs his finger around it, finding its surface dry and smooth, no trace of oil. Good. He did a good job cleaning it earlier. He nods to himself. What he was about to say was that such a display would have felt vulgar in a way, that to make so gross a statement about his feelings, or his attitude, seemed too direct, too intrusive. Affection always feels this way for him, like an undue burden, like putting weight and expectation onto someone else. As if affection were a kind of cruelty too.

"But now you're cooking for me."

"So I am," Wallace says, pushing the carton of eggs and a blue mixing bowl over to Miller. "Please break three or four eggs into this. And beat them, not too hard, just mix them up good, please."

Miller nods, accepts the task. Wallace rinses his fingers in a quick spurt of water and opens the flour bag. He tilts it over so that a clump of flour dislodges itself from the bulk and tumbles into a wooden bowl with a soft splat. Flour shoots up into the air, curls as if slowly gesticulating. Wallace considers putting the fish fillets in warm water, though he knows you aren't supposed to do this. You are supposed to warm meat up slowly in the fridge, letting the temperature rise gradually and evenly without the risk of bacterial contamination.

Wallace considers the frozen slabs of tilapia in their individually wrapped, flash-frozen sleeves. He considers putting them in the microwave, zapping them quickly, and then throwing them into the batter and the grease. He considers the relative risk, considers the accumulation of bacteria, the chance of those bacteria colonizing the insides of their bodies, making them ill, making them vomit, making them shit.

He dips the fish into the water. It will be fine. He lets them float to the surface in the large bowl. They will thaw quickly. They are thin, after all, and not like the fatty fish they caught in Alabama and gutted and cleaned. These fish have never seen a river or a pond in their lives. They have been grown to fat contentment in tanks, raised expressly to be eaten, like the people who live in this city, their lives a series of narrowly constructed tubes filled with the nutrient-rich water they consume without even having to think about it. That's all culture is, after all, the nutrients pervading the air we breathe, diffusing into and out of people, a passive process.

Is it into this culture that he is to emerge? Into the narrow, dark water of real life? He remembers Simone, leaning in toward him, the world vast and blue beyond her window, the kindness in her face as she told him that he needed to think about what he wants from life. He remembers the gentleness of her voice, the awful horror of that gentleness. He could stay in her lab and in graduate school. He could live his life on the other side of the glass, watching real life pass him by. Staying would be so simple, requiring no effort at all except to put his head down as if in prayer and let the worst of it pass over him.

Why go out there to be like these fish, like the people at the pier, bloated and commercial and with so little desire in life except to see the next day, nothing except the pure biology of it all, the part of life that must, by necessity, resist death, linking day upon day upon day, time meaningless, like water?

But to stay in graduate school, to stay where he is, means to accept the futility of his efforts to blend in seamlessly with those around him. It is a life spent swimming against the gradient, struggling up the channel of other people's cruelty. It grates him to consider this, the shutting away of the part of him that now throbs and writhes like a new organ that senses so keenly the limitations of his life.

Stay here and suffer, or exit and drown, he thinks.

He dips the battered fish into the hot oil, and it spits and leaps and crackles. He burns the tip of his finger, but it's numb. There are four pieces of fish in the oil now, all of them obscurely shaped and vaguely human, like dolls made of clay.

Miller is still against the counter. He's pulled one of Wallace's oversize sweaters on, and he's wearing shorts without underwear. Miller's body makes Wallace's clothes look childlike. The knobs of his spine are clear in the way he's bent over with his arms folded under his chin. The boyishness in his face is back.

Wallace fries the fish quickly, turning each piece just as it begins to brown so that it is crispy but not dry or burned. They eat the fish hot out of the grease over paper towels, biting into the white flesh, which steams the moment it touches the air. They ought to wait until it cools, Wallace suggests, but Miller, no longer neat, is eating voraciously, chewing and chomping. Grease slides down his fingers and his palms. And Wallace licks it clean, which makes Miller look at him firmly, his eyes glossy with want. They eat sitting next to each other on the counter, their thighs touching, eating because they don't have to talk as long as their mouths are doing something else. And what would they talk about, anyway?

This too could be his life, Wallace thinks. This thing with Miller, eating fish in the middle of the night, watching the gray air of the night sky over the roof next door. This could be their life together, each moment shared, passed back and forth between each other to alleviate the pressure, the awful pressure of having to hold on to time for oneself. This is perhaps why people get together in the first place. The sharing of time. The sharing of the responsibility of anchoring oneself in the world. Life is less terrible when you can just rest for a moment, put everything down and wait without having to worry about being washed away. People take each other's hands and they hold on as tight as they can, they hold on to each other and to themselves, and when they let go, they can because they know that the other person will not.

The fish tastes good—hot, buttery, smooth, salt and pepper and a little vinegar, which was his father's secret. In those years they all lived together, his father did all the cooking, and his mother worked. In those years, his father cooked for him all manner of delicious foods. In those years, his father soothed him with food, with pink-dyed pickled eggs, or sliced strawberries, or mango, or papaya. His father introduced him to all sorts of furry sour fruits, as they sat together on the rickety porch in the summer sun, their skin turning the color of clay, eating off paper plates. How has Wallace forgotten this? The sticky sweetness of those mango slices, the sharp sourness of kiwi as his father taught him to choose the ripest ones, the ones that were firm but not too firm, and perfectly green, prickly in your palms at the grocery store.

Miller offers Wallace the last piece of fish. Wallace clears his throat, shakes his head.

"No, that's okay," he says. "You finish." He hops down from the counter and washes his hands in the sink. Miller watches him. Wallace can feel his eyes sliding over him, checking for something, anything. Wallace smiles.

"What are you thinking about? You're a million miles away."

"I'm here," Wallace says. "I'm here in the world." Miller laughs at him, but Wallace can only think about how true this is, that he is in the world. He is both here in his body with Miller and elsewhere, beyond; that all the moments in his life are gathered up in this moment, that all of it has been for this. He is in the world, everywhere he has ever been and everywhere he will go, simultaneously. Yes, he thinks, yes.

Miller gets down from the counter, too, and comes up behind him, wraps his arms around Wallace. His stomach presses against the middle of Wallace's back. Wallace can feel him, all of him.

"I'm in the world too," Miller says.

"Despite your best efforts," Wallace says.

"What's that supposed to mean?"

"Nothing. Just something to say, I guess."

"Do you think I want to die?"

"No, I don't. Well, maybe you do. But I don't think it."

"Then why would you say that?"

Wallace thinks about this. He's running the hot water over his fingers, its temperature rising steeply, burning his palms. Miller presses him forward so that Wallace can feel the edge of the sink bite into him.

"Why would you say that?" he asks again, his voice lowering, settling deep in his chest. He's got his fingers hard around Wallace's shoulders, has him wrapped up again. Fear, molten, slow, climbs inch by inch in Wallace like rising water. His hands are burning now, stinging, raw.

"I don't know," Wallace says, and Miller puts more pressure on his throat. "I don't know."

"I don't like that very much," Miller says, and the hard stubble on his jaw rasps against Wallace's neck.

"I'm sorry," Wallace says.

"I try to be in the world," Miller says. "I try to be. I am trying to be. It's not fair for you to say that."

"It's not," Wallace agrees. He turns off the water. His hands are pulsing and damp. His palms have gone completely red. Miller puts more weight on Wallace's back, digs hard with his chin into the space between Wallace's shoulders, a tender place that gives in easily. Wallace lets out a startled yelp of pain.

"Tomorrow is Monday," Miller says.

"Today is Monday," Wallace says, swimming around beneath his skin. "It's Monday already."

"So it is," Miller says, and he lets go of Wallace, who feels he can breathe again. "Do you want to come with me somewhere?"

"Where?" Wallace asks, drying his fingers, breathing slowly, deeply.

"To the lake."

"It's the middle of the night. It'll be morning soon."

"If you don't want to go, then say so."

"It's fine, I'll go."

"You don't have to."

"It's fine," Wallace says.

THEY PUT ON their shoes and go out into the cool, humid night. There is a ridge of gray light along the horizon, like a second world emerging from the first. The air hangs close. Wallace has on a sweater and shorts and floppy, soft shoes. Miller is wearing his thick boots and shorts, miles of leg flashing with each step. They plod along the street, then head along the houses that sit huddled near the shore, until they reach the stone steps.

"Come on," Miller says when Wallace lingers at the top of the concrete. He's on the first step, looking up at Wallace. "Come on."

"What are we going to do in the lake?" Wallace asks. "I can't swim."

"You can't swim?" Miller asks. "You're from the Gulf Coast. You're from a state with real beaches."

"I can't swim," Wallace repeats. His mother never let him try. There was a neighborhood pool near his preschool that offered free lessons to every child under the age of seven. He begged her to let him go, to let him try. She told him not to beg, that begging made a person ugly.

A memory dislodges from some dark inner continent and rises to the surface of his thoughts: Miller sitting on the edge of the pier in blue swimming shorts. His skin a little burned. His muscular back, long torso. His hair dark, his mouth wide and red. A sly smile. *Rub it in.* The scent of aloe, wet and clear. The sunscreen cool in his palm. The lapping lake, the laughter of other people ascending, climbing into the air. Clouds on the horizon, white and fluffy, the peninsula green and lush in the distance. Miller, turning toward him, a drop of water caught in the hollow of this throat. That smile broadening. *Rub it in.*

"I'll teach you," Miller says, grabbing Wallace's fingers. "Come on, I'll teach you to swim."

Wallace looks out over the gray shifting water and at the undulating darkness below its surface. The peninsula is in the distance, and he can see just around its bend, the water already gleaming. The row of dark hedges that comprise its body flutter as if they were a murmuration of birds, a mass action cascading.

"All right," Wallace says, Miller's fingers rough around his. Miller pulls on him, and they go down the smooth, slick concrete stairs. The lake rises up the length of Wallace's body as he marches down the steps and eventually into open water. Miller has an easy stroke, pulls them evenly, smoothly along. His limbs slice through the water.

Weightless, Wallace feels unmoored, out of control, but he wills himself to float. Miller takes his wrists, wet and hard. He pulls Wallace close to him. He wraps his arms around Wallace and tells him to breathe, to feel himself getting lighter and lighter until he is nothing at all.

Wallace floats on his back. Occasionally, waves cover his mouth and nose and he panics, feels as though he'll drown, but Miller holds him steady, his smile easy.

The water feels slimy, like they're in the mouth of some enormous organism, its waves like a thousand teeth eating the shore.

"I used to pretend that I was in the whale that ate Jonah," Miller says, floating next to Wallace. "I'd swim and pretend I was in the belly of a whale."

"That's kind of how it sounds," Wallace says, the water echoing in his ears.

"It does," Miller says. "When you're in the belly of a whale, nothing else matters. The whole universe could explode, and you wouldn't know. You're already in a different universe, I guess."

"I used to get scared when I thought about the Red Sea parting," Wallace says. "I don't know why, but when they told that story in church at Easter, I always got scared and sad. Something awful about so much water just hanging over your head."

"I imagine so," Miller says.

"And then it all comes down. Those soldiers who were chasing the Jews, they got drowned in the water."

"They did."

"When they tried to baptize me when I was little, I was so afraid of that—being drowned, like in Exodus—that I cried and cried and fought and eventually they just gave up."

"You weren't baptized?"

"No," Wallace says. "Everyone but me."

"Do you believe in God?"

"Me? No. Well. No, I guess not. Not anymore."

"Science is kind of like God," Miller says.

Wallace is silent on that score. Instead, he asks, "Why did you want to bring me out here?"

"Because I wanted to be inside something else, I think."

"Other than my apartment, you mean?"

"Yes. It was getting suffocating in there. I guess I just needed to be in something bigger."

"I go to the roof."

"What do you mean?"

Wallace turns to him in the water, but loses his balance, plunges down beneath the surface. Below, the world is green and black. There are algae blooming all along the arms of the pier, and just under the water there is a rust-colored film. Miller pulls him up and Wallace breathes, his lungs filling with air.

"Oh," he says.

"Be careful," Miller says sternly. "Don't die."

"I'll try not to," Wallace says, wiping water from his eyes.

"What did you mean, before, about the roof?"

Wallace coughs up lake water and shakes his head to clear his ears.

"I meant, when I feel like everything is closing in, I go to the roof of my building."

Miller nods thoughtfully, then asks quietly, "Will you take me there?"

"Okay," Wallace says. "All right."

IN SOGGY SHOES and dripping clothes, they make their way back across the street and into the building. They get into the elevator smelling strongly like the lake water and algae. The elevator smells like beer and grease. Miller's eyes are red, from fatigue or the lake or both. They're holding hands, dripping onto the dark carpet. Up they go, against gravity. They emerge into a world that is more silver than gray. Morning is brightening. The roof is metallic and gravelly, spiked with antennae. Wallace immediately feels the sense of inverted scope, so high above the world, where everything flattens and becomes smaller. So high up—birdlike—that Wallace feels as if he's floating. He is, at all times, acutely aware of his distance from the ground. At this height he is a little dizzy, but he disguises his discomfort with a wan smile. Miller lets out a low whistle of appreciation.

"Holy fuck," he says.

"Yep," Wallace says, watching as the gravel on the top of the roof darkens beneath their dripping clothes. White pebbles, crushed stones, turn to powder under their feet. Someone has left deck chairs and a little table up here. There is a grill; this is the only place in the building where fire is permitted, which seems counterintuitive. Why would you want to start a fire at the highest point, the place most difficult to reach and extinguish? But there it is, black metal in the corner, near the side of the building that faces the city rather than the lake.

Behind them, the lake is full of luminous water. Miller bends over the edge of the building, its railing waist-high, and he peers down into the world.

Wallace sits on the ground next to him, knees against his chest. He usually comes here alone, to think and be by himself. He comes to feel the sense of the world around him, its forever shifting currents of air, their coldness on him like a comforting hand. He comes to get away. But here he is with Miller.

Miller crouches down next to Wallace, sits next to him. They sit that way for a long time, the stones sticking to their legs, at first painfully, and then numbly, like anything else. They watch the sun come up, its yellow light saturating everything and eventually burning away the mist of morning. They're still sitting that way when the first sounds of cars fill the streets below, and the world turns over itself, to begin again.

10

I t was an exceptionally hot day in July when Wallace arrived in the Midwest, having spent all of the preceding day
cramped on a Greyhound coming up from Alabama. He
had been asleep when they left Tennessee under the cloak
of darkness, and entered that strange realm where the country
suddenly flattens and smooths out into endless plains brooked by
ice and jagged mountains. He had never been out of the South
before, but had been trying for a long time to leave it; now, having finally done so, he felt only a sense of elation and freedom.
Upon getting off the bus, though, he found the air just as heavy
as he had left it down south. He had not known what to expect,
and the stickiness in the air made him uneasy about his prospects.
But that had been yesterday, and today he stood on the edge of
the pier, looking around at all the people.

They seemed friendly enough, he thought, like people anywhere. They smiled at him, and he smiled at them. He was standing in the middle of the sidewalk, and they were polite as they
excused themselves to get around him. Back home, he had stood
on the edge of the ocean and marveled at the vast gray tumult of
its surf. Here, he could see the horizon and the distant shore of
the lake. There were lakes in Alabama, surely, but few of them,

and all smaller than this one, which was rimmed with conifers, pine and cedar. Here, the scope of the lake was startling. This was no glorified pond, as he'd thought of lakes before. It made him nervous to stand on the slippery stone steps, uneasy, as if at any moment he might slip down and be swallowed.

He was here for orientation. Or, rather, to meet some of his fellow students. They would begin orientation on Monday. Before that, though, someone had suggested that they all go out to the peninsula, to sit on its silty shores and make a bonfire. He had never been on a peninsula before. He had never been on a boat before. He stood near the yellow-bellied boats, running his hand over them while they rested on their hooks like sleeping animals. They were smooth but tacky, and his fingers stuck on them. The whole area smelled like rust and lake water and something like rotting plants.

There were tall, attractive people with shining skin and tank tops walking all around him, talking to each other as if they belonged to a world beyond his grasp. It reminded him of his favorite story, about the woman who goes to Madrid in order to force the nature of her character to emerge by virtue of not fitting in, only to discover that her ability to blend in with the Spanish renders her efforts futile. He had considered himself a Midwesterner at heart, that being in the South and being gay were incompatible, that no two parts of a person could be more incompatible. But standing there, among the boats, shyly waiting to discover the people to whom he felt he would belong, he sensed the foolishness in that.

They finally appeared, his fated friends, four or five people, coming toward him along the sidewalk. At first they had not seemed like a group at all, but eventually the rhythm of their footfalls told him that they were coming toward him en masse. Two of them were tremendously tall, another was very short, and there was a woman with a skinny man's arm thrown around her. The skinny man had a silly mustache, but seemed very serious.

"Are you Wallace?" the sandy-haired one asked, sticking out his hand. "Yngve. Pleasure."

"Pleasure," Wallace said, smiling because he couldn't stop himself. These were to be his friends here, the people who looked after him. He had seen them only via the internet, their little portraits and bits of their lives transmitted across Wallace's uncle's shaky wireless.

"I'm Lukas, with a *k*," the red-haired one said. And then, the tallest one nodded from the back of the group.

"Miller," he said somewhat morosely. He was very good-looking, but there was something about him that withdrew even as it advanced. Wallace nodded back.

"I'm Emma—and this is Thom, my fiancé," the girl with the curly hair said. "Happy to meet you finally."

"Happy to meet you," Wallace said, as if he could only repeat what other people said. His eyes were wet, he realized with horror. "Oh, god. I'm going to cry." He laughed and blotted the tears with his hand. "I've been very tired lately."

"I know the feeling," Emma said, stepping forward to hug him. "You're with friends now."

"Hello," someone called from the other direction, and they all turned. Another boy, tallish and fair, came loping up to them. "I'm Cole, hi."

"Hello, Cole," said everyone.

They ended up getting one of the small boats, so it would take several trips to get everyone. Wallace volunteered to go last, both because he was nervous and because he wanted to make it easy on everyone. In the end, it was him and Yngve and Miller, just as the sun was setting. The boat rocked as Miller piloted them out to the tip of the peninsula, where it was sandy and gray and covered with pine needles.

They walked along the shore after tying up the boat, and then scaled an embankment so that they were among the trees. Voices reached out to them in the dark; now and then they saw a flicker of flame as they passed other little gatherings. Yngve was walking very quickly out ahead of them, carrying a satchel with food and other supplies. Wallace and Miller walked apace with each other, quietly, not saying anything.

Wallace glanced up at him—his face was forbidding. Wallace was giddy, almost sick with excitement, to be in this place, among these people—it was the accomplishment of a long-held wish, a dream come true. The trees groaned overhead, swaying. He felt at home among them too; trees had always been his companions.

They arrived at their designated fire pit. The fire was going, and the others were already roasting food. Yngve had brought plates and utensils. Wallace sat next to Cole on a stump and discovered that he loved tennis too. They talked excitedly about that, the fire splashing orange and gold all over their faces.

Someone wanted to make a toast. They popped a bottle of mid-priced champagne. They looked at each other. They smiled. Lukas cleared his throat. "You know, guys, this is it. This is it. Our life. It starts now."

"Hell yeah it does," Yngve said, putting his hand on Lukas's back. "Hell yeah."

"To life," Emma said, raising her plastic cup. The firelight danced through it. Wallace watched it undulate, writhe in the liquid. Golden bubbles rippled up to the champagne's surface. He lifted his cup too.

"To life," they all said, quietly and in their own ways, and then louder, until they were chanting it again and again. To life, they said, imbuing those words with all their hope and all their desires for the future. Their laughter rang through the night and through the trees, and on the shore they had left behind, people were eating dinner and laughing and crying and going about things as they always had and always would.

ACKNOWLEDGMENTS

Thank you, in no particular order, to Meredith Kaffel Simonoff, Cal Morgan, Antonio Byrd, Derrick Austin, Natalie Eilbert, Sarah Fuchs, Emily Shelter, Pam Zhang, Philip Wallén, Noah Ballard, Hux Michaels, Justin Torres, Jeanne Thornton, Monet Thomas, Esmé Weijun Wang, Judith Kimble, Sarah Crittenden, Peggy Kroll-Conner, Kim Haupt, Heaji Shin, Erika Sorrensen-Kamakian, Hannah Seidel, Sarah Robinson, Aaron Kershner, Elena Sorokin, Scott Aoki, Abbey Thompson, and my whole IPiB cohort.